SHADOW MAGIC

SHADOW MAGIC

JOSHUA KHAN

with illustrations by Ben Hibon

DISNEY · HYPERION
LOS ANGELES   NEW YORK

Text copyright © 2016 by Joshua Khan

Illustrations copyright © 2016 by Ben Hibon

First Edition, April 2016

1 3 5 7 9 10 8 6 4 2

FAC-020093-16015

Printed in the United States of America

Library of Congress Cataloging-in-Publication Data

Khan, Joshua.

Shadow magic / Joshua Khan; with illustrations by Ben Hibon—First edition.

pages cm

Summary: "Thorn, a boy sold into slavery who must serve the royalty of Castle Gloom for a year and a day to earn his freedom, and Lilith Shadow, the 13-year-old ruler of Gehenna, who is forbidden to practice the magic that is her heritage, join forces to solve the murders taking place in Gehenna."
—Provided by publisher.

ISBN 978-1-4847-3272-4 (hardback)

[1. Fantasy. 2. Magic—Fiction. 3. Murder—Fiction.] I. Hibon, Ben, illustrator. II. Title.

PZ7.1.K53Sh 2016

[Fic]—dc23   2015015069

Reinforced binding

Visit www.DisneyBooks.com

To my wife and daughters

Give me my robe, put on my crown;

I have Immortal longings in me.

—From *Antony and Cleopatra,*

by William Shakespeare

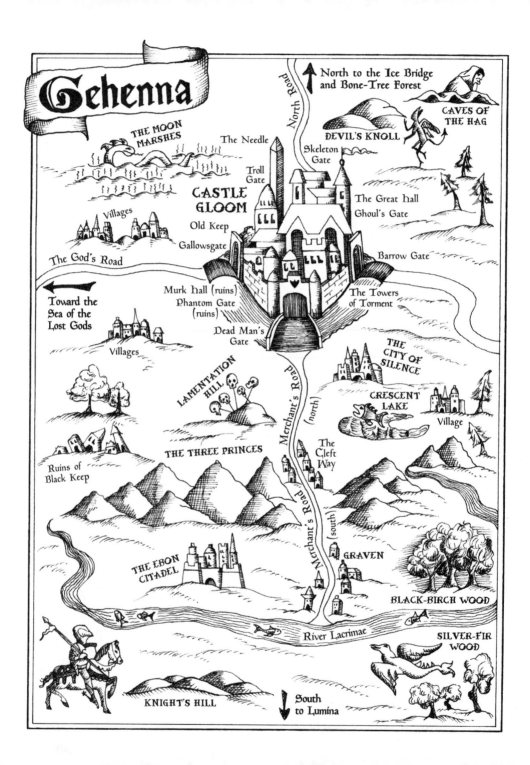

CAST OF CHARACTERS

PORT CUTLASS
Thorn, a runaway boy
Merrick, a wandering minstrel
Lukas, a slave master

CASTLE GLOOM
Lilith Shadow, ruler of Gehenna
Pandemonium Shadow, her uncle
Mary, a servant
Baron Sable, a nobleman
Rose, a servant
Wade, a squire
Old Colm, the weapons master
Tyburn, the executioner

PRISM PALACE
Duke Raphael Solar, ruler of Lumina
Gabriel Solar, his son and heir apparent
K'leef Djinn, a hostage

BEASTS
Custard, a puppy
Thunder, a warhorse
Hades, a monster . . .

PORT CUTLASS

ONE

"How much for this boy?" asked the man, prodding Thorn hard in the chest.

Thorn grimaced, but did nothing.

The slave master, Lukas, wiggled all his fingers.

The man frowned. "Ten? Captain Pike sells his boys for five."

Lukas, born ogre-ugly but turned hideous by the large scar across his face, laughed. "Pike sells them half-starved and diseased." He tugged Thorn forward by his manacles. "Have a good look at him, Master Shann," he said. "Twelve summers and already taller than many men. Straight limbs and a sound chest. And look at these." Lukas twisted Thorn's wrist to turn his palm up. "Good old-fashioned farmer's hands. I swear by the Six, you put him in the fields, and you'll get ten years out of him. Maybe fifteen."

Thorn pulled himself free. They talked as if he was some animal.

The customer, Master Shann, prodded him again. "Open your mouth, boy."

Thorn clamped his mouth shut.

Lukas cuffed the back of his head. "Open your mouth."

Thorn didn't.

"Is he simpleminded?" asked Shann. "I have no use for simpleminded boys."

Thorn should have punched him for that. Shann needed punching. He was big and round and squashy-faced, with a bulbous nose crowded with hairy warts. But hitting a customer would only earn him another beating—the third this week—so Thorn kept his fist clenched and by his side. It wasn't easy.

"Or is he mute? Is that it? I have no use for mute boys, either. Speak, boy. Say something."

Speak? All right.

"Fat. Stupid. Oaf," said Thorn.

Shann blinked.

Thorn spoke some more. "Smelly. Foul. Toad."

The beady, puffy eyes almost vanished into Shann's doughy face. "I have even less use for *surly* boys." He swept around and marched off.

The slave master grabbed Thorn's hair and pulled him so they were face-to-face. "I'll deal with you later." Then he shoved him off his feet before chasing after his would-be customer. "Wait, Master Shann! Wait!"

He was in for a beating later tonight. Maybe it wouldn't be too bad. Even Lukas knew that bruised slaves didn't fetch the best prices.

A shadow crossed over him.

"That was unwise, my young friend."

Thorn looked up to see Merrick, a minstrel the slavers had captured a week after him. Merrick folded his long, skinny legs and sat down beside Thorn.

"I don't care. I ain't no slave."

Merrick shook the manacles around his own wrists. "These aren't bracelets we wear."

Seagulls squawked overhead, and limp green flags hung off the flag-poles. Fishermen sold their day's catch from the quayside, farmers herded sheep and goats along the narrow alleys into pens, and bony dogs searched the rubbish. The air stank of unwashed animals, rotting fish, and too many sweating people, and the sea breeze did nothing to relieve it.

But the foulest smell came from the slaves. Disgorged from the ships' hulls after weeks, sometimes months, of crowded travel, they were now lined up along the platforms. Men, women, and children.

Plenty of little ones. They didn't run as fast, so were bagged first.

"It shouldn't be allowed, stealing people from their homes." Thorn looked down at the clutch of small children. Most had slumped into quiet despair; others still gazed around, searching the crowds, perhaps hoping their parents might appear and save them.

"It *isn't* allowed," answered Merrick. "The Great Houses certainly don't have slavery. But we're a long way from them and the protection they might offer." He brushed dirt off his motley. The patched costume might have been bright once, but life on the road had faded the brilliant colors to a dull and lifeless gray. "I bet you never thought you'd end up here when you ran away from home."

Thorn touched the carved acorn amulet hanging around his neck. "I didn't run away."

"No? So what was it, then?"

"It ain't none of your business."

The less Merrick knew about Thorn's crime, the better. The minstrel couldn't keep his mouth shut; after all, it was his job to tell stories.

And if any of them knew why he'd left home, they'd stretch his neck with a rope.

"Did you commit some dastardly offense?" Merrick winked. "That's it, isn't it? You stole the heart of a fair-faced princess, but her evil father, the baron, had her promised to some weak-chinned son of an earl. She's in her tower right now, pining for you."

"Of course not!"

"What a shame. That would have made a good tale," he said. "So, tell me, why are you here?"

"I don't even know where 'here' is."

"You are in Cutlass," declared Merrick, sweeping out his arms. "The largest port along the Sword Coast. A place where you can buy anything, and I do mean *anything*. Home to slavers and pirates and gentlemen of little virtue."

"Gentlemen of little virtue? Like you?"

Merrick raised an eyebrow. "Ah, so there is a wit under that thatch of straw you call hair."

"I ain't stupid."

"I don't know what you are, young Thorn. Shall we see?" He squeezed Thorn's bicep.

"Hey!"

"You're strong, but then, farmers' boys usually are. You still have all your own teeth and that's a bonus, but you're utterly lacking in charm and, if you don't mind me saying so, not particularly attractive. Can you sing? Dance? No? Come now, you must be good at something."

"I'm good at lots of things," said Thorn. Then he muttered to himself, "Just *bad* things."

Yeah, like spilling blood.

Merrick shook his head. "If you're not careful, Lukas will sell you to the mines. And you don't want to end up there, believe me."

"I ain't going down no mine, and I ain't going to be no slave. Dad said it's better to be hungry and free than a fat slave."

"Fathers, like most men, say stupid things."

"Don't you say that!" snapped Thorn. "You don't know nothing about my dad!"

His dad was worth a hundred Merricks! All the minstrel could do was play the lute, sing badly, and tell stupid stories. Thorn's dad could do anything. He'd taught Thorn how to—

No. Don't think about that. That's what got you here in the first place.

Merrick raised his hands in surrender. "I apologize, my young, irascible friend. I'm sure your father is a paragon of wisdom."

Typical Merrick. An insult hidden in a compliment. His tongue was more twisted than a viper's.

Other buyers walked along the line. One or two stopped to look at Thorn, but he glared back at them and they moved swiftly on. It looked like nobody wanted surly boys.

But one man wasn't scared off.

A swordsman. Thorn recognized the sort; he'd met enough on the road. And he knew to keep well away from them.

The swordsman sat easy on his saddle, elbows resting on the pommel while his horse, a huge black stallion, pulled at weeds growing beside a trough.

He wasn't rich, judging by the plain tunic, muddy cloak, and his worn boots. The sword didn't look like anything special, but it *did* look well used.

And he had dark, dead eyes. Eyes that had seen too much.

The swordsman flicked his reins. The horse tugged the last of the weeds free, and rider and horse sank back into the crowd.

"What about you, Merrick? Ain't you scared of ending up down a mine?"

Merrick waved his long fine fingers. "What barbarian would waste such talented digits on digging rocks? I, who have performed for each of the six Great Houses? I have danced in the mirrored chambers of the Prism Palace and sung in the grim halls of Castle Gloom to—"

"You've met the Shadows?" interrupted Thorn. "The lords of death?"

"I think they prefer the term 'necromancer,' but yes, I am acquainted with the rulers of Gehenna."

Necromancer. Another one of Merrick's fancy words. But fancy words didn't make things any different. Everyone knew what the Shadows were. Dark sorcerers who raised the dead from their graves and had zombies for servants.

"And you came back *alive*?" Thorn checked Merrick's neck. Was that a pair of bite marks or just eager fleas? "Did any of 'em drink your blood? Ain't Lord Shadow a vampire?"

"Lord Iblis Shadow walked in the sun the last time I was there. Not that the country of Gehenna gets much sun." Merrick rubbed his arms vigorously. "Give me the gardens of the south any day."

How many nights had Thorn's dad told him and his brothers and sisters tales about the Shadow family and Castle Gloom, their citadel without windows? How the living and dead danced together at their great balls and feasted on blood and corpses . . .

Thorn remembered the warning his parents had given them all. He must have heard it a thousand times: *Be good or the Shadows will have you for dinner.*

A child screamed.

"Who's that?" Thorn turned toward the noise.

The second scream was louder and longer.

"The twins," said Merrick.

Thorn jumped up, but Merrick gripped his arm. "This is not our affair," the minstrel warned.

Master Shann began dragging Tam away. The boy was six, the same age as Thorn's youngest brother. Tam was crying and reaching desperately for his sister, Annie. The girl sat crumpled in the mud, her own face screwed up in misery.

Thorn's blood boiled as he watched Lukas laughing at Tam's feeble attempts to break free. Thorn had looked after the twins since the day they'd all been caught; he felt responsible for them now.

"Do not get involved." Merrick tightened his hold. "You'll only get in more trouble."

For a second, just a second, Thorn stopped. There'd been nothing but trouble since the day he'd left home. Maybe Merrick was right. He should sit this out. Let Shann drag the boy off. Leave the sister sobbing in the dirt. That's what some would do.

Yeah, some. Not me.

TWO

Thorn wrenched himself free and leaped smack onto Lukas's back, knocking him face-first into the mud. Both tumbled over, punching and kicking. Lukas tried to grab him, but Thorn bashed the slaver's head against the ground.

A boot slapped down beside him, and that was warning enough. Thorn rolled away just as a guard swung his cudgel at him. The knobbly stick cracked the side of Lukas's skull instead.

Thorn scrambled up and rammed his head into the guard's guts. The man went down with a grunt as Thorn skidded beside the girl.

Annie stared at him, openmouthed.

"What are you waiting for? Run!" he said.

"What . . . what?"

Thorn hauled her up and pushed her off. "Run!"

Tam saw his chance and bit Shann's wrist. Shann screamed and let the young boy go. Tam took his sister's hand, and seconds later, the pair had vanished into the busy market.

"After them!" spluttered Lukas. He stumbled toward Thorn, blood dripping from his head, and drew a long, curved knife from his belt. "You're going to pay for this."

This is real bad.

Thorn stepped back, but there was nowhere to run. The guards had just lost two slaves; no way were they going to lose a third.

Why'd I do something that stupid? Risking it all for a couple of skinny kids?

The six guards surrounded him. Each was big, armed with a heavy club, and eager to give out a beating after a long, boring day.

Lukas leered, weaving his blade through the air between them. "It's the mines for you, boy. But first, I'm going to take out those green eyes of yours. You won't need eyes down in the mines."

"I won't need no eyes to beat you, neither. I'll just follow the stink," said Thorn.

He balled up his fists. He was going down, but not without a fight.

A horse snorted.

"Ten sovereigns for the boy."

A black stallion pushed past the guards and stopped in front of Thorn. He gazed up. Past the stirrup, the well-worn boots, and the sword hanging from the rider's hip, into a pair of cold black eyes.

It was the swordsman who'd been watching him earlier. He dangled a small leather purse. "Ten."

What was going on? Bewilderment and wild hope fought in Thorn's chest. There was a chance: a small, mad chance he might survive this. *Might.*

"Get out of here," snarled Lukas. "And take that mangy donkey with you."

"Ten."

"Are you thick or something? He's not for sale." Lukas gestured to the guards. "Maybe I should have my lads knock some sense into you, just so you understand."

Thorn's hopes faded. It was seven against one. The swordsman didn't stand a chance.

"Excuse me! Hello! Hello, there!"

It was Merrick, waving at them.

What was the foolish minstrel up to now?

Merrick performed a wild bow, arms flapping everywhere, and bending so low his nose almost touched his knees. "It's a pleasure to make your acquaintance again."

The swordsman nodded. "Merrick, isn't it? It's a shame to see you in chains. Though not much of a surprise."

Merrick beamed. "I am flattered you remember me, Master Tyburn."

The name hit the guards like a battering ram. A couple of them retreated, and Lukas's face turned ashen. "Ty-Tyburn?"

They're scared of him.

Tyburn tossed the bag to the ground. "Have the boy cleaned up and brought to the Mermaid Inn, tonight. And shave his head. I can see the lice dancing from here."

"Hey! I ain't got no lice!" Thorn shouted. He'd only washed his hair last month!

"The boy needs to be made an example of. He needs to be punished," said Lukas, scowling.

Tyburn leaned forward, his fingers casually brushing his sword hilt. "Did you say something?"

Lukas gulped and shook his head.

They ain't scared; they're terrified.

Merrick cleared his throat. Loudly.

"I'll take the minstrel, too," added Tyburn. He fished out another coin. "Here's a crown."

Just a crown? A crown don't buy you a skinny pig.

But the slave master didn't complain. "Unchain the minstrel," he muttered.

The guard blinked, confused.

"Do it!"

Thorn couldn't believe it. He was free. Just like that.

Or was he?

No one paid ten sovereigns without wanting *something* in return.

"Think you've got off lightly, don't you?" said the slave master as he undid Thorn's manacles. "You have no idea."

"I know you ain't putting me down the mines."

"There are worse places than the mines."

Thorn rubbed his now free wrists. They hurt, but it was a good hurt. "No, there ain't."

"Do you know who Tyburn is?"

"Never heard of him till now." Thorn grinned. "But I saw how you wet yourself when he looked at you."

"You really are as green as grass. Tyburn's an executioner."

"Executioner?"

"Every Great House has one. It's the executioner's job to eliminate any threat to the ruling family. Sometimes that's done by heading up an army, but that's not Tyburn's style. He'll put a drop of poison in your cup or a knife in your back. He's a man without honor."

"That's almost funny—a slaver talking about honor like he knows what it means." Still, that wasn't exactly good news. Thorn looked over at Tyburn. "Why does he want me? Who does he serve?"

Lukas smiled, and it wasn't pleasant. "Look at him. What color does he wear?"

Tyburn's clothing was old, comfortable, and muddy, but from his boots to his tunic to his gloves it was all just one color.

Black.

The slave master was right. There *were* worse places than the mines.

Tyburn served House Shadow.

THREE

"Sit." Tyburn pushed a plate across the table. "Eat."

A whole roasted chicken, its skin crispy golden, sat in a gravy sea surrounded by islands of peas and turnips. The smells made Thorn's mouth water and stomach growl.

"As good as new and lice-free," said Lukas, rubbing Thorn's now hairless head. "That coat is fur-lined. And those boots are as stout as any you could hope for. He could walk a thousand miles in those boots." Lukas smacked his lips loudly. "Thirsty work, climbing that hill. Could do with something to wet my gullet before the long trek back down. What d'you say, Master Tyburn?"

"Get lost," replied Tyburn.

Lukas hesitated, as if he couldn't believe what he was hearing.

"You still here?" asked Tyburn, not even looking up from his own meal.

"Yeah, you heard him," added Thorn. "So just hurry up and get lost. Now."

Lukas's eyes darkened, then he left, slamming the door behind him.

Tyburn glanced at Thorn. "I said, sit. Eat."

Thorn sat. The gravy was chocolate dark and thick, and the chicken's skin was thinner than pastry flakes. The smell made him dizzy. He picked up his fork, trembling with excitement.

Then he put the fork down. "Why? Why all this food?"

"You're not hungry?"

"You're trying to fatten me up, ain't you? Make me round and plump so you can feed me to your masters, the Shadows. Am I gonna be served with gravy, too?"

Tyburn frowned. "You think the Shadows eat boys like you?"

"Don't they?"

"Of course not." Tyburn tore off a strip of chicken. "The Shadows have delicate palates. You'd only give them food poisoning. Now eat."

That wasn't the answer he wanted, but hunger won over caution. Thorn grabbed a drumstick and bit into the juicy white meat. His taste buds, overwhelmed by the first decent food in months, burst with fire, and he gulped down a mug of watery mead. His tongue swam within the honey-flavored drink.

Thorn shoveled in peas and wedges of turnips, barely drawing breath between mouthfuls. As soon as he emptied his mug, it was refilled, and he guzzled that down, too. When he finished one plate, another landed, just as mountainous with hot food. Thorn attacked it like a wolf at winter's end.

His belly ached, but that didn't stop him. Gravy dripped from his fingers, and he licked them clean. *More* food arrived—a raspberry and apple pie with pastry thicker than his thumb and coated in custard. He broke the pie apart with his spoon, and his eyes followed the steam rising out of the cracks before he scooped a large bite into his mouth. The pie burned, but he didn't care.

"Where's Merrick?"

"Gone."

Thorn gulped. "Gone? Where's he . . . gone?"

Tyburn smirked. "You want to know if he's gone or . . . *gone?* Do I have that right?"

"Yeah. Gone to get some bread, or gone to rest in the dirt for a real long time?"

"I haven't killed him, if that's what's worrying you."

Thorn shook his head as he kept downing peas. "Don't you want him as your minstrel?"

"Have you heard the man sing?" asked Tyburn.

Thorn smiled. "Sounded like a bag of cats."

"Then you know why I don't want him as my minstrel."

As he ate, Thorn cast sidelong glances at Tyburn, sizing up the man who had bought him.

Tyburn didn't look like much. Stringy hair, a scarred face, and a cropped gray beard over a hard, bony jaw. He stood not much higher than Thorn—Thorn's dad was taller—and had a wiry build. He was old, too—over forty. Where Thorn came from, that was graveyard old.

But there was a saying back home, one his grandpa used a lot: *There's a bit of wolf even in a mongrel.*

"Seen enough, boy?" asked Tyburn. "Or d'you want to stare some more?"

"I ain't staring," snapped Thorn. He lowered his gaze and went back to the serious task of stuffing his face.

He only stopped after his third helping. He groaned as he tried to give his belly room to stretch out.

The executioner's own plate was empty, and he sat, pipe lit, watching.

"How old are you?" asked Tyburn.

"Twelve, Master."

Tyburn pointed to the amulet around Thorn's neck. "What's that?"

Thorn slapped his hand over it. "It ain't worth nothing."

"It looks like a carpenter's mark. Is it?"

Slowly, Thorn lowered his hand. Tyburn didn't want it; he was just interested in it. "Yeah. My dad carved it for me. Me and the rest of our family."

"Your father a carpenter, then?"

"Woodcutter. Does a bit of carpentry. Doors, wagons, and the like. He puts this acorn design on 'em so folks know who made it."

That wasn't Dad's only trade, but Tyburn didn't need to know about the *other* one.

"D'you earn enough just chopping down trees?"

"We got a few animals," said Thorn. "Chickens and swine and such. We help the local farmers a bit. Picking apples, gathering hay. Clearing the ground for the plow. It ain't hard work, and it puts bread in our bellies."

"That all? Nothing on the side?"

"No," lied Thorn.

"Show me your hands."

Thorn laid open his palms. Tyburn held each, pressing his thumbs against the hard calluses. "So you're used to axes—that's obvious. And these. Archers have similar lumps."

Thorn didn't like these observations. They were too close to the truth. "And so does every person who uses a shovel."

"What about a quill? You know your letters?"

"Never had no need. Trees don't write and pigs don't read."

He wished he did, though. His sisters had learned to read and write, but Thorn hadn't been interested, not when there were trees to climb and streams to fish in. Now? If he had his letters, he'd be able to write back home. And hear the news. News he *needed* to know.

Thorn pulled his hands back. "What do you want from me?"

"This and that."

"That ain't no answer."

Tyburn dug his thumb into his pipe, raising a glow from the smoldering tobacco. "Do you know what an executioner does, boy?"

"Is this a trick question?"

"I deal with threats to House Shadow, the family I've sworn to protect. Some are easy to spot; others are hidden. So I ask questions and listen to answers. I listen *very* carefully. That's how I know what's a threat, and what's not. You understand what I'm saying?"

"That you think I'm a threat?"

"That I know when I'm being lied to." Tyburn stood up. "Get some sleep. We've a long journey ahead of us."

They went northwest along the Cliff Road, above the crashing waves and below a sky dripping cold drizzle. Tyburn high up on his saddle, and Thorn tagging along on a donkey. The boy buried his chin deep into the fur of his coat. By his reckoning, it was late September. Back home, the heat of summer would still be lingering in the breeze. Here, farther north, the wind already carried the bite of winter. They traveled, one day into the next, in silence.

Thorn understood silence. He and his dad would sit in the forest, waiting, not saying anything from dawn till dusk.

But Tyburn's silence was different. It weighed on Thorn, making him want to fill it. He kept his mouth firmly shut the first few days, but by the fourth, he needed to speak, just to hear a sound between them. So, as he and Tyburn were having breakfast at a roadside inn, Thorn spoke.

"Where are we going?" he asked.

"Home."

"Home?" Thorn blurted. His heart jumped. "To Stour?"

"Stour? Is that where you come from?"

You fool. He's not talking about your *home; he's talking about his.*

"Yeah, Master," said Thorn cautiously. "It's a village in the Free Duchies. It ain't big."

But it had everything Thorn wanted. Trees with the reddest, juiciest apples in the world. A river to swim in during the summer and skate on when the snow fell. A pond he and his brothers would spend whole days at catching frogs, and his home: a small, two-room timber house with a straw-thatched roof built by his dad when he'd married his mom.

"Near Herne's Forest, isn't it?"

Why was Tyburn so interested? "I suppose."

"Best you forget it," said Tyburn. "You've a new home now. Castle Gloom."

"Is it far?"

"We take the old road into Raven's Wood. After a fortnight or so, we'll cross the River Styx, and we're in Gehenna."

Gehenna. A country of misty forests and craggy mountains, where the sun never shone and the dead walked.

Why couldn't he have been rescued by one of the Solars? Now *that* was a great Great House. Ancient enemies to the Shadows, their knights were the noblest of all men. The ruler, Duke Solar, had twelve daughters and each was the most beautiful woman in all of the world. That didn't make a lot of sense, but Merrick, who said he'd met them, swore it was true.

Thorn could never become a knight, but he'd make a good squire. He'd look after the horses, clean the armor, and tend the weapons. He'd cheer his knight at jousts and tournaments, and he'd serve at feasts and see these beautiful daughters for himself.

That would be a good life.

But what was he doing instead? Heading off to a land of tombs and graveyards, where he'd probably be sent to work in the kitchens, chopping up corpses for the oven.

"What's Lord Shadow like?" asked Thorn. Merrick hadn't said much about Gehenna's ruler.

"Dead." Tyburn's eyes narrowed. "He was killed five months ago. Gehenna is ruled by his daughter now. Lilith Shadow."

"Lilith? What sort of name is that?"

"It means *Mother of Monsters*."

Thorn gulped. He could picture her. A hideous troll with a long warty nose, green skin, and iron teeth. Probably ate children for supper.

Tyburn dropped a few pennies onto the table. "Let's get going."

Into Raven's Wood. Sounded big.

Thorn smiled. He liked woods, and the bigger the better.

Tyburn was half-right. Stour wasn't just *near* Herne's Forest; it was connected to it, a part of the world's oldest, largest forest.

Almost from the day he was born, Thorn had accompanied his dad into the woods, and he had learned more than just how to cut down trees. *Much* more.

Castle Gloom his new home? Never.

Stour was home. And he'd been gone long enough.

It's time I went back, and no executioner's gonna stop me.

FOUR

I'll wait till he's asleep. Real good and snoring.

With any luck he'd get a half day's head start before Tyburn even knew he was gone.

They'd left Cliff Road, turning away from the sea and into the trees. By lunchtime the scent of brine was gone, and now the air was thick with pine and the smell of damp earth and rotten bark. They followed a rivulet that twisted and frothed between mossy rocks and fallen branches. The dense canopy cast their route into twilight, and that suited Thorn fine. With the ferns and the uneven ground, you could disappear within ten yards.

Tyburn stopped his horse and looked around him. "You hungry?"

Thorn nodded.

Two months of living on slop not fit for pigs had left Thorn with a gnawing, constant hunger. Sometimes he wondered if he'd ever feel full again.

Tyburn squinted. "My eyes aren't so good in this light. Tell me what you see."

Thorn jumped off his donkey, thankful to stretch his legs and shake the ache out of his backside. He searched the ground and picked up some dark rabbit droppings. Fresh. "It's a trail. There must be a warren nearby." He looked along the shallow trench through the tall grass. "They must take this path down to the stream to drink."

"You know how to set a trap?"

"No, Master," lied Thorn.

Tyburn slid off his own saddle and inspected the reeds along the bank. He plucked out a handful. "Strange, a woodcutter's son who knows so much about the habits of rabbits but not how to catch them."

Me and my big mouth. He did that on purpose.

Speaking of traps, Tyburn had laid one for him, and he'd run straight into it.

Thorn tried to cover up his mistake. "We should have bought the fish from that fisherman we passed a while back."

"I've spent a month on the Sword Coast. I'm tired of fish. I want rabbit."

Tyburn twisted the reeds into a loop, using grass stalks for string. He tied one end to the top of a flimsy branch, then he bent it down, wedging it into place with a simple wooden peg. Tyburn sprinkled grass around the loop so it couldn't be seen. The whole thing took a few minutes. It was a good snare, but Thorn would have put it another few yards closer to the stream; rabbits were less wary when they smelled water.

Tyburn brushed the dirt off his trousers. "We'll camp down by the stream. Off this path."

So, by nightfall, Thorn and Tyburn sat eating spit-roasted rabbit.

The stars made their appearance between the cracks in the rain clouds. The moon was a sharp sickle, a silver blade slicing open the blackness.

There's the High King's Crown. And the Manticore's Tail.

The stars here were the same back home. For a moment, lying under his blanket with the campfire warming his face, Thorn could close his eyes and almost, almost, imagine he *was* home.

The donkey and horse wandered nearby, drinking and snacking as it suited them. The campfire flickered red and crackled as Tyburn fed it more twigs. Then he settled down, head resting on his saddle and blanket pulled up over his shoulders. His sword lay beside him.

Thorn knew what would happen next. A meal, a warm fire, and then, under a thick blanket, Tyburn, like all old men, would begin nodding off.

Soon enough the executioner's eyes drooped, his chin fell down to his chest, and after a few minutes, his breath was murmuring through his mustache.

I'll give him a bit longer, just to be sure.

At last, the only sound in the night was Tyburn's soft snores.

Hardly daring to breathe, Thorn drew aside his blanket and got to his feet. His eyes stayed on Tyburn, watching for the slightest flicker of his eyelids.

Thorn's boots creaked, and he froze.

Tyburn shifted, grunted, and that was all.

Phew.

Now what?

It would take coin to get home, but Tyburn's purse was on his belt. No way could Thorn get that. He needed something he could sell at a market.

The sword?

Swords sold for plenty, even plain ones.

He crept across the small camp, lowering each foot slowly, wary of twigs, just like his dad had taught him. The branches bent, but did not snap. He followed the first step with another, then another. It seemed as though the sun would come up before he reached the sword, but better slow and quiet than fast and loud.

Finally, he crouched by the executioner's side.

Tyburn didn't move.

Thorn's breath trembled in his throat. His hands, sweaty, tightened around the leather-bound hilt, and he lifted the sword. It was heavy.

Thorn rested it on his shoulder, the same way he carried his father's ax.

Sell the sword and buy passage back to Stour.

It didn't matter how long it took. Mom and his three brothers and two sisters would be there, that was for sure.

He should have stayed and looked after everyone, like his dad had told him to. It was Thorn's job to put meat on the table, something to add to the pot along with turnips and onions from Mom's vegetable garden. He'd been gone too long.

And maybe, *maybe*, Dad would be there, too.

I'll hug him and tell him how sorry I am for everything.

Things would be different this time around.

Tyburn's horse, Thunder, nudged Thorn, wanting to know where he was going. Thorn rubbed his muzzle. "Shh. Let your master sleep. You stay here and be quiet, all right?"

Thorn really wanted to take him, but a peasant riding a warhorse would attract all the wrong sort of attention.

He moved cautiously, using what little moonlight there was to avoid trenches and twigs and potholes. A twisted ankle now and his plans would be ruined.

An owl hooted.

Thorn glanced back. Even the glow of the campfire had disappeared. He smiled. Tyburn would never find him.

I'm going home.

He checked the moss on the tree trunk. It always grew on the north side. The Cliff Road was to the south. Not far.

A branch creaked ahead of him.

It wasn't the wind. It wasn't a deer exploring at night. Animals weren't so clumsy.

A twig snapped, and a man muttered a foul curse.

Slowly, inch by inch, Thorn sank down behind a bush, down onto his haunches. He slid the sword off his shoulder and laid it on the earth.

Foliage rustled ahead of him. Moonlight glinted on the edge of a steel blade. Men skulked along the path.

"Where are they?" asked one.

How many were there? It was hard to tell in the shadows.

"The fisherman said they took this path," came the reply. "He tried to sell them some fish."

"This is Tyburn we're talking about," said another. "I've a bad feeling about this, Lukas."

Lukas? Oh no.

Finally, Thorn could make them out. There were seven in all.

The slave master grabbed the guard's collar. "He's just one man. And he doesn't know we're coming."

They brandished swords and axes, and each wore some piece of scavenged armor—a dented breastplate or a rusty helmet. Two carried loaded crossbows. When they came for slaves, they brought clubs, nets, and chains.

They ain't here to catch Tyburn; they're here to murder him.

"Think about it, lads," said Lukas, his scarred face ghoulish in the moonlight. "We'll be the fellas what killed Tyburn." He held up his knife for all to see. "And the boy? Him I'm gonna skin alive."

FIVE

"Remember, there's seven of us, and two of them," said Lukas. "Easy pickings."

Steel scraped against steel as weapons were drawn. Armor jangled as a man shrugged.

"Quiet now, lads," warned Lukas. "We don't want to wake them if we don't have to."

They're gonna kill him in his sleep. Cowards.

The bough of the tree groaned, and leaves rustled. The slavers moved away from Thorn, the sound steadily smothered by the foliage.

Thorn listened. Nothing. How far had they gone?

Now what?

He should keep going. They wouldn't find him. Not the slavers and not Tyburn.

Forget Tyburn. He'll be dead in a couple of minutes.

Thorn didn't owe him anything.

The man was an executioner. Tyburn's job was to go looking for trouble. He must have known, sooner or later, trouble would find *him*. The best thing for Thorn would be to stay well out of it.

But something bothered him, like an itch between his shoulder blades. It didn't seem right, letting a man be murdered while he slept, even a man like Tyburn.

Maybe he'd wake up. The slavers were making plenty of noise, so it seemed. Tyburn's camp was off the path. Maybe they'd miss it.

Just go. Leave them to it.

That was the sensible, *smart* thing to do.

No. Never gonna happen.

It didn't matter who Tyburn was. Murder was murder.

Thorn needed to get back. He winced each time a branch rustled and a brittle twig snapped underfoot, expecting a battle cry or an ax in the dark. But he met no one and soon reached the edge of the campsite.

The fire was down to a few glowing embers, but he could just see the form of Tyburn, still asleep under his blanket, his face turned away.

"Tyburn," Thorn whispered from behind a bush, "wake up." He scanned the trees anxiously. Lukas had to be nearby.

"Wake up," he said, a little louder this time.

What was wrong with Tyburn? Maybe it was his age. Old men slept longer and deeper. Thorn picked up a stone and tossed it. It struck Tyburn's back, but the man slept on.

"Wake up!"

I'll throw him his sword. Then he'll have a chance.

Thorn looked all around him. Where *was* the sword? He thought he had it with him!

Cold horror rose from his belly. He'd put it down when he'd hidden from Lukas. And left it.

The bushes opposite rustled. Shadows moved and steel shone.

"Tyburn!" Thorn yelled.

Lukas and his men rushed into the camp. The crossbows thrummed, and two quarrels flew true into Tyburn's body.

"Tyburn!"

One of the guards, a big brute with a black beard, buried his ax in the sleeping man. "I've got him!"

Lukas stabbed down hard, snarling like a rabid dog.

Thorn backed away. He'd acted too late!

"Well done, men." Lukas swung around, face gleaming with sweat. "Now where's the boy? I heard him shout."

Thorn held still, every muscle motionless and holding his breath so not even the leaves beside him moved.

They killed Tyburn, and I let it happen.

He was only a few yards away. They'd find him, and it would have all been for nothing.

Lukas laughed and kicked the remains. "Not so tough now, are you, Tyburn?"

The guard with the ax grinned. "Let's have a look." He lifted up the torn blanket.

The grin froze. His eyes widened. "Lads . . ."

There was no body under the blanket—just a pile of clothes and the saddle arranged to resemble a sleeping man.

Tyburn stepped out from behind a tree, a thick branch in his hands. He swung, swung like a woodcutter chopping down a stubborn tree, all shoulders and hips to give the blow as much force as possible. The branch smashed the man's skull with a sickening, wet crack.

Tyburn heaved the branch up, shattering the jaw of another man and lifting him clean off his feet.

The remaining five surrounded him, swords, axes, and daggers in their sweaty palms. Tyburn held the branch loosely in his.

"Run or die," said Tyburn. "Your choice."

That spurred them into action.

Nothing more I can do here.

Thorn ran.

Shouts broke out behind him. Yells and violent roars and the sounds of weapons clashing. Something large and heavy landed in the stream with a mighty splash.

Thorn stumbled through the woods, not caring which way he was going as long as it was away from the fighting.

A man screamed.

Thorn heard a loud thud. The screaming stopped.

He knew the sounds of the forest. Leaves rustling and twigs snapping as something fled in a panic. It might be a deer that smelled wolf or saw a hunter, but here it was a man, fleeing for his life. His eyes wide in fear of what was behind him.

Steel bit wood. Thorn had heard that a million times before. But this wasn't his dad chopping down a tree. Someone had tried to chop down Tyburn with his sword. And missed.

Bad mistake.

The next sound was a sharp crack that made Thorn wince. That was no branch breaking—that was bone.

The ground gave way, and Thorn tumbled head over heels, plowing down a mud-slicked slope. He banged his head and skinned his chin as he rolled down into a deep trench, coming to a halt in a pile of soggy leaves.

Ow . . .

He lay there, panting, his head spinning. The only noise was his own breath.

Was the fight over?

Thorn tried to grab hold of the earth on the side of the pit, but it crumbled away. The few roots sticking out were too slick. He was stuck down here.

Great. Just great. How much worse can it get?

Thorn heard footsteps approach.

Clearly a LOT worse.

Someone had won, but who? Slaver or executioner?

Knowing his luck, which had been bad since the day he'd left home and had grown worse with each mile, it would be Lukas. By tomorrow, he'd be back in chains working down in the mines with no eyes.

A silhouette appeared at the top of the ridge.

Tyburn looked down at him, bruised but very alive, and holding a blood-spattered branch. "Need a hand?"

"You . . . you killed 'em all?"

"How many were there?" asked Tyburn.

"Seven."

"Then yes, I killed them all."

Seven armed men killed with nothing but a stick. No wonder everyone's afraid of him.

How could he act so . . . normal? When he had so much blood on his hands? "Don't it bother you none? Killing those men?"

"Does cutting down trees bother you?"

"It ain't the same."

"One day you might think differently." Tyburn reached down. "Grab hold, and I'll pull you up."

"No. I like it down here," said Thorn.

"Don't be foolish. Come take my hand."

"Then what?"

Tyburn frowned. "What do you mean?"

"I ran off. I ain't coming up if you're just gonna bash my brains out."

"You came back. That's . . . not what I expected."

"I ain't gonna let a man be murdered in his sleep."

"Even a man like me?"

Was Tyburn smiling? If so, then it was the scariest smile he'd ever seen.

"So you gonna let me go?" He'd tried to save Tyburn, even if the executioner hadn't really needed saving. "That would be fair."

"Unfortunately, life's not fair, so I'll be hanging on to you a while longer." Tyburn tossed the branch aside and raised his empty hands to show he was unarmed. "How's that? Make you feel better?"

"No, not really." But what choice did Thorn have? He did as Tyburn asked, and a moment later, they were standing side by side at the lip of the trench.

Tyburn faced him, his hands on his hips. "Planning to run away again the moment I turn my back?"

"No, Master. No, I ain't."

Tyburn snorted. "You're a poor liar, boy."

All those months of misery boiled over as Thorn glared at the executioner. "Yes, I'm going to run! You might have bought me, but where I come from, men are free. And that's where I'm going. Back home."

"How?"

"I'll get a ship. Sail across the sea."

"Which sea?"

"There's more than one?" Was the world that big?

"You're brave, I'll give you that. But you're stupid. You barge into trouble with no idea of how to get out of it."

"So?"

"So what'll happen is this: even if I gave you a bag of gold and a fond farewell right now, you'd be robbed or end up back where I found you. These are lawless times, boy." He eyed Thorn curiously. "They can make even good men desperate."

"Then what can I do?"

"Tell me the truth."

Thorn bit his lip, unsure if the truth would make things better, or worse. Was Tyburn his friend or his foe? "Give me one reason to trust you."

Tyburn jerked his thumb over his shoulder, back toward the campsite. "I can give you seven. If I were your enemy, you'd be over there, with them."

He had a point.

"All right," said Thorn, "I'll tell you the truth."

Where to start? Then he saw Tyburn's blood-spattered branch. "I did something bad—real bad." He closed his eyes, and he could picture the day so clearly, as if he was standing there again, the blood fresh and wet on his hands.

"I did it, but my dad took the blame. I should have said something. I should have told 'em it was me what did it." Thorn wiped his face of the tears he'd held back for months. "But I was afraid. I . . . was a coward."

"Then what?"

"They were gonna hang him." Thorn gulped as he remembered the soldiers throwing a rope over a tree bough. "But my dad got away. That's why I left home. I had to find him. I went from village to village asking, but no one had seen him. Then one night the slavers got me. They bundled me on a ship, and that's how I ended up here."

Tyburn's gaze didn't leave his. His dark eyes were two pieces of obsidian, giving nothing away.

He's waiting for more. He knows I ain't telling him everything.

"That's the whole story," said Thorn, crossing his arms defiantly.

"So now you're going home, without finding your father?"

"I weren't meant to be gone this long. I thought I'd find him before the end of summer." Thorn felt the cold wind upon his neck. It was autumn already. He was the oldest of six children, and if Dad wasn't back by now, it was his job to look after them. Mom had her hands full looking after the little ones. He'd promised the local farmer he'd help bring in the harvest in exchange for five sacks of flour, enough to make bread throughout the winter. But the harvest was last month and he'd not been there.

"I'll make you a deal," said Tyburn. "There are no slaves in Gehenna. You serve as my squire for a year and a day, and I'll give you gold and safe passage home."

"A year?" Way too long. "Six months."

"A year and a day."

"Eight months. Eight months is fair."

"A year and a day." Tyburn started walking back toward their camp.

Thorn kicked a pile of leaves in frustration. "Why me?"

Tyburn called over his shoulder. "I have my secrets, too."

CASTLE GLOOM

SIX

"Get up, Lily."

"No." Lily pulled her heavy quilt over her head. "I'm sleeping." She nestled down deeper into her cocoon, deeper into the comforting darkness.

"It's late," said Mary, her nanny.

Lily peeked out. "It's dark."

"Ha! Of course it's dark. This is Castle Gloom. Listen to me, Lilith Shadow, you will get up *right* now." The nanny tossed the quilt onto the stone floor.

"Mary!"

"Up. Now."

Lily thrust her head under her pillow. "Don't. Want. To. Get. Up!"

"I swear by the Six Princes, you're getting up if I have to drag you by your hair," said Mary. "You know what day this is?"

"Don't care."

Lily felt a scrabbling on her pillow and something wet—a nose—pressed against her own. A pair of big brown eyes gazed at her.

"And what do you think, Custard?" asked Lily.

Now that he had her attention, her three-month-old black Labrador puppy began wagging his tail and jumping up and down on the bed. Lily gathered him into her arms. "You're right. Mary is a mean old woman." Custard yapped and licked her cheek.

"Get that slobbering beast off the bed," said Mary as she examined Lily's tangled hair.

"Ouch!" cried Lily, shying away. "What are you doing?"

"Tsk. Will you look at this?" Mary brandished a twig she'd just pulled from a snarl. "You've been climbing the apple trees with that servant boy, what's his name . . . Wade?"

"I don't know what you're talking about."

"And what if you'd fallen out and broken your neck, my girl?" Mary sighed. "It's not that I'm bothered in the slightest, but a lot of people depend on you."

"Don't care." Lily rubbed Custard under his chin. He really was a silly dog with a silly name. "*Ow!*"

Mary inspected a second twig. "'Don't care.' 'Don't care.' That's all I ever hear from you nowadays. You have responsibilities."

"Really? I thought all I had to do was sit still, look pretty, and keep my mouth shut," said Lily. "My responsibilities are stupid."

"You? Keep your mouth shut? That'll be the day." Mary drew a lock away from Lily's ear. "People look up to you. What you do, what you say, matters. They want to be proud of you and now, with . . . with your father and brother gone, it's up to you to bring them into better days. The Six know how much our realm has suffered." Mary stroked Lily's arm. "It's your job to look after the people of Gehenna, and it's my job to look after you."

Lily took Mary's hand. She knew her nanny was right. "You shouldn't worry about me."

"Not worry? Child, I've worried about you since the moment your cries first filled this very room. If I don't look after you, who will?"

Mary's skin was thin. Lily drew her fingertip along a blue vein. She gazed up at the lined face, into the sparkling eyes that now sat deeper within the wrinkles. Lily brushed a strand of silver hair aside. "And who looks after you, Mary?"

"I don't need looking after. Anyway, who'd want to look after an old crone like me?"

"I would," said Lily, deadly serious. "I'd never let anything happen to you."

Mary laughed.

"What's so funny? I am descended from the Six Princes. I have the blood of the greatest sorcerers flowing through—"

"And what's this doing on the floor?" said Mary, picking up her dressing gown. "I've only just washed it, and it's got paw prints all over it."

"Mary! You're not listening!" snapped Lily. "I might have awesome magical powers, and you're just—"

"Magical powers? Don't talk nonsense. A girl with magical powers. I've never heard such a thing."

"I *could* have magical—"

"Sulking is not a magical power."

Lily glared.

Mary was not impressed. "Your father—may the Six Princes guard his soul—looked at me with those same eyes whenever he had to do something he didn't like. As gray as storm clouds, with a lot of lightning behind them." Mary snapped her fingers. "Rose, lay out Lady Shadow's clothes."

"Yes, miss."

Rose? Lily hadn't seen her maid working quietly in the corner. The girl was—had been—Lily's best friend. Back when she was plain Lily Shadow, with no prospect of becoming a future leader. The two girls would dress up in each other's clothes and pretend to be sisters. That friendship had ended five months ago, when Lily became Lady Shadow, ruler of Gehenna and mistress of Castle Gloom. Now all she got from Rose were curtseys and "Yes, m'lady" and "No, m'lady."

"Rose, are the clothes ready?" asked Mary.

"Yes, miss."

"What about the Mantle?"

"Yes, miss." Rose nodded to the corner where, lit by two huge iron candelabras, there stood a mannequin wearing what looked like swirling black smoke.

Lily groaned. "The Mantle of Sorrows? But it's itchy."

"Don't care," mimicked Mary as she carried a taper from candle to candle, shielding it from any stray draughts.

Soft amber light blossomed, illuminating the corners and the carved niches in the ancient walls, the faded tapestries and cobweb-coated statues. Mary blew out the taper. "There. That's better."

"I don't belong here," Lily said to herself. This was her parents' bedroom. The table was where her father used to sit, the old armchair creaking as he moved to dip his quill in his inkpot. Her mother would stand in front of the full-length mirror with its frame of black iron. Lily had loved to watch her mother get ready, weaving a string of black diamonds into her hair. She'd told Lily that one day those diamonds would be hers. A day Lily had thought would be far, far in the future.

The cold gems now lay waiting for her on the dressing table.

Lily didn't want to wear any of her mother's jewelry. It felt as if Lily was robbing her tomb.

"Will you hurry up and just sit in front of the mirror?" said Mary, waving a silver-handled hairbrush. "I've still got to get the rooms ready for our visitors and sort out tonight's feast."

Lily did as she was asked and threw herself down on the chair.

Mary set to work.

"*Ow!* That really hurt!" Custard growled on his owner's lap. "I don't know why I still have you, Mary. I'd be better treated by a . . . a zombie!"

"Oh, is that right?" Mary snorted. "Like the one your grandfather had? What was his name?"

"One-Eyed Ron."

"More like One-Eyed, One-Legged, One-Armed, and finally No-Headed Ron. I was always sweeping up pieces of him." Mary gave Lily's hair another violent, eye-watering yank.

"I said, '*Ow!*'"

"Just sit still. Your mother never fussed like you. Honestly, child, think about who you are, what you represent, before you open your mouth. How many times have I told you? You're Lady Shadow now."

"I'm not." It still hurt, remembering what had happened to her parents and brother. "I was never meant to be."

Mary put her soft, warm palm against Lily's cheek. "I know, child. But you are, and that cannot be changed."

"I would rather practice magic. If I could hear their voices again, just once, Mary . . ."

"Hush, sweetheart. Don't upset yourself."

"I dream about them," said Lily.

Mary smiled. "I sometimes see my boys in my dreams, too. Even though it's been five years, they haven't changed. Still causing trouble."

"There are *other* ways you could see them. . . ." started Lily. She was House Shadow and the blood of necromancers *did* flow through her veins, no matter what Mary thought. "To speak with the dead, even visit—"

The hairbrush clattered on the floor. Mary stared at her, horrified. "You want to enter the Twilight? Have you lost all sense?"

"Grandfather did it. He went and spoke to—"

"And look what happened to him." Mary glared at her. "Now you listen to me, my girl. I do not want any more talk about . . . such things. Ever."

"But, Mary—"

"Ever."

There was no point arguing. Not when Mary had her "war face" on. Lily sat still as her nanny brushed through her black hair in long, smooth strokes, moving from the scalp down to the very tip until it shone like a raven's wing. Lily closed her eyes. She felt the pull and slide as Mary took out the tangles and knots.

I could sit like this forever. Just hide in this room with Mary and Custard. Leave all the horrible world outside. This would be perfect.

"You're as beautiful as your mother," said Mary.

"You always say that."

"Because it's always true."

Lily sprang up and kissed Mary's cheek.

"What was that for?"

Lily blushed. She hadn't meant to act like a little girl. She straightened to all her thirteen years' worth of height, a whole six inches above Mary. "Oh, I just want you to know that I . . . that I'm quite fond of you. After all these years. Yes. Quite fond."

Mary sniffed loudly. Too loudly. "*Quite* fond? How I've longed to hear those words. I think I might faint. I am *quite* overcome. Emotionally." She pointed to her eye. "There. I think that may be a tear."

"You may think you're funny, Mary, but you're not." Why did Lily ever bother trying to be nice to this impossible old woman? She decided to change the subject. "Is Tyburn back yet?"

"Not that I've heard. Do you want me to send a bat?"

"No. Leave it." Why was it taking him so long to track down one man? Or had something happened to him? Something bad?

Don't be foolish. Bad things don't happen to Tyburn. Bad things happened because of Tyburn.

Mary tapped the brush against her palm. "I've got to get down to the kitchens. I've left the red ledger with the cook, and I don't trust her. She can't count to twenty without taking her socks off." She waved toward the clothes Rose was spreading out. "So I need you to get washed and dressed. Your guests will be arriving soon."

"I don't want to see them." She'd been dreading today. She had to find a way out of it. "Tell them I'm sick. Diseased."

"Not see them? What sort of talk is that? You will get dressed and be in the courtyard before sunset. After all, don't you want to meet your new husband?"

SEVEN

A hazy drizzle fell upon the courtyard of Dead Man's Gate. Lily and Mary waited on a newly built podium with a few other nobles—allies to House Shadow—under a wide black canopy. The rest of the household were lined up in the mud, miserable and wet.

The only one having fun was Custard. The puppy yapped and dashed among the impatient lords.

"This is lovely," said Lily. "Standing in the cold rain. Enjoying the icy wind. And the mud. Nice, deep, and squelchy. I'm so glad you forced me out here, Mary."

"You're not standing in the mud. The servants are," Mary replied. She stood beside Lily, clutching the red ledger against her chest. She carried that accounting book everywhere.

"You're right. We should let them go back in and get warmed by the fires. This is pointless. Our guests are late. Cancel the feast."

"Enough," snapped Mary. She rubbed her temples. "You'll be the death of me, my girl. You're marrying Gabriel Solar, and that's that. It's . . . it's for the good of Gehenna."

"Why can't it wait?" asked Lily. "I'm thirteen, Mary."

"Other noble houses often arrange early weddings between their off-spring. In the Sultanate of Fire, they do it at birth." Mary picked a stray thread off her gown. "Anyway, this is merely the engagement feast. You won't actually marry for another three years."

"But I don't even know Gabriel."

"You've seen his portraits. And what about the minstrels' stories? They have only praise for the young lord."

"Give a minstrel enough silver, and he'll tell you a frog is a prince."

"We'll know soon enough." Mary glanced at Lily. "I wish you'd wear a *little* color. Just some red lipstick. Who would really notice?"

"We are House Shadow, black is our color."

Black for her heritage.

Black for mourning. For Father, Mother, and her brother, Dante.

And the Mantle of Sorrows did itch. Really badly.

"They're only here for three days," said Mary. "I only need you to be polite and smile and keep that sharp tongue of yours under control for three days."

"I'll *try*."

A host of bats swirled overhead, emerging from their hidden places along the castle walls and towers. Big and small, they flapped and shrieked as they chased insects in the twilight. Other noble houses used birds for hunting and message carrying. She couldn't understand why. Bats were beautiful and smart.

"I wish they'd get a move on," grumbled Baron Sable. The gruff old man was smoothing down his walrus mustache, a sure sign of annoyance. "I should be out on patrol."

"How goes your progress, Baron?" asked Lily.

"Badly, m'lady. There have been raids along the River Lacrimae; farms have been burned. Some grave robbing, too."

"Grave robbing? Do you know who's doing it?"

"Bandits, mainly. Now that there's peace between us and the Solars, the countryside is filled with unemployed mercenaries. It doesn't take long for them to turn into brigands." He stroked his mustache, twisting the tips into points. "It's usually outsiders who break into the tombs. They've heard that we bury our dead with gifts, so they think they're filled with gold and jewels. They'll be lucky to find more than some old furniture and a few pieces of cracked pottery."

"Make sure these thieves are punished," said Lily. Things must be bad if people were stealing from the dead. "What of the pirate raids?"

"Ah. Now that is strange. They've stopped." Sable smiled. "Captain Barracuda is dead."

"Good news at last."

Sable wasn't finished. "Stranger still was the manner of his death. He drowned."

"Sailors drown, Baron. It doesn't seem strange to me."

"In his bathtub, m'lady. In the port of Cutlass. I understand Tyburn went to Cutlass."

Lily said nothing. She'd learned long ago that it was best not to dwell on the activities of her executioner.

Sable got the hint. "Still, it's going to be a harsh winter for some."

"Give the farmers grain from our stores," said Lily.

"That grain was earmarked for Glimmer Hall, m'lady," replied Sable. "It's coin we sorely need."

"The needs of my people come first."

"Of course." Sable bowed. "I'll see to it."

The needs of my people.

Her people. It still didn't feel right, thinking about the Gehennish like that. They'd been her father's people. After that they should have been Dante's people. Anybody's but hers. How could she be expected to look after a whole country? She had her hands full looking after Custard.

Could they see how scared she was? How lonely?

Everyone was too busy to see. Mary fussed about the castle keeping track of the maids, and the money being spent by the cook, and whether they could save on candles. Good old loyal Baron Sable had the borders to guard. And Tyburn . . . he was Tyburn. Did he truly feel anything?

There were plenty of people ready to give her advice, but in the end, *she* was House Shadow now and she was expected to *rule*. If they knew how lost she really was, it would all fall apart.

And that's why I must marry Gabriel Solar.

For peace. The two countries had been at war for generations. House Shadow against House Solar. Darkness against light. It had gone on so long that everyone just thought that was the way things were. Every family here had lost someone. Both of Mary's sons had died fighting against the Solars.

Do they think I'm betraying them by making peace with our enemies?

There had been little celebration at the news of the proposed match, more weary resignation. Better to join the two houses through marriage than be conquered.

Maybe it *was* for the best. Life could improve. Solar gold would allow people to rebuild their farms, buy grain and livestock. She might even repair Castle Gloom. Lumina had better access to the sea, so trade would flourish. They'd have goods and minstrels traveling up Merchant's Road again instead of penniless beggars and crippled soldiers.

Everyone knew that face-to-face, sword-to-sword, Gehenna could never defeat Lumina. The Solars had too many troops, too many horses, too many of everything.

Gehenna wasn't rich. It had craggy mountains whose peaks lay in mist all year long, and summers here were short. Its ground was hard and stony—too poor for crops—and the population was sparse and thinly spread.

Its power had never lain in its armies or wealth. Its power was in magic. Iblis Shadow, Lily's father, had been a great sorcerer, and his magic had protected Gehenna's borders.

Now he was dead, leaving the country all but defenseless.

If only Father had taught me magic alongside Dante. Then things would be different.

But it was the eldest son's duty to learn the magic of darkness and be the next Lord Shadow. From Lily's first scream at the world she'd been given a very different destiny. Because she'd been born a girl.

Women could not practice magic. The law was ancient and the penalty simple: death.

So House Shadow, one of the six ancient families of sorcerers, was now reduced to a thirteen-year-old girl and a handful of servants.

Castle Gloom had once housed tens of thousands. It wasn't so much a castle as a huge, walled city. Now most of it lay in ruins, home to spiders, bats, and mice.

And Lily loved every inch of it. Every tumbledown wall and tottering tower and dusty statue. She'd named each gargoyle on the Great Hall and climbed up to visit them on their pretend birthdays. She and Dante had spent endless nights feeding baby bats in the caverns under the castle.

How could she not love it? It was her home. It had been her parents' home, her grandparents' and theirs before that, going all the way back, thousands of years, to the time of the Six Princes.

Castle Gloom was as much part of her as her own bones, and she would do anything, *anything*, to protect it.

Even marry her enemy.

"I wish we had more soldiers here," said the baron. "It would make a better impression."

Twenty men stood by the gatehouse, dressed in black armor and trying to look fierce while rain dripped off their noses.

The famous Black Guard. The greatest knights of Gehenna. Lily and her brother had been raised on tales about them. Dante had convinced his father to have a suit of armor made for him, identical in all but size to the one worn by the great Sir Ironside. Legend was that Ironside was eight feet tall and could carry a warhorse on his shoulders. Lily had always had to play Lady Lamia, Ironside's true love. Sometimes she was imprisoned in a tall tower, sometimes in a cave or mighty castle, waiting to be rescued. Lily smiled at the memory. She'd never minded being saved by her big brother.

There were no Sir Ironsides in the Black Guard now. No Sir Blackblades nor Skull Knights.

Just old men and beardless boys, their old armor rattling as they shivered in the icy drizzle.

But Gehenna wasn't only defended by the living. . . .

"Where are the Immortals?" Lily looked around. She knew something was missing. "We have a battalion of them."

Sable shook his head. "The zombie soldiers? None left. It was only your father's magic that kept them going. With his passing, they just . . . fell apart."

"Couldn't we find some ghosts? Just to wail about the gates a bit? I hear there are a few still in Gallowsgate."

"I'm sorry, m'lady."

A door crashed open, and a man stumbled out. He steadied himself against the wall and belched.

Mary sighed. "Your uncle's drunk."

"When is he not?" said Lily.

The man tried to close his wine-stained jacket around his swollen belly. He belched again. Then he saw Lily, and his blotchy face broke into a stupid grin as he stumbled up the steps of the podium. "My dear niece. What a vision!"

"Good evening, Uncle."

Earl Pandemonium Shadow's bloodshot eyes brimmed with tears. "Beautiful. Your parents would be proud." He kissed her cheek, and Lily held her breath so she wouldn't be choked by the fumes.

Light flashed on Merchant's Road. Drums echoed in the wind.

Mary squeezed Lily's hand. "They're here."

EIGHT

Pennants flapped on long white wood lances, and the armor of a hundred knights shone with the brightness of polished mirrors. Their horses were pure ivory with manes of silver.

"The paladins," muttered Baron Sable. "The Solars' elite cavalry."

Then came the musicians and foot soldiers with spears and shields, and ladies in white fur cloaks and silk. Wagons rolled along the rear, drawn by massive draft horses. Wagon after wagon.

"Why are there so many of them? How are we going to feed them all?" exclaimed Mary.

"They want to dazzle us with their strength," said the baron.

The procession wove its way along Merchant's Road between two mounds: Lamentation Hill and the City of Silence.

The City dominated the eastern side of the road and spread all the way to the border of Spindlewood. It had never been measured, but Lily reckoned it was as big as Castle Gloom and within another hundred years would be larger. It was the family graveyard, and every Shadow was buried there, sometimes reluctantly.

Lily knew how the other Great Houses dealt with the dead. They cremated them in the Sultanate. House Typhoon performed sky burials, putting their dead on towers to be devoured by vultures and other carrion birds. House Coral tipped the bodies into the sea.

How could you honor the dead like that?

The Gehennish built tombs. Even the smallest hamlet had homes for the dead. Houses with tables and chairs within, beds made of stone, and portraits or statues of those that had passed into the Twilight and beyond. And the City of Silence had the grandest tombs of all.

Her parents were housed in the newest, along with her brother. Not six months had passed since she'd left food, drink, and gifts within and sealed the doors. The sound of the great stone doors closing forever still echoed her heart.

Bats flocked around Lamentation Hill. They hung off the spindly, twisted trees like so much rotten fruit. Even from this distance, Lily could make out the five tall poles rising up out of its summit and their dreadful decorations. She turned her gaze away.

What did it say about her kingdom that the only main road ran between a place of execution and a graveyard?

"A new age is dawning, Niece," said Uncle Pan with a sigh. "An alliance between the House Solar and Shadow. Between light and darkness. We shall make Castle Gloom great once more."

If you don't squander it all on drink and wild schemes.

That wasn't fair. It had never been easy for her uncle. As firstborn, he should have been ruler of Gehenna. But try as they might, no tutor had been able to teach him even the simplest of spells. Instead, his brother, Iblis, had become Lord Shadow.

Mary spoke. "I'll need to send for more sheep. Two dozen at least, and the farmer will want double for the short notice...."

It would all go in the red ledger. The number of guests and horses, and how much they'd need for food, and what servants they'd be allocated if they hadn't brought their own. She'd even count out every chest and crate, marking down what each contained and the value of every item. As well as the ledger, Mary carried a heavy ring of keys. There had to be a hundred of various sizes and shapes, and they opened every door in the castle.

Every door but one.

Mary ran the household now, and no one thought it strange that a nanny should be in charge of the ancient citadel. After all, few had lived here as long as Mary.

Oversight of the castle had been Lady Shadow's responsibility. Lily had watched her work by candlelight making long lists within the red ledger. She'd often asked Lily to sit with her and help, but Lily had found it much too boring.

All that time she could have spent with her mother was forever lost now, never to be regained.

In rode the paladins, their horses' hooves pounding on the old, thick wood of the drawbridge. Each man was tall and handsome, as if sprung fully formed from a maiden's romantic vision.

Lily looked out over her own troops, her Black Guard. The men wore hand-me-down armor, faded tabards more brown than black, and there wasn't a straight spear among the lot of them. She sighed.

But if the serving girls were swooning over the paladins, Custard was not impressed in the slightest. He was scurrying back and forth along the podium, teeth bared and growling his little growl.

"Someone take control of that animal," snapped Mary. "He's going to get trampled if he's not careful."

Lily bent down and looked sternly at Custard. "Now don't be a naughty dog. You heard Mary."

He leaped into her arms.

"Give him to a servant," said Mary.

Lily hugged her puppy closer.

Mary glowered, but Lily knew she wouldn't risk an argument while all the guests were arriving.

The next rider through Dead Man's Gate was a plump, round-faced boy, the same age as Lily. Dark-skinned, with long, wavy black hair, he wore a long crimson cloak embroidered with wild images of phoenixes and fiery spirits. Gold and amber-studded rings covered his fingers. Surrounded by the Solars, he looked like a blood drop on the snow.

"Why's he shivering?" said Lily. "What's he scared of?"

"He's not scared; he's cold," said Mary.

"Cold? Call this cold? It's practically summer." She peered more closely. "Who is he?"

Uncle Pan frowned. "That's K'leef. He's the fourth son of Sultan Djinn."

"He's from the Sultanate of Fire?" Of course. Look at all that red. Now she was really intrigued. The Sultanate was a thousand miles south of here. "What's he doing in Gehenna?"

"He's a hostage. The Solars captured him some months ago. The duke's keeping him close until a ransom's been paid for the boy's safe return."

"Poor child," said Mary. "No wonder he looks so miserable."

"Put him in the Eclipse bedchambers," said Lily. They were the best guest rooms, and she felt sorry for K'leef. He might be a prisoner, but she could make him comfortable while he was here.

"I'll prepare them myself," said Mary.

"The duke," whispered Pan.

The approaching horseman wore armor that didn't merely shine, but glowed. The breastplate was studded with diamonds fanning out from a silver heart, and sweeping white feathers crowned his helmet. A cloak of glistening silver rested across his shoulders.

Duke Raphael Solar.

No color blemished his skin, and his eyes were a pair of silvery mirrors. His mouth was wide, closed, and humorless, and even though Lily knew he was over seventy years old, he seemed like a young man: straight-backed, sure, and arrogant.

Mary looked around. "Where's the herald? Give him the signal."

Lily nodded to the old man waiting at the end of the podium.

The herald cleared his throat and bowed deeply. "Lords and ladies, may I present Lady Lilith Shadow, scion of the great House of Darkness. Mistress of Castle Gloom, ruler of Gehenna, guardian of the boundary between the lands of the living and dead. Daughter to Lord Iblis Shadow. Granddaughter to Charon Shadow, known as the Twilight Walker. Child of the first and oldest of all the six Great Houses . . ."

"He's pouring it on a bit thick, isn't he?" said Uncle Pan.

Mary spoke. "It's important to remind our guests of who we are."

Good old Mary. Lily smiled as she remembered her family motto: *First there was darkness.*

The herald continued. "M'lady Shadow bids you rest and comfort. May your dreams be fulfilled and your nightmares soothed." He bowed again.

The courtyard fell silent as Duke Solar dismounted and marched up to the podium. He lowered his head in a polite bow. "M'lady Shadow."

Mary nudged Lily, who shook her head, blinking and bewildered. The lord of light was literally dazzling. Lily came to her senses. "Dear Duke, welcome to Castle Gloom. Consider our home . . . yours." The words almost stuck in her throat, but she had to say the formal greeting.

"I was sorry to hear about your misfortune." He made it sound like she'd lost a doll rather than her family. "Despite our history, I had immense respect for your father. Lord Iblis Shadow was a great man. I hope, one day, you will look on me as your new father."

Lily merely smiled. *Yes, when I see pigs flying.*

The duke turned to the knight beside him. "May I present my son, Gabriel?"

Gabriel Solar bowed. Some of her housemaids were giggling behind their hands as they gazed at him.

A glare from Mary shut them up.

The minstrels hadn't been wrong.

All right, he's handsome. Even beautiful.

Gabriel's white-gold locks were held in place by a silver band, and his eyes were sapphire bright. Diamond earrings hung from his ears, and his armor was encrusted with gems. It wasn't armor for a knight but for an actor, theatrical instead of practical. He reached for Lily's hand.

Custard growled.

Gabriel backed away. "What a vile beast. I hope he's not rabid." Then he remembered himself and gave a courtly bow. "Lady Shadow, I am honored to meet you. I look forward to being your lord and master." He coughed discreetly into a white silk handkerchief. "I mean . . . your husband."

NINE

The Great Hall echoed with laughter, music, the voices of hundreds of guests, and barking dogs. The white outfits of the Solars mixed with the black of the Shadows, creating a moving checkerboard over the vast chamber. The feast was in full flow. Custard, the greedy pup, was wandering from table to table, looking up at the guests with his big imploring eyes until they tossed him a lamb chop or a sausage. All were enjoying themselves.

Except Lily. She felt like she was at a funeral: hers.

She sat at the high table at the head of the hall, right in the middle, with Gabriel on her left and Uncle Pan on her right. The suitor wore garments of perfect white, and a bejeweled longsword dangled from his hip. The sword was just like its owner: handsome, but useless.

"Imagine my relief when I finally saw you," said Gabriel, smiling at her. "No one would call you truly beautiful. Your eyes are too large and your nose—a lady should have a small, delicate nose—but still, I am pleasantly surprised!"

Lily smiled even though she was screaming inside.

Gabriel made a sweeping gesture with his arm. "This will all have to change when I rule Gehenna. Windows, the castle shall have windows. Everywhere. And mirrors. Plenty of mirrors. It's all rather gloomy." He snorted. "Did you hear what I just said? Castle Gloom, gloomy? Rather witty, even if I do say so myself." He laughed loudly.

"Very witty," said Pan. "Don't you think, Lily?"

"Half-witty," Lily muttered.

Gabriel wasn't finished. He inspected Lily from head to toe and let out a theatrical sigh. "And your outfit—I've seen better-dressed peasants. I shall have dresses sent from Lumina. I can't have my bride looking like some farmer's wife. They'll be white, of course."

"I am House Shadow. Our color is black, as you well know."

Gabriel answered with a sly smile. "Ah, but you won't be a Shadow once we're married, will you?"

Lily gripped her fork so tightly her knuckles turned white. Would it be so bad if she stabbed him in the neck?

Others around the high table—those dressed in white—joined in with Gabriel's braying. There was a group of white-costumed squires with him, and even though they couldn't have heard him, they laughed long and hard. Gabriel rose and walked over to them.

Thank the Six Princes.

Lily relaxed and lowered her fork. The feast was truly awful, but it had given her a chance to make an important decision.

"I cannot marry Gabriel."

Pan blanched and almost spilled his wine. "Why—why not?"

"I hate him. In fact, I really don't think I've ever hated anyone quite so much, quite so quickly."

"You've only just met. Give it time, and I'm sure—"

"I'll only hate him even more."

"He's just tired after a long journey." Pan offered a sickly, desperate smile. "Be patient. Tonight is merely the engagement feast. The actual wedding isn't until you're both sixteen, three years from now. By then I'm sure Gabriel will be a sensible young man."

Lily faced her uncle. "Cancel the engagement."

"And then what?" Pan's face darkened.

"What do you mean?"

"Grow up, Lily." He shook his head. "I love you like a daughter, but you need to face reality. We are weak. If we don't go through with this, by next week the duke will have his armies at our gates. Within a fortnight the turrets of Castle Gloom will be covered in white flags, not black. You will lose Gehenna."

"Couldn't we sign a peace treaty instead?"

"We have. It's called a marriage contract." He looked into his wine cup. "This is what your father wanted. He arranged this marriage with the duke, just before he died."

The Black Ford Truce. She should have been there when her father and Duke Solar had met along the banks of River Lacrimae, the natural boundary between Gehenna and Lumina. But if she had been present, along with her mother and brother, then she wouldn't be here now. "The marriage was meant to be between Dante and one of the duke's daughters. That was the original plan."

Pan nodded. "Lady Angela Solar. A beauty and a tender heart. She and Dante would have been a fine match. But it was not fated to be."

"It wasn't fate that killed Dante, Uncle. It was brigands."

"And now their heads decorate Lamentation Hill. Tyburn dealt with them."

Lily's gaze hardened. "Tyburn dealt with *some* of them. There's still—"

"The dead are dead, no matter how we might wish it otherwise. It is time we looked to the future, Lily."

"So that's my choice, marriage or war?"

"The needs of your people come first, Lily," said Pan. "How can you subject Gehenna to more war, just because of what you do and do not like? I know you're not that selfish."

How far into the past did the hate go? Everyone knew the legend: Prince Shadow and Prince Solar were twins. They should have been the closest of all the Six Princes. Yet one worshipped the dark, and the other the light, and that difference had led to countless wars through the ages.

The people of Lumina thought the Gehennish were evil for the way they treated their dead, raising them from their endless sleep. Lily knew what it really meant: that the dead were not forgotten—they were still wanted, valued.

The Gehennish thought the Lumineans were warmongers and land-grabbers who believed that anyone who didn't follow their way should be destroyed. How many other lands had been crushed by Solar armies, their languages and cultures wiped out?

There was no point in trying to argue with a Solar. They couldn't understand why everyone else didn't want to be just like them.

"I could defend Gehenna if I'd been allowed to study magic," she said.

Pan groaned. This was an old debate. "You know the law as well as anyone. Women cannot study magic. You might as well ask the sun to rise in the west."

"There has to be a way," said Lily, determined not to give up so easily.

"Don't you think I've tried?" blasted Pan. "If there was another way to become a sorcerer, don't you think I would have found it?"

"I'm sorry, Uncle." She could see the hurt in his eyes. It would be there until the day he died. "Let me marry anyone else. Anyone but Gabriel."

"There is no one else."

Her corset seemed too tight. She pulled at the bone and cloth entrapping her, breathing deeply to clear the dread swelling inside.

"Hey, K'leef!" Gabriel shouted from down the table. He waved a sausage in the air. "Close your eyes and open your mouth!" He tossed the sausage at K'leef's face. It smacked the boy on the cheek.

Gabriel howled with laughter. "Did you see that? Give me something else!"

Lily gritted her teeth.

Gabriel picked up a carrot. "Don't forget your vegetables!"

Lily stood up. She wasn't going to let Gabriel get away with this.

Pan held her wrist. He looked at her pleadingly. "Please, Lily, sit down."

Blood raged in Lily's head as she watched Gabriel's cronies join in, tossing food at K'leef. She pulled herself free of her uncle. "Stop it," she hissed.

Gabriel piled peas onto his spoon and flicked them.

"Stop it."

Gabriel didn't hear her. He rolled a lump of bread in his plate until it was dripping with gravy.

"Stop it!" Lily slammed her fist down.

The blow burst out like a thunderclap. It reverberated between the stone walls over and over.

Everyone, noble and servant, Solar and Shadow, fell silent. Even Custard stopped barking.

All eyes were on Lily.

Gabriel gazed at her, too. "What did you say?" he asked with quiet menace.

This is how wars start.

Lily pushed her lips into a fake smile. "The servants need to clear the table," she said. "It's time for dessert."

Mary clapped, and the servants leaped into action.

"Music," commanded Duke Solar. The orchestra hesitated, then started up again. The murmurs returned and soon the guests were all talking. About her.

"I'm proud of you," whispered Uncle Pan. "That could have gone badly."

"If he's like that now, imagine what he'll be like in three years. In ten."

Pan cleared his throat loudly as Duke Solar sat down beside her. "You look unwell, m'dear."

"She's just excited," said Uncle Pan.

A servant approached and placed four crystal goblets before them, one each for Lily, Gabriel, the duke, and her uncle. Duke Solar raised his. "Consider these an early wedding gift. I hope we shall be celebrating many toasts for years to come. Of anniversaries. Of children."

Lily tried not to vomit.

"To peace," said Duke Solar.

"To peace," said Lily, and she raised the goblet to her lips.

TEN

"Wait," said Uncle Pan. "Listen. They're playing the *Danse macabre*."

The noise of chatter dropped as the orchestra took up the tune. The lute fell to a low, haunting melody, and the drums were steady but soft, the beat of a sleeping heart.

Lily put down her goblet without taking a sip. She knew this tune better than she knew the sound of her own breath.

This was House Shadow's dance. Legend was, the first Lord Shadow had danced it with his wife, a princess he'd rescued from the land of the dead. It was about immortal love, and Lily's parents had danced to it at their wedding.

Oh no. They expect me to dance with Gabriel.

She looked down the table.

There he was, smoothing back his hair.

"Go on," said Uncle Pan. "Dance with him. Show there's no bad feeling between you."

"I have . . . er . . . I have a pain in my leg," said Lily. She rubbed her knee. "Ow. It really hurts. I need to sit down or it'll fall off. Honestly."

Mary poked her from behind. "Get going, my girl."

Gabriel waited. Everyone waited.

Mary poked her harder. "Get up. Now."

Custard sniffed at her plate and grabbed an abandoned lamb chop. He shook it in his jaws, growling.

"I have to take care of Custard," Lily replied. She reached for her puppy. "Bad, bad dog."

Mary leaned closer so she was whispering in Lily's ear. "If you don't stand up this instant, I am going to drag you onto the dance floor by your ear. And don't think I won't."

Mary wasn't bluffing. Lily had seen Mary tell off her father in front of a roomful of ambassadors for not eating his greens. Someone had laughed until Mary had stared at them. Her gaze could silence an emperor.

"All right," said Lily. "Look, I'm getting up." She slowly rose, pushing her chair back a few inches. "See?"

People started clapping to the rhythm. Others beat their mugs against the tables.

When she reached him, Gabriel smiled. "You look worried. Don't be. I've been taught by the best dancing masters in all of Lumina. They think I'm brilliant. I've invented a few special moves myself. Perhaps I'll teach them to you."

Lily glanced back. Both Mary and her uncle were urging her on.

Gabriel took her hand. "Just do as I tell you, and you'll be fine."

She inhaled sharply and pulled away. "I'm afraid I can't dance with you. I've already promised K'leef."

"Wh-what?" stuttered Gabriel.

Uncle Pan leaped in. He cleared his throat and laughed, awkwardly. "Give us a moment, m'lord." He pulled her aside. "What do you think you're doing? You can't dance with K'leef. Solar will take it as a great insult."

"Good." Lily ripped herself free and swept over to the end of the table, where K'leef sat. "Come on."

"What?" said K'leef.

"You and I are going to dance. Now." She glared at him. "Remember? Like we agreed?"

"Dance?" K'leef didn't resist; he was too confused. "To this?"

"Of course." This was her favorite tune. "It's perfect."

"For a funeral."

"Ha-ha-ha. You're so funny," said Lily sarcastically. She pulled him out of his chair. "Just get up."

Lily headed toward the steps, dragging the red-robed boy behind her. She didn't look back, but she heard the gasps. She hurried to the open dance floor before Mary could stop her.

The music faltered. The conductor looked uncertainly toward the high table.

"You," ordered Lily. "You with the baton."

The conductor pointed at himself. "Me, m'lady?"

"Start again. From the beginning."

Lily and K'leef stood utterly alone in the center of the Great Hall. Hundreds of people watched them, not one speaking. The clapping and banging had stopped.

Lily glared at the conductor. "Well?"

He winced, but then he turned around to face his musicians. One or two smiled at the trouble Lily was causing.

"I don't know how to dance," admitted K'leef.

"Of course you don't; you're a boy." Lily sighed. She had to make this work, somehow. "Just don't tread on my toes or bump into any furniture. Your left hand goes in my right, and your right goes around my waist."

K'leef frowned. "Like this?"

The music began.

They danced. Or more accurately, Lily dragged K'leef across the floor, trying to make sure he didn't step on her gown.

"Is this right?" said K'leef after a minute of slowly moving around the dance floor. "Isn't the man meant to lead?"

"I don't see why."

So they danced, K'leef dressed in a sweeping robe of red and orange and Lily in glistening black.

"Stop gripping my hand so tightly," said Lily. "Your rings are really tearing into my fingers."

"Sorry."

She looked at the rings on his hand, on every single finger. "And why are you wearing so many, anyway?"

K'leef wore not only rings, but a necklace, bracelets, and earrings. He dripped jewelry, all of it made from amber. Even his buttons were of the orange stone.

He scowled. "The duke wants everyone to see what a rich prize I am."

"If you were that rich, shouldn't you be wearing rubies? I thought the ruby was the favorite gemstone of House Djinn."

He shrugged. "I'm the fourth son, so I have to wear amber. Only the eldest son, the heir apparent, wears rubies. At least I'm not the tenth. My brother, Saleem, wears jewelry made from sandstone."

"What's it like living in the Prism Palace?"

"The Solars' home?" K'leef's gaze darkened. "The duke is a tyrant, and Gabriel is a cruel, petty idiot."

"It can't be that bad, can it?" It couldn't be. She would be living there one day. "You're just saying that because you're their prisoner."

"Perhaps. But soon you'll be their prisoner, too, won't you?"

Lily faltered.

"I'll be Gabriel's wife. That's different. I think."

"I'm sure you're right." K'leef met her gaze. He must have seen the doubt in her eyes. "You don't want to marry him, do you?"

"Would you?"

K'leef smiled. "I don't want you marrying him, either."

"Why not?"

"Think about it. Solar's lands are in the middle, with Gehenna to his north and the Sultanate of Fire to the south."

She understood. Duke Solar wanted peace with House Shadow. Once he knew his northern border was safe . . .

"He'll declare war on you," said Lily.

"Last summer's attack was just the beginning," said K'leef bitterly.

"What happened?"

"I was leading a caravan. We had stopped at an oasis to rest and water the camels, and we didn't have enough guards. His paladins ambushed us. Afterward, he said it had been a mistake, that his men thought we were smugglers. He says I'm his *guest*, but everyone knows I'm his hostage."

"Your father didn't retaliate?"

"The duke has made it clear that if the sultan does anything, my head will be removed."

Lily gulped. "I'm sorry."

"He wants our wealth and lands, Lady Shadow. Your houses joining would be a disaster for my family."

"So what's the answer? Should I marry you instead?"

"Wha . . . what?" K'leef stumbled. His heel came down on her toe. "Ow!"

"Er . . . sorry," said K'leef. He looked down at his feet as if he wasn't quite sure what to do with them. "Do you want to start again?"

Lily caught sight of Gabriel. He stood watching, his hands clamped into fists and his face blotchy with rage. "He's going to take this insult out on you," said Lily. "I'm sorry. I shouldn't have dragged you out here."

"It was worth it," said K'leef, slowly resuming the dance. "How about you? Are you sure you won't get in more trouble for dancing with me?"

"I am ruler of Gehenna, you know. I should be able to dance with whomever I like."

"Looks like your dog is causing trouble, too."

Custard was jumping across the high table, snapping at plates and knocking over cups. Duke Solar had red wine splashed all over his oh-so-pristine white tunic. Lily smiled. That stain was never coming out.

Lily laughed, loud and pure, and for this moment, she was happy. K'leef smiled at her and she giggled as Custard sprang away from Mary, knocking over Lily's new crystal goblet. He sniffed at the liquid and began lapping it up.

Other dancers began to drift onto the floor. The *Danse macabre* continued, rising in tempo so feet moved swiftly, and the women's gowns, black and white, silk, satin, linen, and radiant with jewels, created a world of whirling beauty. Lily was dizzy. She clung to K'leef as he twirled her faster and faster.

"Stop it, K'leef!" she cried. "I'm going to be sick!"

Mary screamed.

Everyone froze in midstep. Lily craned her neck over the crowd to see what the problem was.

Custard was stumbling on the table, his tongue hanging out of his loose jaws. Green froth bubbled in his mouth.

Lily ran to him, pushing dancers aside. "Get out of my way!"

She reached the high table. Mary looked at her helplessly and handed him over. Lily cradled Custard in her arms.

The puppy's eyes rolled wildly. His mouth and nose were covered in green gunk. He gazed up at Lily and gave a feeble yap. The short stubby tail wagged.

"What's wrong with him?" asked Lily. "What's wrong, Custie?"

She gazed into his big brown eyes. Custard stared back, confused and wanting her to make him better, like she always did. The trust was total. He was hers, and she looked after him. He wagged his tail and snuffled against her.

He coughed once, and his tail stopped wagging.

"Come on, Custie."

The puppy lay unmoving.

She hugged Custard tightly, praying for a heartbeat or a breath. "Come on, Custie."

But there was nothing.

Duke Solar touched the puppy's mouth. He rubbed the emerald froth between his fingers and sniffed. Then he scowled and wiped his hand clean. "It's poison."

ELEVEN

"Life-bane," said Duke Solar. "A rare poison. Expensive, and very effective. That mongrel saved your life, Lady Shadow."

"He was not a mongrel," said Lily, her voice as empty as the Great Hall was now.

Custard is dead.

Lily sat, hands on her lap, feeling like a part of her was missing. If she tried really hard, she could still hear his yapping. When she closed her eyes, she could see him prancing on her bed, slobbering over her sheets and wagging his tail. He would never do that again, and that was what she found hardest. That things could change so suddenly and so completely. Again.

He was mine, and someone took him from me.

The feast had ended in an uproar, everyone frightened that their food might be poisoned. The Solar entourage had practically run out of the Hall, the paladins glaring all around them, hands ready on their sword hilts. Lily's own soldiers had been equally ready for some Solar plot. It was a miracle that no one had been killed.

The lights had been put out across the Great Hall, leaving only the few lit candelabras along the high table. The shadows now owned the vast, empty space. Lily stared into the candlelight, lost.

"An assassin," said Tyburn, "here in Castle Gloom."

Tyburn. As usual, he had shown up when things were at their worst. His boots had left muddy prints across the floor, and he stank of his weeks on the road.

"There weren't any assassins here before the Solars arrived," said Lily, staring at the duke with all the hatred she'd hidden until now. "You want Gehenna and will get it any way you can. Well, you can't. It's my home, and you'll never, ever have any of it. Not a brick, not a blade of grass."

Pan stepped between them. "Lily, dear, you're upset. You should leave this to the grown-ups."

But she wasn't finished. Not by a long shot. Someone at the high table had been sly and cruel enough, vindictive enough, to poison her drink. "What about Gabriel?"

"What did you say?" said Duke Solar, his voice dangerously quiet.

Pan butted in. "What Lady Shadow means is, she hopes the young lord is unharmed. He did faint, did he not?"

Right after Duke Solar had declared the cup poisoned, Gabriel had screamed and collapsed into the arms of one of the maids. His squires had ended up carrying him out.

Not really the action of an assassin, was it? Fainting at the mere mention of poison. Or was it all just a clever disguise? Perhaps Gabriel *wasn't* that puny, arrogant, and cowardly.

"Hmmm." Duke Solar poured out a glass of wine. He stared at the drink but left it untouched. "I promise you, it was none of my people." He turned to Lily. "You are wrong, Lady Shadow. I don't want Gehenna. *I already have it.* I had it the moment you agreed to marry my son."

"No," Lily replied, barely able to believe what she was hearing. "It's my home, not yours."

"I need you alive," continued the duke. "If you die, there will be no wedding. Your family line will end, and the citizens of Gehenna will go to war with Lumina again. Why would I want that? For that reason, I think it best we move you to somewhere safer than Castle Gloom."

"And where would that be, m'lord?" asked Tyburn.

"The Prism Palace," said the duke. "We'll leave tomorrow morning."

"I will not leave my home," Lily insisted. He might as well cut out her heart.

Duke Solar met her gaze, and Lily saw her frightened expression reflected in his mirror eyes. "There is an assassin here in Castle Gloom, m'lady. He tried to kill you tonight and almost succeeded. Do not give him another opportunity. You will leave with us, at dawn."

"Uncle? Tell him!"

Pan glugged down a goblet of wine. If it was poisoned, he was willing to risk it. "Lily . . . I think the duke might be right. He'll look after you."

"As I would my own daughter." The duke smiled at her. There was no affection or kindness in it.

"I am not your daughter! You are not my father!" Lily screamed.

Tears leaked from her eyes.

I will not cry. I won't give Solar the satisfaction. I'd rather die than leave Castle Gloom.

Her mind raced. She didn't have armies or skill with a sword or magic, but somehow, somehow, she needed to beat them. She needed time.

"Wait, what about Halloween?" she said, clutching at a straw. "I can't leave. Not before Halloween."

Solar scowled. "Why is that so important?"

"It's Gehenna's big annual holiday, and we throw a huge masquerade ball. It's been held here since the first stone of the castle was laid. *If* I'm to leave, I need to say good-bye to everyone, and that will be the best time to do so."

"A masquerade? Why a masquerade?"

Pan spoke. "In the olden days, when magic was common, Halloween was the night when the barriers between the lands of the living and dead were at their lowest. The dead would rise from their graves and join the living. Masks were worn so that no one would know who was alive and who wasn't."

"A dance is held in every village, and people wear masks and dress up as ghosts and ghouls," added Lily. "Families have midnight picnics at the graveyards and leave food and drink so their dead know they're not forgotten. We have a big weeklong fair leading up to it, just outside the castle walls."

"Today is the nineteenth. Halloween is almost two weeks away," said the duke. "I cannot stay that long. I have duties that cannot wait."

"You can leave anytime you want. I promise as soon as Halloween is over, I'll come *straight* to the Prism Prison . . . I mean, Prism Palace." Lily gave him her widest smile, showing him all her even white teeth. She just hoped he couldn't see that she was lying straight through them.

The duke almost laughed. "I must depart tomorrow morning to visit my domains on the border. However, I will return for this Halloween Ball. It sounds fascinating. In the meanwhile, I shall leave my paladins here. All the better to protect you, m'lady."

"What about Gabriel?" asked Lily. "Surely he'll be wanting to come with you?"

"Ah, no. I think he'll stay. It will give you a chance to get better acquainted. Won't that be nice, m'dear?"

"So very nice," said Lily, biting off each word.

Pan clapped. "Marvelous! Why don't you invite the lesser houses to attend, your grace? The Glimmers, the Shards, the Lightbringers. We shall have a grand ball. All the great families of Gehenna and Lumina gathered under one roof!"

Twelve days until Halloween.

Twelve days to come up with a plan to stay in Castle Gloom.

She knew that Gabriel was behind tonight's poisoning. Everything she'd seen of him tonight, especially the way he'd treated K'leef, warned her that he was spiteful, selfish, and utterly lacking in honor. Exactly the sort to pour life-bane in her cup just because she'd danced with the Solar hostage instead of him. After all, the duke had said it was expensive, and who else but someone like Gabriel could afford it? If she could prove it, then there'd be no reason to leave Gehenna, would there?

He'd killed Custard. She wanted him punished for that, wanted it more than anything. But you couldn't punish the heir apparent of Lumina for killing a mere puppy.

But he'd tried to kill Lily, and she was ruler of Gehenna. That was treason, and there was only one punishment for that and it was as bad as bad could be.

Death.

A chill, dreadful thought crept through her mind.

Could I do that, even to someone like Gabriel?

I . . . I don't want to have to make that type of decision. Someone else should decide. Anyone but me.

But there was no one else.

Tyburn stood there, watching in his quiet way. Strange, the air always felt colder when he was in the room.

If Gabriel was guilty, then she would have work for her executioner.

TWELVE

A tumultuous cloud of bats swirled above Thorn. High-pitched shrieks tore through the torchlit courtyard, and leathery wings whipped the air furiously.

He didn't know much about bats, but something wasn't right.

Other bats clung to Castle Gloom's walls like a bristling cloak, crawling along the stones, twitching, and using the hooks on their wings to hold themselves in place. Their red eyes shone in the torchlight. Their needlelike teeth glistened.

The gargoyles along the high walls of the castle looked almost alive; Thorn thought he'd seen one turn its head as he and Tyburn had entered the courtyard just an hour ago.

Creepy. But calling Castle Gloom creepy was like calling the sea damp.

The castle was ancient and derelict. The towers rose crookedly into the sky, and empty halls with caved-in roofs squatted around muddy squares. The outer walls were covered in black ivy so shiny it looked as if it had been washed in oil.

Still, he hadn't spotted any zombies along the battlements, nor had he seen any vampires. Which was good.

And there was no Tyburn, which was even better. The moment they'd dismounted, a soldier had come running up to them and spoken to the executioner. Tyburn had tossed Thorn his reins and run off toward the main keep, leaving him to take care of their hoof-sore mounts.

Fine by him. Thorn much preferred horses to executioners. He patted Thunder's neck. "How can you stand it here?"

Tyburn's horse replied by lifting his tail and plopping a large, moist lump of dung on the ground.

"Oh. Thanks. Very much."

The bats weren't the only ones who looked out of sorts. The many people milling about did, too, and they all had swords.

"None of my business," Thorn muttered. This time he was going to stay well out of it.

Steam rose from the pile of dung. There were bits of straw sticking out of it. And it stank. Thorn needed a broom.

A pack of squires barged out of a door. They were half carrying a boy with blond hair and a nasty scowl.

One of the squires said, "Air! He needs fresh air!"

"I'm fine! Let me go!" the boy shouted. "I did not faint. I was . . . checking under the table!" He pushed them off, straightened his tunic, and dabbed his forehead with the lace cuff of his sleeve.

Wow. I didn't know clothes could be that white.

The boy's blue eyes met Thorn's. "What are you staring at?"

"Nothing."

The boy pushed two of his cronies out of the way to stand face-to-face with Thorn.

"Do you know who I am?"

There were a lot of them and just one of him. They were bigger and noble-born and Thorn was a mere peasant, but he really, *really* couldn't stop himself. "Dressed like that? The court jester?"

"You scum!" The boy reached for his longsword.

It was a man's weapon, and the boy's arms were too short to unsheathe it quickly. Thorn gave him a second to get properly tangled up.

Then kicked the boy's feet from under him.

The boy yelled—and dropped face-first into the horse dung.

"Oops," said Thorn.

The boy spluttered and gagged. He tried to wipe his face but just spread the dung over more of it. "What are you waiting for? Get him!"

Uh-oh.

Thorn backed away, clenching his fists. The squires drew out daggers.

"C'mon, lads. That ain't fair," said Thorn.

"Fair?" said the biggest. "What's fair got to do with it? This is about winning."

A voice called out from the darkness. "What's going on?"

Thorn didn't dare take his eyes off the squires, but someone was approaching. All he could make out was someone in black.

A *she* someone in black.

The girl shoved the biggest squire aside so she stood between them and Thorn. "I asked a question."

The dung-covered boy got to his feet. "That maggot attacked me! I demand he be whipped!"

"First person who touches me loses their teeth," threatened Thorn.

"Do shut up," the girl said to him. She faced the boy. "You're mistaken, m'lord. You slipped."

"What?" said the boy.

"What?" said Thorn.

The girl shook her head. "Surely you're not saying that a defenseless, *unarmed* stable boy defeated you? If word got around that the duke's son, armed and surrounded by his guards, was beaten by a commoner, then think of the embarrassment. Not just for you, but for your father."

Whoever this girl was, she was clever. Maybe too clever.

The boy's eyes narrowed. He seemed to be thinking. Slowly, but hard.

"Yes . . . I slipped. It is too dark here. You should have more torches in the courtyard. See to it."

The girl curtseyed. "Of course, m'lord. As you wish."

The boy and his cronies all stormed off.

Thorn unclenched his fists. "I suppose I should thank you."

"Are you a total idiot, or merely suicidal? You must be, to insult Gabriel like that," said the girl.

"Important, is he? This Gabriel?"

"Only heir apparent to House Solar. So, yes, fairly important."

"Oh." Insulting the powerful was becoming a habit. "But as my grandpa would say, 'He started it.'"

"That's the most stupid thing I've heard all night."

"Look, I've thanked you already. Now go away." He gathered Thunder's reins. Where were the stables?

"Don't turn your back on me."

"Did you hear something, Thunder? No? Me neither."

She grabbed his arm and pulled him back around.

They glared at each other.

Look at her. Some stuck-up snob dressed in jewels and pearls and acting like she owns the place.

"Will you just get lost?" said Thorn. "I have work to do."

"I am Lady Shadow," she said, "and when I give an order, you follow it."

Ah. Maybe she does *own the place.*

"You're Lady Shadow? Nah, you can't be. She'd be someone more . . . cackling."

"Cackling?"

"Mad old woman sort. Y'know, cackling and brewing potions and with only one tooth in her mouth. Real wrinkly."

"What's your name?" Lady Shadow asked.

"Thorn"—he bowed like he'd seen Merrick do—"Your Princessness."

"Are you ill?" she asked.

"Ain't that how you do it? Bow, I mean?"

"Only if you're an octopus." She waved dismissively. "And you call me 'm'lady.'"

"You ain't a princess? Where I come from, you can call yourself a king if you've got two fields. An emperor if you've got four."

"Well, where *I* come from, no one uses royal titles. Not since the time of the Six Princes. It's bad luck."

"What about the Coral king?" asked Thorn. "He uses a royal title."

"Him? He's half man, half fish. Who cares what he calls himself?" She pointed at Thorn's head. "So what happened to your hair?"

Thorn rubbed his palm over the two weeks' worth of bristles. "Lice. Tyburn had it all shaved off."

"You came with Tyburn?" She looked surprised.

Thorn wrinkled his nose. That dung was unbelievably smelly. He found a shovel up against the stable door. "Yeah. I'm his new squire."

Now she looked shocked.

"What?" asked Thorn.

"There must be something very special about you, Thorn. Have you slain a dragon recently?"

"Nooo. . . ."

"Troll? Ogre? An army of giants? Something equally heroic?"

"Caught a couple of rabbits. Does that count?"

"I'm just trying to understand why Tyburn picked you to be his squire. You *do* know who Tyburn is, don't you?"

"Yeah. That's been pointed out. A lot."

"And he lets you look after his horse?"

Thorn brushed the forelock from the horse's eyes. "Thunder? He's just a big old softie."

"The last squire who tried that almost had his hand bitten off." She went to touch Thunder, but the horse snapped his teeth at her, and she backed away. "Er . . . nice horsey."

Thorn shrugged. "I've always been good with animals. Like my dad. I once saw him scare off a wolf just by whistling." He looked her over. How could she be wearing so much jewelry and still be standing? "So how long have you known Tyburn?"

"All my life."

"What's he *really* like?" They'd been riding together for two weeks, but Tyburn had kept conversation pretty much limited to "Get up," "Eat," and "Sleep." "Y'know, on his days off, when he's not being an executioner?"

"Tyburn never has a day off. Tyburn's always Tyburn."

"He can't be. What's his first name?"

She shrugged. "I don't know. No one's ever been brave enough to ask him."

And this was the man he had to serve for the next year? Just great. What sort of world was he in? Bats in swarms as thick as clouds. A windowless castle bigger than any city he'd ever seen, one-name killers, and all ruled by this girl.

They were interrupted by another boy, this time dressed in black. He carried a small bundle in his arms. "M'lady, I've got him."

Lady Shadow took the package and cradled it in her arms. "Thank you, Wade. You may go."

The boy, Wade, glanced over at Thorn. "Are you sure?"

Lady Shadow nodded, not taking her gaze from the bundle. Wade shot another suspicious look at him, then bowed and left.

"What's that?" Thorn asked.

Lady Shadow's face fell, and tears glistened in her gray eyes. "It's Custard, my dog."

He could hear the pain in her words. The way they almost choked her. "I'm sorry. You're going to bury him?"

"Yes. In the Night Garden." One of her hands gently stroked the bundle. "Gabriel's been humiliated twice tonight. He's not going to let either insult go. You'd better come with me."

"I can handle Gabriel easy."

"It's not him that'll be the problem. It'll be the ten others he'll bring with him."

Thorn ducked as a bat screamed overhead, its wing tip brushing his ear. He shook his head as other bats darted past before rising up into the night.

Lady Shadow laughed. "They're harmless. Just ignore them."

"Harmless? *Look* at 'em. They're huge. How big do they get?"

"You have no idea."

THIRTEEN

"Who's that?" Thorn asked Lady Shadow.

Ahead stood a black marble statue, twelve feet tall and wearing a cloak that was made of bats. Hundreds of them.

What was it about House Shadow and bats?

The statue's face was gaunt, and there was clearly a family resemblance. "One of yours, I suppose?"

"Lazarus Shadow. He planted the Night Garden." Lady Shadow brushed her fingertips along a row of rosebushes. Their petals were shiny black, as though freshly painted. The scent was . . . drowsy, as if someone had perfumed them with dreams. "These roses only grow here. They unfurl at night."

Pebble-strewn paths branched out in all directions, and there were bushes, flowers, and trees. Thorn didn't recognize many of the plants, even though he'd grown up beside a forest.

Everything's strange in Gehenna. I left "normal" behind long ago.

Thorn adjusted the shovel he'd found, swapping it from his right shoulder to his left. "Lazarus Shadow? I've heard of him. Wasn't he a vampire?"

"He just fell in with the wrong crowd when he was younger."

"This crowd being vampires?"

"Mm-hmm."

"I saw this puppet play last year at midsummer's fair," Thorn said. "*Lazarus and the Silver Warrior, Michael Solar*. Lazarus kidnaps Solar's love, and there's this big fight and he gets his head chopped off."

"Just because he was a vampire doesn't make him a bad person," she said.

"Er . . . I think it does."

"That's because you only hear the Solars' side of the story. They always made us the villains. Look around you. Everyone forgets what a great gardener Lazarus was."

"Didn't he use the corpses of his victims for fertilizer?"

"Waste not, want not."

There was a splash from up ahead.

Lady Shadow tightened her grip on her puppy as she peered into the darkness. "Who's there?"

Thorn hefted the shovel. Was it Gabriel? If it was an ambush, he'd fight.

"Who's there?" Lady Shadow repeated.

A flame flared into life, bringing brightness and color to the night. "It's me—K'leef."

A dark-skinned boy in a long red robe stood beside a pond, rolling fire between his many-ringed fingers.

Magic. He knows magic.

The flame transformed in hues, ranging back and forth through the rainbow and casting weird, mesmerizing patterns across the pond's surface.

Thorn stared at it, spellbound. He'd never seen real magic before. "Can you teach me that?"

K'leef looked him up and down before answering. "I doubt it."

"What are you doing here, K'leef?" Lady Shadow joined Thorn by the water's edge.

"Throwing pebbles. Watching the ripples." K'leef looked up. "And you?"

"I'm burying Custard." She gestured toward Thorn. "This is . . . Spike?"

"Thorn."

"That's what I meant to say," replied Lady Shadow. "This is K'leef. He's from the—"

"The Sultanate of Fire. I know," Thorn said to K'leef. "That trick of yours was a bit of a giveaway. It's really amazing."

K'leef blushed, and the flame vanished. Smoke twisted between his fingers for a moment before drifting off in the faint night breeze. He took Lady Shadow's hand. "I'm really sorry about what happened tonight, Lily."

He calls her Lily.

Of course he would. The two of them were alike, what with their jewels and rich clothes. They were nobles and Thorn was a peasant and so it was "Lady Shadow." That's how things were.

So why did it suddenly bother him?

Lady Shadow pointed to a spot of bare earth between two tall rose-bushes and told Thorn, "Dig there. Make it deep."

She and K'leef stood silently as Thorn dug the grave. The dirt was damp and soft. It didn't take him long. Soon he scooped the last of the soil and stabbed his shovel into the ground. "There. It's done."

"Thank you," said Lady Shadow. She knelt beside the grave. "Good-bye, Custard." She kissed the puppy and laid him in the hole. "Go find Dante. My brother will look after you."

After Thorn had covered the grave, Lady Shadow put roses over the earth. She stared at the spot and bit her lip, trying to hold back her tears.

Why not allow herself to cry? Thorn could see that the puppy had meant a lot to her. Maybe it was one of those rules nobles had. They weren't supposed to show they were upset and cry. It might make people think they were just like everyone else.

"What happened to him?" Thorn asked.

"Poisoned," said K'leef.

"Who'd want to poison a puppy?"

"They were trying to poison me, not Custard." Lady Shadow stared at the grave and sniffed loudly.

"Oh." No wonder Tyburn had run off like that.

K'leef brushed his fingers. It's not like he had any dirt on them; Thorn had done the digging. "Any leads, Lily?"

"It was a poison called life-bane. You've heard of it?"

K'leef shook his head.

"I have," said Thorn. He might only be a peasant, but he knew things, too. "You make it out of berries that grow in Herne's Forest. Dry 'em and grind 'em up into a powder, then sprinkle it on some old meat. We use it to kill rats. Wolves, too."

"Who taught you that?" asked Lady Shadow.

"My dad. He didn't want us kids scoffing the wrong sort of berries. You need to know what's safe and what ain't." Thorn leaned on the shovel. "What happens next, m'lady?"

"What do you mean?"

"Seems to me, someone owes you a dog. I don't know how you do things here, but where I come from, if someone does you wrong, you make 'em pay for it."

"I know who did it," said Lady Shadow.

K'leef looked up. "You do? Who?"

"Who do you think? Gabriel." Lady Shadow frowned. "But how do I prove it?"

Thorn grinned. "Easy. The best way to find out a secret is to go where you ain't allowed, listen to what you ain't meant to hear, and see what you ain't meant to see." Thorn gazed at the walls, towers, and battlements that surrounded them. A place like this would have *thousands* of secrets.

K'leef nodded knowingly. "You'll have to be careful, especially after insulting Gabriel tonight."

"She insulted Gabriel, too? How?" Thorn was impressed. Maybe there was more to this girl after all.

"Lady Shadow refused to dance with him," K'leef said proudly. "She danced with me."

"And that's an insult? Riiight." He'd never understand nobles.

"Exposing Gabriel won't be easy."

"If life was meant to be easy, then carts would have square wheels," said Thorn.

"What?" said Lily.

"That's not a saying around here? My grandpa used to say it all the time. It's about how making square wheels is easier than round ones, but—"

"I know what it *means*," said Lady Shadow. "I can't be sneaking in corridors and spying at keyholes." She kicked a pebble angrily. It sounded to him that sneaking and spying were *exactly* what she wanted to be doing. "There are rules."

"Stupid ones," said Thorn. Nobles. They weren't like normal people. He scraped the mud off the shovel. "I should get back. I wouldn't want no one else falling into that dung."

"Wait," said Lady Shadow.

"Yeah?"

Lady Shadow faced Thorn. He could almost hear her heart racing. "If it were up to you, what would you do?"

"Them rules of yours?" said Thorn, smiling. "I'd start breaking 'em."

FOURTEEN

For the squires, every day began the same way. With a predawn run.

Today it was out through Dead Man's Gate for a lap around the hill, then back for weapons training. Last boy home went without breakfast.

Thorn ran alongside K'leef. He wasn't sure how the pair of them had ended up together. It was probably because they were strangers in Gehenna and no one knew what to make of them, yet.

Thorn wished K'leef hadn't come up to him at the gate. He didn't have anything in common with him.

But he was stuck with him, and there was nothing he could do about it.

And *stuck* was right. The Sultanate boy was plowing unsteadily through the mud, gasping with each breath. He'd already fallen once, face-first. In his rich, red-colored robes and dainty embroidered shoes, he wasn't exactly dressed for running. At least he had dumped his rings and all his other jewelry.

He probably doesn't want to be weighed down any more than he has to be.

"You're not helping yourself wearing that. Couldn't you borrow some clothes from one of the squires?"

"I belong to House Djinn. I dress in red."

"Right now you're dressed in mud." Thorn sighed. "Here, let me help."

K'leef gave Thorn a weary, grateful smile and grabbed his hand. Between Thorn pulling and K'leef crawling, they managed to get him out of the quagmire of a ditch.

"I'm surprised they let you out," said Thorn. "Ain't Solar worried you're going to run off?"

"Of course not. I gave my word not to attempt to escape."

Thorn laughed. "You're joking, right?"

K'leef stared at him so angrily, Thorn worried he was going to catch fire. "You're *not* joking?"

"When a noble gives his word, he keeps it," said K'leef with a huff. "It's a matter of honor."

Thorn shook his head in amazement. Nobles and their stupid rules. "What are you doing out here, anyway? Nobles don't need to run; you've got horses. My dad told me the best horses in the New Kingdoms are the fire breeds from the Sultanate."

"He's right," said K'leef. "But we also have flying carpets. Much more comfortable."

"Flying carpets? Really?"

K'leef laughed, or maybe he was having a heart attack. Thorn wasn't totally sure. The boy's face was a dangerous dark red. Eventually K'leef started breathing normally. "No, Thorn. Used to, but all I've got back home is a cushion that floats a foot or so off the ground."

Back home. Thorn saw the brightness in K'leef's eyes when he spoke about it. Maybe he and this noble weren't so different after all.

"This run was Gabriel's idea, not that he'd take part himself. He thought it would be funny." K'leef spat. "There's nothing he'd like better than to see me carried back on a stretcher. But I'm not going to give him the satisfaction."

"Funny, I don't see Gabriel here. Nor any of his cronies."

"He may be an idiot, but he's not stupid. Gabriel's probably sitting by a warm fire tucking into his breakfast."

"That reminds me. If we want our own breakfast, then we'd better get a move on."

There were two hills beyond Dead Man's Gate. Thorn hadn't noticed them when he'd arrived last night. "Which one do we go around?"

K'leef, panting, pointed at the western one. "Lamentation Hill."

"I've never seen a place so grim." The trees were twisted like the bones of old men. "The local picnic spot, is it?"

"It's where they execute criminals, Thorn."

"And what's the other one called? Let me guess: Really Sad Hill?"

"No. That's the City of Silence. It's the Shadow family's graveyard."

Now that the mist was clearing, Thorn saw that the crest was covered with tombs and the slopes were lined with countless gravestones. "It's bigger than Castle Gloom."

"The Shadows have been here for thousands of years," K'leef explained. "It's no wonder, then, that the home of the dead is greater than that of the living."

"Nice place, Gehenna. Massive graveyard to the left, and execution ground to the right." Thorn peered up at a row of poles. "What's on top of those? Birds?"

"Heads."

"Oh." He wasn't shocked. Heads on spikes were a pretty common sight in some places. He counted five in all. "Whose?"

"The brigands who killed Lily's family," K'leef replied. "What I heard was that Lord Shadow, his wife, and his son had gone to sign a treaty with the Solars. The Black Ford Truce, they call it, and it's the first time the two houses have had peace in a hundred years or so. Lily's brother was going to marry one of the duke's twelve daughters."

"But I thought the duke and Lord Shadow hated each other."

K'leef tapped Thorn's forehead. "Think about it. The duke's grandchild would one day be ruler of Gehenna. We belong to ancient families, Thorn; we take the long view."

"Then what happened?"

"The deal was done and Lord Iblis, Lady Salome, and their son, Dante, were on the way back when they were ambushed. They were robbed and killed. The brigands even burned the bodies, hoping that no one would recognize them."

"Where was Lady Shadow during all this?"

"Back here. The official line is that she was ill that day. . . ." K'leef winked at him. "But I heard the true story from her maid, Mary. Lily had had a fight with her father earlier that week, so he'd grounded her."

"Why does that not surprise me?" Thorn had only met her last night, but there was a stubborn look in those gray eyes of hers. "Still, that argument saved her life, didn't it? So how did the heads end up on them poles? I'd have thought the brigands would've made themselves pretty scarce after what they'd done."

"What do you think? Tyburn found them. That man would chase you to the very gates of hell if he had to. The brigands still had Lady Salome's jewels on them. Tyburn killed five, but one got away. The executioner's been searching for him ever since."

Thorn understood. His village, Stour, suffered bandits like most places, and they'd lost the occasional chicken or sheep. Men got desperate. But stealing was one thing; murder something else.

K'leef glanced back at the ragtag bunch of boys approaching. "Let's push on. We don't want to be last."

They weren't. Last was a boy named Pedder.

Old Colm, the weapons master, stomped out, dragging him along. Despite his wooden leg, Old Colm moved fast.

"I wasn't last, sir! I wasn't!" Pedder complained.

Old Colm shoved the boy down the steps into the courtyard. "No food and water for this one today. Maybe he'll be quicker with an empty stomach."

The squires lined up in the courtyard of Dead Man's Gate. The mud was stiff with frost, and Thorn's breath came out as a big white cloud. Thorn noticed how the others looked his way.

"What are they so interested in?" he muttered.

K'leef mimed something smacking his face. "They've heard what you did to Gabriel last night. Which was *very* excellent, by the way. Remind me to buy you a palace the next time you're in the Sultanate of Fire." K'leef raised his hand. "And before you ask, let me tell you that Gabriel isn't the sort fellow to hold a petty, vindictive grudge and come after you in the middle of the night with a mob."

"Really?"

"No, I'm lying. I'd sleep with my eyes open from now on if I were you."

Thorn scowled. "And next time we go running, I'm just gonna leave you to drown in the mud." The day was getting worse and worse.

Old Colm looked them up and down, shaking his head. "By the Six Princes, I've never seen anything so pathetic. You all couldn't fight a cold. You're not squires, you're trolls. What are you?"

"Trolls, sir!" they all shouted.

"Say it like you mean it!"

"WE'RE TROLLS, SIR!"

It was a well-known fact that Old Colm hated trolls. Story was, a troll chieftain had ripped his leg off in a battle. Old Colm had grabbed it and used it to beat the troll to death.

The weapons master waved at the bundle of unstrung bows against the wall. "Now take one each."

The boys looked at each other, uncertain.

"What are you waiting for? String them," ordered Old Colm. He handed a large iron key to one of the older boys. "Tom, go get some more arrows from the armory. I reckon we'll be losing plenty over the wall."

The hay targets stood two hundred feet away, up against the wall of the Black Keep and below the watching gargoyles. In the center of each bale was the red bull's-eye. From where Thorn stood, it was the size of his thumbnail.

The squires struggled. The bows wouldn't bend. One sprang up, smacking the boy on his forehead. Another cried out as he cut himself on the thin bowstring.

Thorn hooked the bottom of the stave around his ankle and back of his leg. The stave ran up behind him, against his shoulder. He gripped the horn tip and bent down. The wood creaked and pressed hard against his back, desperate to spring back straight. With his right hand, Thorn flipped the bowstring loop over the tip, then relaxed. He plucked the taut bowstring. Ready.

"How did you do that?" K'leef asked him as he wrestled with his own bow.

"Use your whole body to bend it, not just your arms."

"I get it. Thanks."

"I'll tell you what," said Old Colm, holding a silver crown between his finger and thumb. "See this? I'll give it to the first boy who scores a bull's-eye. Halloween's eleven days away, but the fair's already setting up on Devil's Knoll. A lad with silver in his pocket could have a fine old time at the fair." He winked. "Know what I mean?"

The boys laughed, but there were plenty of hungry eyes on the coin. A crown was a man's weekly wage.

The boys lined up in four columns, each facing one of the targets. Thorn was last in line. Arrows flew. Some hit the hay, others the walls, and plenty skimmed across the courtyard floor. One boy put his through his boot, and the foot within it, and was carried off to the infirmary, howling. None hit the bull's-eye, and Old Colm's coin remained unclaimed in his pocket.

Thorn reached the front. He picked a good arrow, one that was straight and its fletching neat and smooth. He nocked it and hooked his thumb around the bowstring.

"What do you think you're doing?" said Old Colm.

Thorn looked down at his thumb. "This is how my dad taught me."

"Oh, did he? Now tell me, troll, was your pa a legendary archer? Perhaps he was taught by elves, was he? Your fingers not good enough?"

"No, sir." Thorn blushed as the boys snickered. He rearranged his grip, holding the bowstring with his fingers, like everyone else. One above the notch, two below.

"No, no, no," said Old Colm. "That won't do at all. Gather around, trolls. Let the new boy show us how's it done. With his thumb. What do I know? I've only been teaching archery fifty years." He folded his arms. "Come on, troll, show me. Please, teach us all how to shoot."

Thorn's heart beat rapidly, and he felt the gaze of the other boys. A few laughed, and they jostled one another. They liked it when a new boy got humiliated.

Old Colm nudged him. "The target's over there."

Thorn took a deep breath. He turned side-on to the target. He relaxed his shoulders and blocked out the giggles and noise around him.

He hooked his thumb around the bowstring, raised the bow, drew the string to his chin, and saw down the line of the arrow, the target a haze beyond.

Don't worry about the target, Dad would say. *Make the arrow do the worrying. You just send it on its way straight and true.*

Thorn let the bowstring go. The arrow flew.

He heard the *thunk.* He didn't need to look. The gasp from the boys told him everything.

Bull's-eye.

Old Colm scowled. He handed Thorn another arrow. "A fluke. Do it again."

Thorn took it.

There was someone watching from the steps that led to the main doors. Thorn saw a match flame and a glow settle within a pipe.

Tyburn. The warm red light lit his stark, hard face. The boys murmured among themselves. A few inflated their chests, and others stood straighter, all wanting to impress the executioner.

But not Thorn.

He should do what his dad had told him.

Keep your head down. Don't attract attention. Stay out of trouble.

Thorn's archery was what had landed his father in so much trouble. Thorn's archery and arrogance.

I'll miss.

That was the sensible, clever thing to do. Make his first shot seem like sheer luck. A fluke.

Miss.

Go on. Just miss.

Why was it so hard? The bull's-eye was right there, just waiting to be hit. It seemed huge.

I . . . can't miss. I don't want *to miss! Why should I?*

Miss!

Thorn nocked the second arrow, drew, and loosed.

The arrow sailed high. Well over the targets. It flew upward and toward the keep wall.

It buried itself down the open throat of one of the gargoyles. It went clean in, so only the white goose-feathered fletching remained visible, jutting out between the gargoyle's fangs.

Thorn had missed. Spectacularly.

K'leef stared at it. They all did.

"Well, I'm not going up there and getting it," muttered one of the boys.

Old Colm grunted. "As I thought, a fluke. Now everyone, line up. Watch Harry. He'll show you how to shoot *properly.*"

Tyburn puffed out a smoke ring and went back inside the keep.

While the other boys were distracted, Old Colm tossed Thorn the crown. "Here, catch. I don't know what you're up to, troll, but I don't appreciate being made a fool of."

"A fool, sir? I don't understand. I missed."

"Did you?" He looked up at the gargoyle. "In which case that's the best worst shot I've ever seen."

Thorn drew the brush over the horse's coat.

Why had he made that shot?

Stupid. All it did was make everyone suspicious. Especially Tyburn.

Practice had gone on until well after sunup, and Thorn had made sure not to be too good, but it was too late. At breakfast everyone was talking about two things: the poisoning at the feast and Thorn's shooting. As soon as breakfast was over, Thorn had escaped to the stables.

And that suited him fine. Thorn enjoyed grooming horses. Especially ones like Thunder. His coat was so black it held all the other colors. Purples and blues and even shades of green rippled within it. They'd had a cart horse back home, and Thorn had spent a summer learning to ride on it. It had been equally big, seventeen hands, but it had been slow, docile, and not too bright. Thunder was different. Despite his size he looked nimble enough to dance on a penny.

Thorn picked out another stone from the horse's hooves. This was his sort of work. Not too complicated and no surprises. As long as you fed one end and cleaned the other, you couldn't go far wrong.

Out of the corner of his eye, Thorn glimpsed a squire heading toward him.

Now what?

The squire stopped a healthy distance away. "That's Thunder, isn't it?"

"You want something?" He looked at him properly. "I met you last night, didn't I? You brought the puppy. What was your name?"

"Wade." The boy was dressed in a black outfit fancier than Thorn's, but he looked nervous, and his eyes darted about like a mouse in a kitchen. "It's just that I was over at the lesser hall, where the Solars are? I heard Gabriel talking. He isn't happy."

"Of course he ain't. He probably saw himself in the mirror."

"He was talking about revenge. For what you did to him."

Thorn frowned. He'd hoped that K'leef had been wrong about Gabriel. No such luck.

"Mean little toad, ain't he?" Thorn looked over at the other stable boys, all dressed in black, like him. They were pretending not to eavesdrop. "You come over to help me, Wade?"

He shook his head. "Don't you get it? Gabriel's going to marry Lilith Shadow. We can't risk making an enemy of our future ruler."

"Then why are you telling me this?"

"Come on. We all know what you did to him. Every one of us would have loved to do the same. But we're—"

"A bunch of cowards?"

"We're not stupid," answered Wade. "I'm sorry, but you're on your own."

On his own. Some things never changed.

"How long have I got?"

The barn doors swung open, and Gabriel and a dozen of his white-clad squires marched in. Some had cudgels, others daggers. Gabriel had his longsword out and wore a shiny steel breastplate. He saw Thorn and grinned.

"Not long," said Wade.

FIFTEEN

"Think you can make a fool of me, peasant?" Gabriel snarled. "Think you can get away with what you did?"

"You mean shove your face in manure?" Thorn grinned. "Yeah, I reckon I can."

Gabriel smiled maliciously. "I'm going to teach you a lesson about respecting your betters. I'm going to *carve* it into you so you never forget it."

Wade and the other stable boys were gone. No last-minute help coming from them. Gabriel's cronies blocked the door. The only thing nearby was a broom.

So Thorn grabbed it.

Gabriel tightened his grip on his longsword. "Pathetic."

Thunder stamped his hoof. He whinnied and shook his head. He knew Thorn was in trouble.

"Get him!" ordered Gabriel.

Thorn grabbed hold of the horse's mane and swung himself up, broom still in his other hand.

"Go, boy!" shouted Thorn, kicking his heels.

The horse charged.

It didn't matter that they had clubs and knives. It didn't matter that there were more than ten of them. What mattered was they were on foot and Thorn was on a massive, muscular warhorse trained to trample *everything* in his path. Seventeen hands high, he was built to carry a fully armored knight into battle. With hooves that could cave in skulls and teeth big enough to snap off hands, Thunder crossed the small gap between his pen and the stable doors in a second.

The squires dove aside. Two weren't quick enough, and the horse glanced them with his shoulder, sending them tumbling.

Thorn couched the broom handle under his right armpit and aimed the brush at the biggest target he could see.

Gabriel.

The broom smacked dead center with a deafening clang. Gabriel flew twenty feet through the air, flipping over and over like a tin chicken, then smacked down in a fresh mound of horse dung.

"Whoa, boy!" Thorn tried to get control of Thunder, but the warhorse had his own ideas.

Thunder spun around, searching for more enemies, and that was too much for Thorn. He wasn't a horseman. Fighting off squires with a broom and staying on was one job too many.

So he fell off.

Solar squires spilled out of the stables. Others got to their feet after having dived away from the charging Thunder, their white tunics filthy with mud. A couple dragged Gabriel out of the fly-infested mountain of brown stuff. His breastplate had a big broom-shaped dent in it.

"Get him!" yelled Gabriel, frothing at the mouth. "Get him!"

No way was Thorn going to win this. He dragged himself up out of the mud and ran. He dashed toward a gap between a tower and a wall. He didn't know where he was running to, but it had to be out of the courtyard.

He ran between tottering walls and leaning towers and over crumbling walls and under half-demolished bridges. Sometimes the cries of the squires faded away to almost nothing, then suddenly they'd be at his shoulder.

Thorn ran as fast as he could, not looking back, deep into the labyrinthine paths of Castle Gloom.

He ran until his legs burned and his chest ached. He found an alcove, just a break in the wall, and stopped to catch his breath and look around.

He was totally lost. None of Castle Gloom made sense. It was a hodge-podge of buildings, all in different styles from different centuries, made of marble, granite, brick, and who knew what else. All of it ancient. Breath caught, Thorn raced on. Down an alley and around—

Disaster struck.

Thorn hit a dead end.

A wall blocked his way. It was high, more than fifty feet, and covered in stiff black ivy. The squires were closing in.

Thorn took hold of a vine. It was brittle, and he didn't have any idea how strong it was.

This wasn't like climbing trees back home. There he could just glance at a branch and know if it would take his weight.

Would they kill him? Back in the courtyard, with others standing there, someone might have stepped in to make sure things didn't get out of hand. But now, in the alleyway, with no one else around? Led by a guy like Gabriel?

If they catch me, I'm dead.

He began to climb. As quickly as he dared. A thorn jabbed into his palm, but he ignored it. He was going to get a whole lot more punctured if he stayed down there in the alleyway.

Thorn reached up and his hand came down flat on roof tiles. He pushed himself through the last few inches and slid across the roof on his belly.

"He's up there!"

Thorn glanced down. A group of squires stared up.

He waved at them. "Hard luck, lads. You can get lost now." No one was going to risk climbing after him. Not unless they were stupid. He kicked a few loose tiles off. "Oops."

The squires jumped as the tiles tumbled down, shattering at their feet.

Then, huffing and puffing, Gabriel caught up to his squires. His eyes bulged when he saw Thorn. He shoved one of the boys against the wall. "What are you waiting for?"

"It's not safe. He's throwing tiles down on our heads!"

"I don't care!"

"But, m'lord—"

"What are you, scared? It's not high! I could climb that with one hand! It's easy!"

"Then why don't you?" snapped the squire, unable to help himself.

Gabriel slapped him. "*I* give the orders. Or shall I tell my father that you didn't obey me?"

The squires began to climb.

Thorn picked up another broken piece of tile, dragging his fingertip along its sharp, jagged edge. He was tempted to throw it; he couldn't miss at this range. But these squires weren't his enemies; they were being bullied by Gabriel into coming after him, and they didn't deserve a chunk of slate in their foreheads. Thorn put it down and took off again.

When will they give up?

The roof went on and merged with another. Castle Gloom stretched off in all directions. A life spent climbing trees and running along boughs gave Thorn a sure and light foot, and he moved swiftly across the roof.

He dropped onto a second roof, one patched with holes, and the tiles underfoot creaked. The old timber supports groaned as he stepped forward.

Not good.

Thorn reached the end of this roof and realized there was a gap between it and the next. The width wasn't the problem—only about five feet. It was the depth. Fifty feet straight down and . . . kersplat.

Maybe there was another, safer route?

Just then the first of the squires reached the top. The boy shuffled warily toward him. He saw that Thorn was trapped and drew out his dagger.

Thorn's heart pounded. He focused on the spot in front of him. The morning dew shone on the black slate. Putting one foot in front of the other, he swung his arms to build momentum.

Then he jumped.

As he landed, his left boot slipped. His back hit the roof, knocking the wind out of him. His head cracked a few tiles, and they fell away.

No, no, no . . .

He started to slide down the roof feetfirst, faster and faster with each second. He dug in his heels, trying to slow himself down, but he was already going too fast and the slope was too steep.

Somewhere far below he heard tiles smashing on the cobblestones.

His stomach lurched as his feet slipped over the edge into open air. Thorn just had time to cry out before he fell off the roof.

SIXTEEN

How do I prove Gabriel was the poisoner? And how do I prove it before they cart me off to Prism Palace?

She needed to be sneaky. If Uncle Pan found out that she was doing her own investigation, he'd probably keep her locked up in her rooms until Halloween. And if Mary did? That would be much, much worse.

Anyway, that wasn't going to happen. Deviousness was going to be her middle name. Which was a lot better than her *actual* middle name, Hecate.

Father wouldn't have just sat around waiting for others to sort it out; he'd have done it himself. "Leading from the front," he called it.

I'll be leading from the shadows.

So, where to begin?

At the beginning.

In the cellars, where the wine for the feast was stored and opened.

Lily approached one of the servants, the boy who had carried in the goblets on the night of the engagement feast. She knew that he'd already been interrogated by Tyburn, but she had a few questions of her own.

"Hello," she said.

The boy almost dropped the wine bottle when he saw her, pale and darkly dressed, standing right behind him.

"Looks like you've seen a ghost," said Lily.

"Er . . ."

"So, what's your name?"

"Um . . . David?" He stepped back. Then bowed. "M'lady."

"Ah, David. Do you work here?" She looked around the cellar. Plenty of the racks were rather empty-looking. That couldn't all be due to the feast, could it?

Or was it Uncle Pan? Even he couldn't drink *that* much.

"Er . . . yes, m'lady?"

"Good. It's just . . ." How could she put this? "I'm trying to work out who tried to poison me. It wasn't you, was it?"

"Aargh . . ." David turned ashen. And started shaking.

"That was just a joke. Of course it wasn't you. I know who it was but just need your help proving it."

"Urrgh . . ."

"Now, you can tell me—it was Gabriel, wasn't it?"

"M . . . M'lady?"

"Gabriel Solar? Dresses all pretty but with the face of an imbecile? My fiancé?" How that word made her want to vomit! "Did he put something in my goblet?"

"M'lady, I don't know anything! The steward gave me the tray with the goblets already filled! I just carried it up from the cellar!"

"Ah, the steward. Of course. And where is he, this time of the morning?"

"The kitchens, m'lady," said David, still pale and shaking.

Despite the seriousness of the situation, Lily had to admit this was more enjoyable than being stuck in her rooms. If it carried on like this, she'd probably be finished by lunch.

Well before Lily reached the kitchens, she heard the noise of it: pots and pans clanking, and the cook bellowing orders. The smells followed: bread baking, soups simmering, onions and garlic sizzling, and a hundred other herbs and spices mixing with the roasting meat.

A maid rushed out of the kitchen door with a tray of toast and marmalade. There was a bottle of wine, too, and Lily guessed it was on its way to her uncle. She took a deep breath and entered.

The cook waved her rolling pin at the baker, then the butcher, and next the boy who was struggling with fresh loaves piled in his arms as he wove between the tables and scurrying maids. She ruled the kitchen, a general in an apron.

Waves of heat rippled across the flour-covered floor as oven doors crashed open and slammed shut. Over the spit turned two big sheep carcasses, the fat hissing as it dripped onto the coals.

Now which one was the steward?

She stopped a servant as he lumbered past, a sack of flour on his back. "Excuse me, but I'm looking for the—"

"Can't you see I'm busy, girl?" The man adjusted the load. "Though I'd never thought I'd see the day we'd be feeding the Solars and their kin."

"I was just wondering—"

"I said . . ." He looked up and glared angrily at her. Then he froze, and the anger flipped into terror. "M'lady, I didn't know it was you. Er . . ."

"The steward. Where is he?"

"Over there, with the ladle." He forced a stiff smile up onto his frightened face. "What I was saying about the Solars . . . I meant it's a blessing by the Six themselves that we've such fine guests. They light up the room, as it were. And I've never seen a more handsome lad than Gabriel. Ridiculously handsome."

"Yes, Gabriel is certainly ridiculous," Lily replied. She spotted the steward and left the servant with his flour.

The steward was testing the soup, sipping delicately from an iron ladle.

"Morning," said Lily as brightly as she could.

The steward spluttered. "M'lady?"

Why had everyone stopped working? She tried to ignore all the eyes upon her.

Devious. She had to think devious. Devious and subtle.

First, she needed to put him at ease. She wasn't entirely sure how to speak with servants, but it couldn't be that hard, could it?

"Nice weather we're having, isn't it? For this time of year. And those socks you're wearing, pure lamb's wool? I bet they must keep your toes *very* snug."

The steward stared at his socks, then back at her. His expression was pained. "Er . . . my socks, m'lady?"

This was working out brilliantly. Now perhaps she should pay him a compliment? Yes, to gain his trust.

"I love what you've done with your hair," Lily pointed at the few tufts around his ears. "Simple, yet elegant."

"My hair?"

There, she had his complete confidence. "So, I was wondering, about last night. You didn't happen to see who tried to poison me, did you?"

The ladle dropped from his fingers and clanged on the flagstone floor.

Lily paused. That seemed rather guilty, didn't it? She pressed her fingertips together and put on her hardest stare. She'd often faced it from her father when she was caught making trouble, and she'd always crumbled under his cold gray gaze. Now it was time for her to try it. "You seem very nervous. Is there anything you want to tell me?"

Was he in on the poisoning? Gabriel wasn't the sort of person to do his own dirty work, not when he could get a minion to do it for him. Maybe he paid the steward to pour the poison into her goblet? Yes, all the pieces were falling into place. Lily bet if she went to his room she'd find a bag of Luminean sovereigns hidden under his bed.

Perhaps he was still working for Gabriel; after all, the poisoning had failed yesterday. He might try again, and when better than at breakfast?

She looked suspiciously at the soup.

"Lilith Shadow!"

Uh-oh.

Mary bustled through the watching cooks and serving girls, one hand dragging a weeping David, the other hand clasping the usual red ledger.

Lily turned to the steward. "I'll deal with you in a minute." She spun around to face Mary. "Do you sleep with that book?"

"I use it as a pillow," said Mary unapologetically. She pulled David up. "What have you been saying to this poor boy?"

"Nothing!"

"So you didn't accuse him of trying to poison you?"

"Of course not!" Lily glanced over to the trembling steward. "Not him, anyway."

Mary let go of David and rubbed her temple. "I can feel it coming on, one of my *special* headaches. You're going to be the death of me, my girl."

Lily took Mary's arm and pulled her to one side. "Shh," she whispered. "Don't tell anyone, but I think I know who killed Custard."

Mary clutched the ledger to her chest. "You do?"

"Right here, in this room."

"Lily . . ."

Lady Shadow tilted her head slightly. "It's him. The steward."

Mary opened her mouth to speak. Then shut it. Then opened it.

Then grabbed Lily by the collar.

"Ow! You're choking me!"

"Come on. We're leaving."

"But what about him?" Lily said loudly, pointing first at the steward and then at the big pot on the stove. "For all we know, he's poisoned the soup!"

Mary spun around and glared at the steward. "Have you?"

"N-no, Mary. Of course not."

"Satisfied?" said Mary.

Lily glowered. "Of course he's going to say that."

Mary snatched a spoon out of a cook's hand and filled it with soup. "Mary, don't!" Lily warned.

Mary swallowed it. She grimaced.

Lily gasped. "What's the matter? Did he put poison in it?"

"Worse."

"Worse?" Oh no! She didn't want Mary to die!

"Garlic," said Mary. She waved the spoon at the steward. "Did I or did I not tell you that the earl doesn't want garlic? It gives him fierce wind! How's it going to be, him sitting at the table next to the duke's son, when he can't control those weak bowels of his?" She flung the spoon at him. "There'll be war!"

So the soup wasn't poisoned. Maybe Lily had been wrong about the steward. She decided to take her leave. There was still plenty of investigating to be done. Better she go quietly, so as not to interrupt . . .

But Mary must have had eyes in the back of her head. "You stay right there."

"I *am* Lady Shadow, you know," said Lily, trying to reclaim some dignity. "You can't order me around."

Mary stood up on her tiptoes so the two of them were, almost, eye to eye. She put her stubby forefinger on Lily's nose. "Did you say something? Or was that a mouse squeaking?"

Lily decided not to say anything more.

"Now listen to me, Lily." Mary's voice dropped to a low and malevolent whisper. "You will go straight back to your rooms. You will stop bothering my staff, and you will leave this business to the likes of Tyburn. Do I make myself clear?" She raised a hand before Lily could answer. "No, don't speak. Just nod."

Lily nodded.

"Good girl. Now go. Chop-chop." Mary inhaled deeply through her flared nostrils. Then she gazed around the silent kitchen and clapped once. "What are you all gawking at? Get back to work!"

SEVENTEEN

Lily stomped back and forth in her bedroom, her boots beating hard on the vast mosaic that covered the floor. She stopped on the face of her ancestor, Baal Demon-scourge, a sorcerer who had overseen the construction of the Great Hall.

Why couldn't she be more like Baal? Even the lords of hell had feared him.

Who feared her? No one.

Instead, Mary ordered her about like some scullery maid!

Lily kicked her chair. It wasn't just Mary. No, there was Duke Solar, too. And Uncle Pan. She would have thought her own uncle would try to help her, but he was just like the rest. They wanted Lily to sit quietly, look pretty, and not make a fuss. They didn't want a ruler; they wanted a silly little girl.

Lily threw herself onto her bed.

What can I do?

She stared at the ceiling, at the painting of dancing skeletons and ghosts looming over tombs and gravestones. Zombies, of course. So many of them.

Count the bones. Her mother often told her to do that when she couldn't sleep.

That's what they wanted: for her to stay here and do nothing. Sleep and sleep until her wedding day.

Wasn't there some story about a princess who'd slept a hundred years, waiting for her prince?

What. An. Idiot.

Lily jumped up.

I need another plan.

She wasn't going to give up. Maybe, just maybe, it hadn't been Gabriel. But if not him, then who?

Lily went to her desk. She would make a list of suspects. Start there. Then investigate each person until she figured out who the poisoner was. She pulled out a sheet of parchment and dipped her quill into the ink.

There was a tap at the door.

"Go away. I'm busy." She poised the nib over the parchment. She needed a name to go at the top.

The door opened a crack. "Hello?"

It was Rose, carrying a tray. "I brought you a nice meal. I've got lamb broth, some fresh bread, and I thought you might like some chocolate, what with all that's been going on."

"I said I'm busy." She couldn't think of anyone to put on the list. Not a single person. Maybe she wasn't clever enough to do this. Maybe she was just the silly little girl everyone wanted her to be.

No. That can't be true. I won't allow it.

Rose put the tray down beside her. "But, m'lady, you need—"

Lily flung her arm across the desk, hurling the tray and all its contents across the room. "I AM BUSY!"

"I just thought—"

"*Thought?*" snapped Lily, fury washing over her. "You *thought*, Rose? You? Quick, write that down in the castle histories: *Rose thought!*"

"I'm sorry, m'lady." Rose curtseyed. "I'll clean up this mess and go."

Why am I angry with her? She hasn't done anything wrong. . . .

Lily blushed with shame. "I'm so, so sorry, Rose. Let me help."

"That wouldn't be right. Leave it to me. I don't mind."

"Stand up, Rose." Lily spoke firmly but more gently this time. She took Rose's hand and raised her so they faced each other.

They both had pale skin and black hair. Rose had "black blood"; that's what they called it. Somewhere in Rose's family's past there was a Shadow ancestor.

But fate had made Lily ruler of Gehenna, and Rose a servant.

"Sit down," said Lily, pointing at the chair by the dressing table.

"M'lady?"

"Only if you'd like to."

Rose frowned, then slowly walked over to the dressing table and sat down meekly with her palms on her lap.

Lily picked up the chocolate, unwrapped it, and broke it in half. "Go on."

"I couldn't."

"Come on, Rose. When was the last time you had chocolate?"

"Your tenth birthday. Mary let me lick the spoon she'd used to make your cake." She looked longingly at the dark brown block. "All right . . . just a nibble."

Three years ago.

"No, not just a nibble." Lily put the half slab in Rose's palm.

They sat and ate. Lily watched how Rose's eyes widened when she took her first bite, heard Rose's groan of pleasure when the cocoa and sugar melted in her mouth.

Why doesn't it taste that good to me?

I haven't waited three years for it.

"Now that you've eaten my chocolate, you owe me something," said Lily.

Rose looked frightened.

Lily met her gaze with steel. "This is important, Rose. Do you understand?"

Too scared to speak, Rose nodded.

"You must call me Lily." She put up her hand before Rose could protest. "*Lily*. Say it."

"Lily."

They both laughed.

Rose galloped around the room. "You should have *seen* him, Lily!" She swung a hairbrush left and right. "Charged straight at them on the back of Tyburn's horse!" She neighed and galloped around the room a second time.

"Thorn rode Thunder?" Lily couldn't believe it. "How?"

"No idea, but one minute, he was surrounded by Gabriel and his squires, and the next, they were being chucked this way and that. I saw it all from the storeroom door." She swiped the hairbrush. "*Thwack!* Thorn hit Gabriel right center, sent him flying a hundred feet in the air, I swear he did!" She collapsed on Lily's bed. "It was brilliant."

"That Thorn's a boy of mystery," said Lily. "He rode Thunder? *Really?*"

"And you've seen that arrow in the gargoyle, the one with the broken ear?"

"You mean Chip?"

Rose nodded. "Thorn did that."

"They said it was a lucky shot."

"Right after he hit a bull's-eye? No one's that lucky."

"And what were you doing up so early in the courtyard?"

Rose blushed. "Mary . . . she needed some fresh flour. From the storeroom. It's not my fault that's when the squires do their training." She grinned. "And in the summer when it gets too hot, they all take their shirts off."

"Rose! I'm shocked!" Lily laughed. "You're a woman of mystery yourself." She leaned closer. "Any particular one you have your eye on?"

Rose looked down shyly before confessing, "Fynn. He's a guard at Skeleton Gate."

"I know who you mean." Lily nodded. Big, friendly. Not too bright. "Good choice."

Rose suddenly became serious. "People don't notice servants. That don't mean *we* don't notice things."

Was that a dig at Lily? It was true. There'd been plenty of times when Lily had forgotten that Rose was standing right next to her. A shadow of a Shadow. "What is it?"

"I . . . I don't know."

"There're only us two here, Rose."

Rose sat up. "It's about the feast."

"What about it?"

"I was there, Lily. I was mostly busy keeping Baron Sable's flagon filled. But I was there."

And no one noticed. Including me. "What did you see?"

Rose looked anxious. "I haven't told anyone. I didn't because who would believe a servant over a duke's son?"

"This is about Gabriel?"

"He's evil, Lily. Really evil. You need to watch out for him."

Lily laughed. "Gabriel's a stupid fool."

"It was the crystal cups," said Rose. "I saw what he did when you went off and danced with the Sultanate boy."

"What did he do?"

"He put something in your cup, Lily."

Lily caught her breath.

I told them from the beginning, and they didn't believe me.

Lily stared. "Are you sure? Totally sure?"

Rose nodded. "It was Gabriel who tried to poison you."

EIGHTEEN

I hate this place. Really, truly HATE it.

Every cobweb and every stone. Even the sound of it. The way the air moaned out of secret vents, and the echoes that decayed like the breath of old men.

Castle Gloom was unnatural, hard and lifeless, the opposite of the world that Thorn had grown up in.

Instead of a forest of great, leaf-wrapped trees, there were endless columned corridors all covered in dust. Instead of soft grass and moss, there was hard, dead marble. Instead of sparrows, falcons, pigeons, kingfishers, crows, and a canopy filled with birds, there were bats, bats, and more bats.

And Castle Gloom went on and on. Forever.

He hadn't encountered any zombies, which was good. But he hadn't found a way out, which was bad.

He'd fallen off one roof and right through another, knocking himself out in the process. He had lain among broken beams and shattered tiles for hours and only awoken after dusk.

No sign of Gabriel and his cronies, fortunately. They must have seen him fall and assumed he'd broken his neck.

Bruises and cuts covered his body, but amazingly, he hadn't suffered anything worse. Thorn's head was thicker than most.

There'd been no way to climb out of the hole in the roof, so he'd gone exploring instead.

That was *hours* ago.

Thorn clawed through walls of cobwebs and wandered through corridors thick with untrodden dust. He strayed down hallways where the faded faces in the portraits seemed to move in their frames to watch him go by. Once or twice, strange sounds had reverberated from somewhere hidden and dark and, his heart racing and his hands clammy, he'd hurried on to the next vaulted chamber.

It was obvious to him by now that large sections of the castle were empty except for the moaning wind and him.

And, of course, the bats.

A slice of moonlight shone through the collapsed ceiling high overhead. Bats flew in and out of cracks in the castle walls in waves. Their wings fluttering in that uneven, frantic way that bats flew, as if they weren't really sure about this whole wing thing.

What was the point of bats?

Thorn was lonely, aching, and starting to feel weak from hunger. Would anyone come looking for him? Old Colm? Tyburn? Maybe even Lady Shadow?

Don't be daft.

They wouldn't waste their time on a nobody.

Thorn sat down, weary to his core.

Everything had gone wrong. The more he tried, the worse it got.

Ever since that day he'd gone hunting alone in Herne's Forest. It seemed so long ago, and so far away, like it had happened to someone else.

The nobles called it poaching. He called it not starving.

One deer. That's all he'd taken. A two-year-old doe. No one would miss her.

He'd been proud of the shot. Late in the evening, with poor light, and plenty of foliage in the way. A distance of over a hundred yards, and he'd hit true at a target smaller than his palm.

After that? One disaster after another.

You can't beat 'em.

Maybe he was one of life's losers.

Just give up.

The bats circled above him, shrieking hideously.

They came and went as they wanted. In and out of the broken roof, through the vents, and into the sky.

If they can get out, then so could he.

Thorn gritted his teeth and rose to his feet.

He'd show everyone. He'd show those royals that even if they had their castles and magic, he had more. Jewels and shining swords didn't mean much down here. Not as much as guts.

The roof openings were too high up, and climbing in the dark was beyond stupid. He needed to find an opening lower down.

There, a break in the wall. He watched as bats swooped into it.

He peered in. It was dark, but he could hear the echoes of beating wings.

Thorn found a tapestry and ripped it into strips. He tied them in a bundle around a broken chair leg and, after a few minutes of striking his pocket flint against the floor slab, created a small fire. The cloth took a while to catch, but eventually he had a smoking torch. Good for an hour or two, he reckoned.

He slipped through the crack.

He shimmied sideways and downward until he found himself in a crooked passage. He passed tall black statues of hooded men, horned demons, and skull-faced women. The stone creaked, and Thorn's heart beat faster.

Where was he? Below the foundations of the castle? The walls were crude, bare rock, and the chambers were natural caves rather than brick-built halls.

The floor was pitted with shallow pools and boulders. Stalactites hung from above, some as sharp and fine as needles, others with bases thicker than oak tree trunks.

Bats swooped among them.

The air trembled. A breeze, strong and earthy with the smell of damp fur, blew over him, causing the torch's flame to waver and smoke.

Something above him hissed. It let out a long, waking breath that made the hairs on the back of Thorn's neck rise.

A shape moved overhead.

Thorn lifted his torch.

The light shone on one of the huge spikes of dark stone above him. Water trickled down over its folds and creases, and Thorn saw it move. Bristles stood up along it, and it shook.

That ain't no pillar.

It unfurled its sail-sized wings. The creature shivered and droplets of water showered down on Thorn.

The wings kept opening. A dozen feet wide and not half open. Then twenty or more.

Thorn moved behind a boulder, hunter-quiet, his eyes never leaving the waking monster.

Blank eyes opened and a mouth widened to reveal saber-like fangs. Its fetid breath stank of things long dead. It snapped its jaws, and in one bite, swallowed a host of smaller bats. It sniffed the air through its flared nostrils.

Stalagmites had begun to form upon it, long strands of limestone that cracked and splintered as it loosened itself. How long had it slept to become encased like that? Decades? Centuries?

It jumped down. Despite its immense size, it landed with barely a sound and lapped water from a pool.

Thorn stood, utterly motionless, staring. The fur on its body was as spiky as pine needles, and the wings were oily black and lined with veins.

Thirst quenched, it raised its head and searched with its high-pitched shriek.

It's still hungry.

Snacking on the small bats wasn't going to fill its belly, not after a long hibernation. Thorn crouched a little lower in his hiding place. The bat was big enough to swallow him whole.

The monster beat its wings. The leathery skin slapped like sails catching the wind.

It needs to get out and hunt.

But how? The bat was gigantic. Its body was over a dozen feet long, and each wing stretched at least fifty.

The bat turned around, its ears twisting in all directions. Thorn could see long, old scars through the fur on its back.

It's looking for a path to the sky.

The bat's attention locked onto a deep, crooked tear in the chamber's ceiling.

Was that an opening?

The bat flapped its wings and rose to its claw tips.

Thorn was a few feet behind it. His heart beat like it had never beaten before. He was terrified and yet thrilled. The bat shrieked again, louder and clearer. It was a declaration.

This has to be the stupidest plan of all time.

But stupid is better than none.

He had to decide right now. Stay and find his own way out . . .

. . . or hitch a lift?

The bat beat its wings harder and hovered a few feet off the ground.

It's leaving.

It's now or never.

Thorn leaped on just as the bat launched upward.

NINETEEN

Thorn dug his fingers into the bat's fur as he slammed against it, and hung on for all he was worth.

The bat shot upward.

Thorn screamed as it swooped along the chamber's ceiling, weaving in between the jagged stalactites.

This is insane!

The bat threw itself in wild directions, tumbling and spinning as it tried to shake him off. Thorn flattened himself against the hairy back, smothering his face in the thick, stinking fur.

Faster and faster it raced along secret paths through underground halls and caverns. It shrieked, and Thorn heard its thundering echoes. Sometimes they hit him almost instantly, meaning the rock was close; other times the sound returned after a few seconds, telling him the walls were farther away.

He hung on, listening and praying.

Then, suddenly, the echoes didn't return at all.

Thorn opened his eyes. He saw a slash of stars in the darkness ahead.

Sky. It was sky.

He just had time to gasp as the bat burst out of the cave mouth. It accelerated with every beat of its massive wings, now fully unfurled.

Thorn's heart filled his throat as the bat flapped, rising higher and higher toward the moon.

Could he fly all the way there? It was a wild thought, but before he could urge it on, the monster peaked, arched backward, and tucked in its wings. For a moment, they paused in the sky.

Then they plummeted back toward the earth.

Thorn gripped tighter and felt the bat's heartbeat thumping against him. His own heart seemed ready to burst with the sheer thrill of it all. The ground rushed toward them.

Then the bat threw out its wings and skimmed over trees, its claws brushing the tops.

Despite the icy wind biting his face, Thorn grinned. He was faster than the wind!

Spindlewood. We've come out of Spindlewood.

Could he fly all the way home? Over the woods and sea and into the morning sun. Stour was somewhere to the east. . . .

But the bat had its own ideas about where it wanted to go, and moments later, they swooped over Castle Gloom. They flew across the battlements and the petrified soldiers, between spindly towers and smoking chimney pots.

Wind tore at Thorn's face, biting cold but fresh and *free.*

With a twitch of its left wing, the bat banked toward the animal pens. A stink hung over the large courtyard, and there was a central patch of thick mud where the pigs lay. The cows were in the sheds, but the sheep roamed within a fenced square.

The bat hissed and plunged.

It smashed the fence into splinters and piled into the panic-stricken flock.

For the second time that day, Thorn was thrown off his mount. He smacked down among the sheep, reducing his world to spinning sky and hooves and smelly wool. The sheep were panicking, and he got a kick in the head.

"Get off me!"

The sheep weren't listening. They trampled over him, eyes wide with terror as they surged toward the gap in the shattered fence.

Bruised, bleeding, and with a mouthful of wool, Thorn let himself collapse.

I've just ridden a giant bat.

He grinned.

I bet even high-and-mighty Tyburn hasn't done anything like that.

Then a sour, troubling thought bubbled up.

Giant bat. Giant hungry bat.

Sheep.

Drat.

Groggy and still not too sure on his legs, Thorn struggled to his feet.

A sheep bleated before the bat sank its fangs into its body. The bat lifted it up and, grinding its jaws, devoured it whole.

Then, suddenly, the sky was filled with wings.

Bats poured out of every doorway, every chimney and vent and crack. They rose from the broken roofs of the abandoned buildings, and a cloud of them descended from Witch's Tower. Not in the thousands, but in the hundreds of thousands.

Thorn watched in awe as they circled above the giant bat like an ebony halo. All animals had a pecking order. An alpha, a top dog. But he'd never seen anything like this.

They've come to greet their king.

The giant bat hissed and grabbed another sheep, holding it down with its claws and ripping off its head.

House Shadow soldiers came running with spears and crossbows and faces white with horror.

Thorn ran in front of them, hands raised. "Don't shoot! Don't shoot!"

The soldiers aimed at the bat.

"Don't shoot!" Thorn shoved one of the soldiers back.

The bat turned to face the line of soldiers and widened its mouth, revealing its bloody fangs and hissing out a warning. It swatted a pair of spearmen aside with a flick of its wings.

"Put your weapons away!" shouted Lady Shadow as she raced across the flagstones, waving furiously. "Put your weapons away!"

Spears dropped and fingers came off the crossbow triggers. The bat picked out his third sheep.

Lady Shadow stopped, panting and flushed. "So, Thorn"—she stared at the bat, her eyes as big as the moon—"who's your new friend?"

TWENTY

"**H**is name is Hades," said Lily, pointing at the name written on the wrinkled page of an old family diary. She could barely contain her excitement. It hadn't even been an hour since Thorn had flown in, and now she sat at the desk in her study with Thorn, Old Colm, Tyburn, and Pan gathered around it. "It means king of the underworld."

"That fits," said Thorn.

Lily tapped the small leather-bound book. "This is the diary of my great-great-grandfather Faustus Shadow. He kept Hades as a pet."

Thorn's brow creased. "A pet?"

"Faustus was a famous alchemist. He . . . *experimented* on Hades. Growth potions. Extended life span, too, it seems." She flipped to another page. "See here? Faustus even rode Hades into battle. He disappeared a hundred and twenty years ago, so everyone assumed he'd died, but it turns out he was just hibernating."

Old Colm sat tapping his wooden leg on the flagstones. He always did that when he was worried about something. "You're full of surprises, aren't you, troll?" he said to Thorn.

Pan dabbed his sweaty forehead. "Twelve sheep that monster ate.

Twelve. We'll have to buy more. Mary will throw a fit." He helped himself to his third glass of wine in as many minutes.

"Where is Hades now, Master Colm?" Lily asked.

"Murk Hall, m'lady. He's settled down for a sleep." Then he growled at Thorn. "So what happened, troll?"

"I got lost," he answered.

Old Colm grimaced. "I heard you got in a fight with Duke Solar's son."

"I got lost. Looking for the privy. Sir."

That sounds like a big, fat lie.

She knew it and so did the others.

"That'll be all," said Pan. "You may go, boy. You, too, Master Colm."

"What about my bat?" said Thorn.

"The animal is too dangerous," said Pan. "Today it ate some sheep. What if it's a village child next time? Or, the Six forbid, one of the Solars?"

"Like Gabriel?" said Lily hopefully. Then she caught Pan's not-amused-at-all look and sunk down into her chair. "Which would be really, really tragic."

"The best thing to do is kill the beast," Pan declared. "Tyburn, deal with it."

"You are not hurting my bat," said Thorn, stepping up to the executioner.

Tyburn merely looked down at the boy.

Lily smiled at Thorn's bravery—and his stupidity.

"Hades is one of the family," said Lily. "We look after our own."

Thorn bowed. "Thank you, m'lady."

Lily almost laughed but saw that Thorn was trying hard to act properly. She returned his politeness with a small curtsey. "You're welcome. There's plenty of information in the diary about how to take care of Hades. You and I will go through it later."

And with that, Old Colm and Thorn left.

Pan slammed the door and glared at Lily. "Stay away from that boy. He's nothing but trouble."

"Someone needs to be on Thorn's side."

"What does that mean?"

"I'm not going to let Gabriel hurt him," said Lily.

"Gabriel Solar is a fool," said Tyburn. "If Thorn can't outwit Gabriel, then he really is of no use to anyone."

"Tyburn, that almost sounds like a compliment."

"The boy's likeable and has many useful qualities."

"'Useful qualities'?" repeated Lily. This was too much fun. The whole castle was in an uproar. Every Shadow squire wanted to be Thorn's best friend. "He just rode in on a giant bat. I think that counts as rather fantastic, don't you? Still, we can deal with Thorn and Hades later," she looked around the room, double-checking that it was just the three of them now. "I want to talk about what Rose told me. She saw Gabriel put poison in my cup, Uncle. What more proof do we need?"

Pan shook his head. "This again? You cannot be serious."

"This is about the Solars trying to take over Gehenna, Uncle. I'm very serious." She would never let that happen. She'd heard that the Solars were already hiring stonemasons to put windows in. Never!

Lily would not be remembered as the Shadow who let light into Castle Gloom.

"Lily, be reasonable. Why would Gabriel want, or need, to do such a thing?"

"But she *saw* him."

"Who knows what that silly girl saw?" Pan grunted. "And the word of a mere servant against the heir of Lumina? No one would believe her. If the duke was here, he'd demand she be whipped for her impertinence."

"No one touches Rose." Lily wasn't giving up. "I don't see why her word means less than Gabriel's, or anyone's, when it's the truth. Gabriel's evil! He tried to poison me, and he tried to have Thorn killed. Wade told me that Gabriel had his squires chasing Thorn with knives, Uncle."

Pan scoffed. "As I said, that Thorn is nothing but trouble."

Tyburn shook his head. "Gabriel is not the poisoner."

"Why not?" she asked.

"He lacks the guile."

"Are you quite sure?"

"It's my job to be sure, m'lady."

Pan folded his arms and considered the executioner. "Then who is this mysterious poisoner?"

"The man I've been hunting for the last five months. The sixth brigand."

It was as if a cold hand had seized Lily's lungs and was squeezing the breath out of her. The pain grew every second as the agony of her family's deaths became fresh all over again.

Pan swallowed his wine. "He must be long gone by now, Tyburn."

Lily's hands shook. Despite the crushing tightness in her chest, she forced herself to speak. "Six men were responsible for killing my parents and brother, Uncle. We found five. Let Tyburn finish."

"Your father's carriage was ambushed in Spindlewood. Why would brigands pick such a spot? There is little traffic in that part of the woods. Little chance of a rich merchant or well-to-do farmer traveling through. No, there are better places, with richer pickings." Tyburn met her gaze. She knew he'd been loyal to her father, but there was no emotion in the man's eyes. No sense of loss or pain. Lily turned away.

Tyburn continued. "They were there on purpose. Not to rob, but to kill the Shadows. No mere brigand would risk taking on a sorcerer as powerful as your father. It would have to be someone special."

Lily whipped around. "They were assassins, you're saying?" Her eyes flashed as the idea sunk in. "A special kind? But you caught five and . . . took care of them. That doesn't sound so special to me."

"Five were pawns, I think. Mere hired hands. The sixth one, though . . . he was injured by an arrow but escaped. We searched Spindlewood with troops and hounds, and we found nothing. No trail, no mark of his passing."

Tyburn paused, resting his hand on his sword hilt. The shadows were heavier in the faint candlelight, deepening the wrinkles and creases in his face. "I have spent months searching and still haven't found him. No man has ever evaded me for so long."

"It was sloppy of you to let him get away in the first place." Pan's hands tightened around the goblet. "I gave you extra men to make sure they were dealt with properly."

"And you think the sixth brigand and our poisoner are one and the same?" asked Lily.

Tyburn didn't answer immediately; he seemed to be weighing his response. Lily knew he didn't like to guess. "Most likely. He would have had to lie low to recover from his arrow wound—that would account for the last few months—and now he is back to finish the job. Remember, m'lady, you were supposed to be in that carriage, too. You were meant to be killed alongside the rest of your family."

Pan put his hand gently on her back. "Enough, Tyburn. Can't you see you're upsetting her?"

"No, it's all right. I need to know this." Lily stared at her hands, clenched fiercely into fists. "I want to help," she said. "I want to know who this man is. I should—"

Pan squeezed her shoulder. "Leave this to Tyburn, Lily."

"They were my family. I owe this to them, Uncle."

Pan spoke to Tyburn. "Do you think he's still nearby?"

"Near enough to put the life-bane in the goblet during the feast. I am questioning the various servants. . . ."

They weren't listening to her. They weren't going to let her do anything.

After five months, she thought her heart had started to heal, but hearing about the man responsible for killing her loved ones had torn it apart again. She *had* to find him, but she knew she'd get no help from Tyburn or Uncle Pan.

It's time to stop playing by the rules.

So now she needed to break them, starting with the biggest one of all.

TWENTY-ONE

The next evening, Lily took K'leef and Thorn off to explore Castle Gloom.

They started with a secret doorway behind a statue of Baron Moloch Shadow, standing at the head of the Corridor of Woe.

Thorn peered down the unlit passageway. "Why do I think this is a bad idea?"

K'leef looked down the same passageway and nodded. "A very bad idea."

Lily glanced back at them. "Don't tell me you're scared?"

K'leef straightened his robes. "Of course not. I was just . . . worried for Thorn."

"I'm a lot less scared than you, K'leef," snapped Thorn. "Back in Stour, Dad and me went hunting—"

"All right. You're both very brave." Lily huffed and tugged K'leef's sleeve. "Come on. I need to find this poisoner."

"Are you sure it's not Gabriel?" said Thorn. "He's a louse."

"Tyburn's convinced it's this sixth brigand. Whoever he is."

So down they went.

"What are we doing here, exactly, apart from getting covered in cob-webs?" asked K'leef, brushing his cloak.

"We're breaking the rules."

They stopped in a small chamber while Lily figured out which way to go. Thorn listened at a door. "Can you hear that?"

"Hmm." *Which arch should we go through? The first one or the second? Or the third?*

"It's just that I can hear something." Thorn reached for the door handle.

"I wouldn't." Lily slapped his hand. "That's the Hall of Forgetfulness. Going in there would be a very bad thing indeed."

"Why?"

"I can't remember." She peered this way and that. "Left, I think."

Lily led them farther into the depths of the castle, down winding stair-cases and through hidden doors, and the air grew staler and the cobwebs thicker.

"Are we there yet?" said Thorn as they marched through another empty chamber. "Wade and the other squires were heading to the fair. I was gonna go with 'em."

"This is more important."

"For you, maybe."

Lily scowled. Why had she brought him, anyway?

"Don't worry, Lily, I'll help you," said K'leef, grinning back at Thorn, who picked up his pace.

A pair of black marble doors barred the way.

Carved into them were leering, monstrous faces and grinning demons, each frozen in terrifying detail.

"This is the Shadow Library, isn't it?" K'leef took a step backward. "Lily, I hope you're not planning what I think you're planning."

"Library?" said Thorn, blushing. "I can't read."

Lily crossed her arms. "This is the only way I can find out what's going on. The only way I can save Gehenna. The only way I can protect it now that my father's gone. I need to learn magic, and you, K'leef, are going to teach me."

Thorn spluttered. "Are you insane?"

Lily poked him in the chest. "It was you who told me to start breaking the rules!"

"Yeah, break the rules, not upset the natural order of the world!" Thorn shook his head. "I ain't having it. I'm in enough trouble as it is. Let's go back before anyone knows we're missing. My grandpa always said—"

"Oh, shut up about your grandpa, Thorn." Lily smirked, and it was sly and more than a little wicked. "Or do you want to stay here for a year?"

"What do you mean?"

"I am Lady Shadow, you know. If you help me, I'll give you a sack of silver and a ship to take you back home. By next week."

"And what will Tyburn have to say about that?"

"Tyburn works for me." Lily looked over at K'leef. "And the same applies to you, or have you gotten too comfortable being Solar's hostage?"

"I gave my word to the duke I'd not try and escape." K'leef frowned. "Anyway, the Solars would catch me before I got a mile from here."

"The duke doesn't know the secret ways through Gehenna, K'leef. This is my country. I could have you back in yours before the snow falls. Provided you teach me magic, that is."

They scowled. They frowned and crossed their arms and kicked the dust, but she had them.

We're all the same, with the same desire: home.

"All right," said Thorn, a slow, big smile spreading across his face. "It's a deal."

Lily turned to the Sultanate boy. "And you, K'leef?"

K'leef didn't have the same smile as Thorn. "I don't know. . . . I gave my word."

"Does your honor mean so much?"

He started as if she'd slapped him. "It is all I have, Lily."

"It's all you have while you're away from home," she clarified. "If you help me, you will gain something much more important: freedom."

He nodded, though he still looked troubled.

Lily drew out a key made of bone, the Skeleton Key, and put it in the lock and turned.

With the sound of grinding rock, the doors unfurled like petals on a giant flower. A stale, cold wind blew out, shaking the dust and cobwebs.

She'd never been inside. There'd never been any need; after all, it was a library of magic, no place for a girl. Lily had always been envious when her father took Dante down for a lesson. Secrets that only father and son could share.

"We could use some light," said Lily.

K'leef blew gently across his palm.

Candles hissed to life. Torches in wall brackets spluttered and bright flames awoke, spreading golden, dancing light on the dark gray walls.

Waves of illumination spread outward as more candles brightened along tunnels and endless corridors, and in alcoves and nooks among dusty parchments and ancient scrolls.

How far back did the library go? She had no idea.

"Wow." Thorn entered, gazing about him. Then he stopped, mouth agape. "Who. Are. They?"

As the candlelight revealed more and more of the library, they suddenly realized that they were standing within a circle of statues.

Not just any statues, but titanic gods of stone, each over seventy feet tall.

K'leef gazed up at them in awe. "The Six Princes."

The ancient founders of the six Great Houses of magic, the first sorcerers the world had ever known, and the most powerful.

"I . . . I never seen nothing like it," whispered Thorn. "They're your ancestors?"

Lily nodded. "K'leef's, too. And Gabriel's."

"We inherited our magic from them," added K'leef.

"Is it true they were brothers?" asked Thorn. "The children of a barbarian king and his elf wife?"

"She wasn't an elf. She was the daughter of a demon lord," said Lily.

"You're both wrong," interrupted K'leef. "She was a desert spirit. She'd been trapped in a bottle, and when he freed her, she fell in love with him. She passed her magic down to their six sons. That's the true story."

"And I bet House Coral will swear she was a mermaid." Lily shrugged. "Elf, demon, or spirit, it just means she came from the otherworld, a place of pure magic."

Thorn just shook his head in wonder.

Lily continued educating Thorn. Her heritage had been drummed into her—and every noble—since the crib. She pointed to a statue of a sorcerer surrounded by birds. A pair of massive eagle's wings rose from his shoulders. "That is Prince Typhoon. Master of the element of air. Those descended from him call themselves the wind lords and live far to the east, beyond the Eagle Mountains."

K'leef joined in, pointing at the next great statue—a merman rising out of cleverly sculpted waves with sharks and dolphins surfing alongside. "Then you have Prince Coral of the element of water." He moved around to a figure wreathed in marble-sculpted flames. "This is my ancestor, Prince Djinn. He founded the Sultanate of Fire to the south."

Thorn faced a figure with bark-like skin and antlers jutting from his forehead. "And this is Prince Herne, lord of the earth, yes?"

Lily smiled. "You know much about him?"

"I grew up next to Herne's Forest. I know plenty. They say he's still alive, sleeping in a deep cave guarded by a black unicorn."

K'leef nodded. "So they say. Herne didn't believe in the more formal traditions, and neither do his descendants. They're called druids, aren't they?"

"We've got one in Stour. You have a sick animal and old Birch'll fix

SHADOW MAGIC

it right up." Thorn shrugged. "No grand palaces or castles for the druids. They're happy sleeping in meadows."

Lily pointed at the last pair of statues. "Prince Solar, lord of light, and finally, Prince Shadow, the founder of my house, my family."

The lord of darkness loomed over them. Carved out of black marble, he was hooded and attended by cavorting skeletons. In the folds of his cloak lurked ghosts and phantoms.

"So, since we're here, can you teach me some magic, too?" Thorn asked K'leef. "It don't need to be nothing fancy."

"Sorry, but I can't." K'leef picked up a book. "You have to have the blood of the princes in your veins to be able to create magic. It also dictates which type of magic you can create. If you're descended from Prince Djinn, like me, then you will only ever cast fire magic. The same goes for the heirs of Prince Coral. They will only ever be water magicians."

Thorn pointed at Lily. "But what if she marries Gabriel? That's light and darkness."

Lily paled at the thought of it.

K'leef continued. "One blood will dominate. Any children would have light *or* darkness, but never both. It's impossible to cast more than one element. And even if you have the blood of the princes, it doesn't guarantee you'll be able to use magic."

"Like my uncle, who can't cast a single spell," said Lily. "The blood's been diluted too much. Each generation is slightly weaker than the last. The blood—and the powers—of the Six Princes runs thin nowadays."

K'leef wove the flames through his fingers. "This is the best I can do. My ancestors were able to turn the whole sky ablaze."

It was similar for Lily's family. The Shadows were once masters of the undead, but it had been many decades since any of them had been able to summon a single ghost or zombie. Her father had tried, and the effort had wiped him out for a week. Iblis Shadow had known three spells, and that was considered a lot in these times. The ancients would have known *hundreds.*

Lily looked up at Prince Shadow. What would he make of the sorcerers of today?

He'd think we were ants.

They moved past the circle of statues and farther into the heart of the library.

There were objects other than books. Armor, weapons. Boxes with no openings, and bracelets and random cups and circlets.

Thorn picked up a sword of black iron. "This is nice."

Lily barely glanced at it. "It's the Sword of Midnight. Prince Shadow used it to cut time into three, thus creating the past, present, and future."

"Wow, does it work?"

"No. It's a fake." She picked up a crown. "Most of this stuff is. My uncle spent years searching for magical artifacts. He lost a lot of gold buying useless bits of armor, weapons, and rings from swindlers and cheats. My father would check each item, then tell him that all he'd gotten was another piece of junk, but it didn't stop my uncle from buying more."

Eventually they reached a circular chamber with a large table and plenty of space around it.

"This will do," said K'leef. He looked around him and up at the ceiling. His face darkened. "I didn't expect to find *him* here."

The painting on the ceiling covered the whole central chamber. A man, masked and armored, dominated the middle.

Zombies, skeletons, ghouls, and ghosts surrounded him, writhing in torment. Behind him were ruined cities, and the skies were a storm of howling spirits.

"Astaroth Shadow," said Lily. "Many of the horror stories you've heard about our family originate from him."

"Let me guess," said Thorn. "He was just misunderstood?"

"No. He was pure evil. He raised armies of the dead. Turned cities into graveyards. All thanks to that mask he's wearing." She gazed up at it. Carved from black stone, it was plain, but coldly elegant. The mouth was part opened into a sneer of contempt and the eyes tilted into a cruel, hateful frown.

"What did it do?" asked Thorn.

"I've heard that he based the mask on the face of Prince Shadow himself and gained some of our founder's power, adding it to his own magical strength. And he was powerful to begin with."

His blood flows through me. His deeds taint my past.

But he was one of the greatest of my family.

Pride and shame mingled uneasily in Lily's heart.

K'leef stared at the image, his face showing an anger Lily hadn't seen before. "It took all five of the other Great Houses to defeat him."

Lily continued. "With the mask, even a common farmer could be a great sorcerer. Certainly greater than any sorcerer alive now."

"Well, that's sorted, then," said Thorn. "Just get the mask and it's job done."

K'leef shook his head. "It was destroyed many centuries ago." He directed Lily to a clear space. "Stand here and close your eyes."

"What shall I do?" asked Thorn. "I can help."

"Not with this, Thorn," said K'leef.

Thorn frowned and took a step back.

Lily did as she was told. "What am I trying to do?"

"Magic is an art, not a craft. It's born out of the heart, not the mind. It's passion, desire. It can be rage, too."

"But shouldn't we be studying the spell books? The library's filled with them."

"No, it would take too long. This is not about copying another's work or method. It's about creating your own." He stood close to her, whispering from behind. "You're Lady Shadow; your element is darkness and all that dwells within it. There are shadows, of course, but there are other things, too. The spirits of the dead. Dreams, nightmares, sleep, and the creatures of night. The moon—that is yours, too."

"It's too much. I don't know where to begin."

"Pick one thing."

"What about Castle Gloom?"

"Good choice."

The castle was darkness made solid. No natural light had entered it since the day Prince Shadow, the original lord of darkness, had built it. The corridors recalled her family's every footstep. The stone walls in the bedrooms had absorbed the dreams of every Shadow.

How many members of her family had been born here? Almost all of them. Her own birthing cries had once filled the castle. Did it remember?

Things had been buried here. Not just the dead, but memories, too. And secrets. And sorrows.

Sorrows most of all.

I never said good-bye.

I saw them and passed them by without a word. If only I'd said something to Dante on that last day. Or even just smiled at him. He was my brother and I loved him and never told him.

Just a single hug would have made all the difference.

The next time she'd seen him, he was lying under a sheet, his body burned beyond recognition.

Had they even wanted her? Her parents had been polite, formal. Her father's priority had been to teach Dante; her mother's was to support her husband. They'd loved each other so much that there'd been nothing left for her.

Lily tightened her hands into fists.

They'd dressed her in silks and given her jewels and dolls, but none of that had been what she'd wanted.

All she'd had was Custard.

Pink and blind and smaller than her palm, he'd been the runt of the litter. She'd fed him from her breakfast plate, and he'd licked her face and slobbered all over her dresses.

Now he was gone, too.

She wished she'd drunk the poison.

Custard. What a silly name for a black dog.

She heard a startled breath. Was it K'leef?

She kept her eyes closed. All the other dogs in the litter had been pure black, but not Custard. He'd had white socks. Maybe that's why she'd wanted him so much. He was the unwanted one, too.

She'd loved the way he yapped. She could hear it so clearly, even now.

"By the Six Princes," said K'leef. "Lily . . . look."

Lily wiped her eyes with her sleeve and opened them.

A gray mist slowly swirled on the black stone surface. There was something inside the mist—an animal. Not flesh and blood, but it had heart and a voice. And a tail, a little stump that was wagging excitedly. The dog met Lily's gaze and jumped up and down.

"A ghost," said Thorn, stunned. "I don't believe it."

"Custard . . . can I touch him?" asked Lily.

"Try."

She reached out. . . .

"Lily!"

Pan stood by the door, staring at them horrified, sword in his hands. Then he gritted his teeth and ran forward.

"*No!*" Lily screamed.

The sword crashed down on the table, and the mist fell away, leaving nothing there.

Her uncle gazed at the empty table, trembling. "Lily, what have you done?"

TWENTY-TWO

"**H**ave you ever seen a person burn?" said Pan. The question slipped out as a whisper. "Have you?"

"Of course not."

"They say the smoke suffocates you before the heat becomes too much to bear, but that's not true. It's not true at all."

Lily said nothing. K'leef and Thorn were gone, pushed out of the library as Pan had dragged her along by her wrist like some little child. She'd heard the doors of the library slam behind her with a brutal finality.

Pan had yelled at servants to get out of the way and had shoved a boy who hadn't been quick enough, sending him tumbling.

They'd marched through the castle until they'd reached her quarters. Pan had booted the door open and thrown Lily in.

She was scared, but not as scared as Uncle Pan seemed. He sagged against the door, sweating and shaking. "I watched her. I watched her hair begin to smoke. I saw the blisters swell and pop all over her. Her eyes, Lily. I saw them bubbling."

"Who was she?"

"Some village woman who knew a few simple spells for fixing bones and curing fevers, but that was enough. She was a witch, and that was the law. They burned her child, too, just to be sure. A child much younger than you, Lily."

"Why? She was helping people. That wasn't fair."

"Lily, do you know what you've done? If anyone found out, you would suffer the same fate. I couldn't save you. No one could. That family friend of ours, Baron Sable? He and his sons would pile on the logs. Tyburn himself would be the one to tie you to the stake and light the flames. Then what about Gehenna? Solar would march in and scrub the Shadow name from history. He would turn your people into slaves. That's what conquerors do. Is that what you want to happen to Mary? To Rose?"

"Why are they so afraid? Men can practice magic, and when they do it, they're called heroes."

"Men can control magic but women can't. There are too many stories of disasters and wild magic, all caused by women who ended up slaves to the very powers they'd hoped to master."

"Stories told by men. That doesn't make them true, Uncle."

"But it does make them *law*. Laws that can't be changed. Not by me and not by you. Things are dangerous enough around here without you summoning . . . whatever it was."

"It was—"

"I don't want to know, Lily!" he snapped. "I thought you were sensible. What's happened to you?"

"Someone killed my family and tried to murder me."

Pan whipped around and glared at her. It was so sudden, so shocking, that she stepped back, afraid of what he might do. Was this her uncle?

Then, just as suddenly, the fierceness fled. His eyes dulled, his shoulders sank, and he stood there, a sad little man. "They were my family, too," he whispered. "Not a day passes without me wishing I had died instead of them. Useless Pandemonium Shadow instead of Iblis. It might have been the one good thing I achieved in my life." He shook his head. "Leave the investigation to the adults. I couldn't bear it if something happened to you."

Lily took hold of her uncle's hand, ashamed that she didn't realize he missed her family, too, that the pain was shared. "I am Lady Shadow now. I can look after myself, Uncle." And she could do more. Much more. "I summoned Custard. You saw it. Look, Uncle, no one needs to know. But what if I could summon other spirits? Or even enter the Twilight?"

The Twilight. The land between the living and the dead. The realm of restless spirits.

All color drained from her uncle's face. "What do you mean?"

"I never got to say good-bye to my mother and father. If I could see them, speak to them, just for a second . . ." It was possible. She knew it now. She'd brought Custard back, and she hadn't even been trying. "We'd do it here, away from everyone! Don't you want it, too? To see Father again?"

"Enough!" Uncle Pan snatched his hand free. "The Twilight? What do you know about the Twilight? What if you'd not summoned . . . whatever it was you *did* summon, but instead brought forth a specter? You know what a specter is, don't you?"

"Of course," she said, head bowed. "The blackest of spirits. The ever hungry." They were ancient ghosts of rage and hate and the most terrible dwellers of the Twilight. If even one had passed into the world of the living, it would have killed and eaten souls, and there would have been no way to stop it.

"Imagine what it would have done to you, Lily." Pan put his hand on her shoulder and made her sit down. "Listen to yourself. Bringing back the dead. Don't they deserve peace?"

"I didn't mean it like that."

"Give me the key, Lily."

"What?"

"The Skeleton Key. Give it to me."

"Why?"

"Why do you think? To stop you from any more foolishness."

Pan was just trying to protect her. He'd brought her up when her parents had been too busy, which was all the time. He'd been more of a father to her than her real father had been.

He'd been her hero, once. Back when his eyes had been bright and his laugh deep, before he'd swapped stories for drink.

"Remember the tales you used to tell me? When you explored the Shardlands, searching for treasure, and fought manticores and hydras?"

"Enough, Lily." He opened up his hand. "The key."

He wasn't going to change his mind, not this time.

She put it in his palm.

Pan sighed with relief. "That's a good girl."

"Is that it?" she replied coldly.

Pan frowned. "One more thing: I don't want you mixing with those two boys."

"Why not?" They were the only friends she had!

"Thorn's a commoner, and you are a noble. How do you think it looks with you running around with an uncouth lout? The boy needs to learn his place."

"You will not touch Thorn."

"And K'leef? Do not trust him, Lily."

"But he's helping me."

"Helping you? By teaching you magic? Are you blind, child? He knows the price you'll pay if you are ever found using it. He wants to brew as much trouble as he can between you and the Solars, because that would give his father breathing space. He'd love it if we destroyed each other."

"Thorn and K'leef are my friends."

"As you said, you're Lady Shadow now," Pan replied sadly. "You cannot have friends."

TWENTY-THREE

Tyburn wanted to see Thorn. The executioner hadn't shown interest in anything Thorn had done since they'd arrived and now, the night after they'd been caught in the Shadow Library, Tyburn wanted to see him.

I am dead.

How would Tyburn do it? Take him up to Lamentation Hill and add Thorn's head to those five up there already?

This is all that Lily's fault.

He should have stuck with Wade and gone to see the fair being set up. Instead, he'd ventured down into the pits of Castle Gloom and . . .

Seen amazing things. Not just the Shadow Library but K'leef weaving fire through his fingers and Lily summoning a ghost. A real made-of-mist-and-memories ghost.

All right, Lily's not so bad.

But that didn't make seeing Tyburn any easier. He trudged up the stairs to Tyburn's quarters, his legs moving as if made of lead and his heart just as heavy.

The door was already open, and Tyburn was writing at a desk. He glanced up. "Come in."

Thorn wasn't sure what he'd expected, maybe skulls and skeletons and walls filled with weapons. Tyburn's quarters were . . . comfortable. A rug covered the bare stone and embers smoldered in the fireplace. Sure, there were a few weapons, but this was a castle after all.

The only sound was the scratching of Tyburn's quill.

"I want you to go to Graven," said the executioner.

"Is that why you called me?"

Tyburn put down the quill and narrowed his eyes. "Were you expecting something else?"

"Er . . . no. Of course not." Thorn hoped his sigh of relief wasn't too loud. "Where's Graven?"

"You know those big mountains to the south, the Three Princes?" asked Tyburn. "On the other side of them. I need you there and back, by dawn."

"Ain't gonna happen. Them rocks are over a hundred miles away. No horse can cover that distance."

"I wasn't thinking about you taking a horse."

"Then what . . ." Suddenly Thorn grinned. "Oh. Hades."

"The bat should have you over the mountains in a few hours. Follow the Cleft Way and you can't go wrong. Graven's the last village before the border with Lumina, on the bank of the River Lacrimae."

This would be a real test of flying. Thorn's escape from the caverns had been more luck than anything. But taking Hades on a journey, navigating, that was special.

Tyburn tapped a pile of sealed envelopes on the desk. "You know what these are?"

"Trouble?"

Tyburn put them in a satchel and handed it to Thorn. "Coded messages. They allow me to know what's going on, here in Gehenna and beyond. My usual messengers are busy with Halloween duties, so I'm asking you. I want these delivered to Captain Wayland. He runs the patrols on the border. He'll have messages for you to bring back."

This was a big deal. Thorn knew it, and Tyburn had to know it, too. Thorn bet he didn't usually trust stable boys with this sort of work. So why was he trusting him? "What's to stop me from just taking Hades and flying off home?"

"You don't know the way and neither does your bat."

"I could ask someone."

Tyburn leaned back and looked at Thorn. "Yes, you could. And who knows, eventually you might even make your way back to Stour. To find me waiting. Can you guess what might happen next?"

Thorn gulped.

"Just get going," said Tyburn. "And keep your eyes open for anything unusual."

"Like what?" There was plenty unusual in Gehenna. What was considered normal at home might be considered weird here. Like parties. Like smiling. Like not summoning ghosts.

"If I knew, then I wouldn't need you to go and have a look, would I?" Tyburn's attention returned to his letters. This conversation was over.

Before long, Thorn found himself in the ruins of Murk Hall.

It was bigger than the Great Hall. How could humans build such things?

Maybe they hadn't. He'd been here long enough now to know that the ancient necromancers had commanded devils and demons and performed magic beyond the boundaries of his imagination.

The roof had fallen in a long time back. There were broken columns lying across the shattered flagstones and a tree grew in the southwestern corner, its roots weaving over rubble.

But even with the sun in the sky, the hall was reluctant to let in the light. Dense shadows filled the corners and alcoves.

"Hades? Are you here?"

The bat unfurled his wings and sniffed the air as Thorn approached. His huge ears twitched and rotated, and he yawned. His ivory fangs glistened. Remains of dinner hung from his teeth, and in between, wedged in the gums, were chunks of stringy flesh.

Thorn rubbed the beast's chin. "All right, boy? Fancy a trip?"

Hades blinked slowly. His eyes were small compared to his head, and he thrust himself closer to Thorn so they were almost nose-to-nose. He sniffed loudly.

"Sounds like a yes to me," said someone from behind him.

Thorn spun around to where Lily sat among the shadows, less than ten feet away.

"Sorry, did I scare you?" she said, smiling.

"You're a strange, strange girl." Thorn frowned. "I wasn't expecting to see you here. Not after what happened in the library."

"This is my castle, Thorn." She stood up and joined him in gazing at the monstrous bat. "Beautiful, isn't he?"

"Not the word I'd use." Thorn picked a string of what looked like sheep's guts out from between Hades's teeth and tossed it aside. "More . . . majestic?"

"Majestic. I didn't know you knew such words. But yes, majestic." Lily didn't come closer; she seemed wary of Hades. "You're going out on him, then?"

"Yeah. Tyburn wants me to take him to Graven."

"Then you'll be needing something to sit on, won't you?" Lily took his hand. "I have just the thing."

She led him over to a large leather object—shiny, and smelling of polish—on the floor. Straps hung from it in loops, and there were buckles of exquisitely engraved silver.

Thorn nodded in appreciation. "That ain't for no horse," he said.

Lily patted the flat, wide seat. "This is Faustus Shadow's saddle. I found it at the back of the armory. The whole thing was tattered and covered with cobwebs. I had it cleaned and repaired. What do you think?"

Thorn inspected it. Now *this* was beautiful. "What are these?" He checked a row of straps on the side.

"Stirrups aren't any good on a bat; you need to buckle yourself in so you don't fall out, no matter what."

"Makes sense. Fall off a horse, and all you get is a bruised backside. Fall off him, and . . ." He whistled. "Kersplat."

"I've read Faustus's old diary. It explains how to saddle Hades. Want me to show you?"

Thorn slung the saddle over his shoulder. "Sure. That way, if it slips off, I'll have someone to blame."

Lily moved closer, but Hades snapped his teeth at her. His eyes narrowed and he hissed.

"Er . . . maybe you should do it, Thorn."

Hades sat patiently as Thorn saddled him. The beast even shifted to make it easier for Thorn to get under his wings to buckle the belly strap, as if Hades remembered the old routine.

Thorn inspected the bat's old scars: puckered white marks where the fur hadn't grown back. There were arrow wounds, cuts from sword and ax. This was one tough flying rat.

Lily watched. "How do you manage it? Being so good with animals? I heard you rode Thunder, too. No one but Tyburn can ride Thunder."

"Got it from my dad. He says we just smell right. I dunno."

"Smell right?"

"Of the earth. Of bark. Of leaves and grass. I've spent so much time in Herne's Forest I think I just sort of became part of it. Carried the smell with me, you could say."

"That must be helpful if you're a hunter."

"Yeah. The best hunters are the ones who blend in." He stepped back to admire his handiwork. "There. All done."

Hades beat his wings and rose to his claws. The wings stirred the dust and fallen leaves into the air, and hordes of smaller bats clouded around him with excitement.

Yeah, I know just how you guys feel.

Thorn checked that his satchel was buckled and buttoned up his coat. "Time to be off."

"Wait, Thorn."

Lily looked up at him with those gray eyes of hers. The reflection of the moon shone in them and starlight, too. They were strange eyes, and just a little frightening.

"Yeah, Princess?"

"Be careful. Not just tonight, but all the time. You've got powerful enemies here. We all have."

"This is about Gabriel, ain't it?"

She patted Hades's chest. "He's near the top of the list. But there may be others. Others we don't know about."

"It's kinda nice, having the ruler of Gehenna watching my back." He bowed from his saddle. "I feel safer already."

Thorn settled himself and felt the bat quiver with anticipation. He ran the reins through his fingers, testing them. The pommel was in the shape of a skull, of course.

What knight ever had such a mount? A lightning bolt of thrill shot up his spine, raising every hair so they stood on end. Any more excited and he'd be covered in sparks. "How do I look?"

Lily's grin split her face from ear to ear. "Not bad. Not bad at all."

Thorn pulled up the reins, pointing Hades skyward.

Hades didn't need to be told twice.

Bats swirled around them and the stone columns blurred past. Cold night wind snatched the breath out of Thorn's lungs. He felt himself slide back, but the leg buckles creaked, then locked him in.

Hades spun as he rose almost vertically toward the moon. Around and around like a corkscrew, turning Thorn over and over. There was no way to fight it, so Thorn surrendered to Hades's joy.

Wings fully unfurled, the bat left his entourage behind.

Thorn glanced over his shoulder and gasped.

Castle Gloom looked so small. Hundreds of tents surrounded it, black and white and every other color there was. Flags fluttered in the wind. It had to be people here for the Halloween Ball, even though it was still over a week away. Nobles from the lesser houses loyal to the Shadows and the Solars, who had arrived early so they could set up near the castle. Campfires dotted the black earth and moonlight glinted on the armor of the Solar paladins as though they were fallen stars.

The greatest concentration of tents was to the north, around the fair at Devil's Knoll. That made sense; people wanted to be near the fun. The first chance he got, Thorn was going to go and spend that coin he'd won off Old Colm. Wade had told him there were jugglers, cake stands, and even a zoo filled with magical animals.

Thorn scratched between Hades's big ears. "Bet they ain't got nothing as good as you."

To the east spread the vast, dark expanse of Spindlewood.

Thorn tightened his grip on the reins and leaned toward the south. The tents were few and far between there. It seemed no one wanted to pitch up beside Lamentation Hill or the City of Silence.

Hades hesitated, then banked, one wing tip pointed to the earth, and the other to the moon at its zenith.

Thorn and Hades flew on toward the triple peaks of the Three Princes.

TWENTY-FOUR

Snow and ice encrusted the upper reaches of the mountains. The peaks of the Three Princes were connected to one another by a gently curved ridge, creating a natural bowl on the southern face. Great clouds of white breath bellowed out from Hades's mouth, and in the night, his fur glistened with gently falling snow.

Lily had been right. He was beautiful. And majestic.

A few hours later, they were circling above what had to be Graven. A light drizzle fell on both bat and boy. Judging by the clouds, Thorn reckoned he still had some time before it turned from a mist to a torrent and, if he was lucky and got his business done quickly, he might be able to beat the rain back to Castle Gloom.

The village was built as a strip along the riverbank. Old stone walls had tumbled in places and been poorly repaired with wooden posts. There was a large graveyard beside it.

Thorn squeezed his knees into Hades's shoulders. The monster responded by closing his wings and swooping downward. The ground rushed toward them and then, just when it seemed too late to avoid crashing, Hades's wings flung out wide and he landed, barely stirring a grass blade.

A horn blew from within the village walls.

Good. They've seen me. I hope they bring me something hot to eat.

Graven didn't look like much. Not the village, anyway.

But the graveyard was something else.

"Did you bury kings out here?" Thorn asked Hades. The tombs were easily twice the size of the village huts and made of old, perfectly worked stone. The statues looked so lifelike he half expected them to wave at him.

The wooden gates opened and a squadron of cavalry rode out. Even from here he could hear the jangle of armor and see the black pennants on the spears.

Hades hissed loudly.

Thorn unbuckled himself from the saddle and slid off. "Hush, boy. They're on our side."

Black-cloaked riders drew up and formed a loose circle around him and his beast. The men stared at Hades and clutched their spears tighter. Hades snapped his jaws at them, and more than one rider had to rein in a frightened horse.

"I'm looking for Captain Wayland," shouted Thorn. "I've some letters for him."

A rider dismounted and tossed his reins to his companion. He wore a single breastplate of steel and a skirt of mail that covered his legs to his calves. He had the easy walk of a man used to armor, and the sword on his left hip was plain, broad, and brutal. He flicked up the visor of his helmet and the face under it was as tough as his blade. "That'll be me."

Thorn held out his satchel. "Tyburn told me to bring you these."

Wayland took the satchel and passed it to another rider without looking at it. He chewed his mustache as he gazed up at Hades. "And who are you?"

"Thorn. I'm Tyburn's squire."

"Squire?" That surprised him. "Things have changed much in Castle Gloom if the executioner's got himself a squire and men are riding bats now." He gestured toward the village. "You have ice dangling from your chin, boy. Come inside. We've a fire and a duck turning over it."

"Much appreciated, Captain."

"What about your mount? I have oats in the stables."

Hades shrieked and beat his wings. He twisted his head as he rose, searching this way and that. Thorn knew the bat well enough now to understand that he was going hunting. Thorn shouted after the leather-winged monster. "Be back before it starts raining! And don't eat any villagers!" Thorn caught the frightened look among the soldiers. Maybe he shouldn't have said that. He gave them his best and broadest smile. "He's harmless, really."

The other men stayed on their horses, but Wayland walked alongside Thorn.

"The graveyard's bigger than the village," said Thorn. "Who used to live here?"

"What do you mean?"

Thorn gazed up at the high iron railings surrounding the cemetery. "Back in my village, when you die, you get a sack, a patch of earth, and a wooden plaque with your name on it—if someone in your family knows how to write."

Wayland smiled. "This is Gehenna. Here the dead have as many rights as the living. All makes sense, in a way. You're going to spend more time dead than being alive, so it stands to reason you need somewhere to stay that'll last a few centuries at least."

"But you're *dead*. You don't need nothing."

Wayland shook his head. "Gehenna was once a country of necromancers. All the old lords could summon ghosts and ghouls and what-have-yous. Whole armies of them."

"Armies of undead? That's evil."

"Is it? Seems to me armies of the living are worse. Think about it. Sons and fathers and brothers going off to war, maybe to die, maybe to lose an arm or a leg. Then what happens to their families back home with no one to plant seeds or reap the harvest? Nothing but starvation and misery. Even those who survive aren't the same. War wearies the soul." Wayland gestured at the graveyard. "A zombie doesn't feel pain. He's already left this world. No one's counting on him back home, are they? Used to be a law that you were still eligible to serve in the army even ten years after your death."

"Why ten?"

"After that, the body's too fragile. Bits falling off all the time."

"Still, seems a fat waste of time and money building tombs like that and leaving it to a bunch of bones."

"There's dead, and there's *dead*. The first kind didn't always stay where they were buried. Nothing worse than Grandma coming back complaining her coffin's too small."

"Don't take this the wrong way, but that's probably the creepiest thing I've ever heard." Thorn lifted up his collar, suddenly feeling colder. He was never going to get used to this place.

Wayland smirked. "Don't worry. That was a long time ago. There isn't that sort of magic in Gehenna anymore. Look over there." He pointed to a fenced-off field beside the main graveyard. "That's what we do with our dead now. A strip of earth, six feet by two. Nobody can afford the big tombs these days."

By the time they reached the gate, there was a crowd of villagers waiting.

"Are you from Castle Gloom?" asked one of the men, wringing his cap in his hands.

Wayland sighed. "Valen, let the boy get some food and warmth."

But the man took Thorn's arm and held it firm. "Are you?"

"Yeah," said Thorn.

Wayland pushed Valen off. "The boy's come a long way. And he's here on real business, not to listen to your ghost stories."

"What ghost stories?" said Thorn. He looked at Valen. "What's going on?"

Hadn't Tyburn told him to look out for anything unusual?

Valen looked at one of the villagers, a woman. "You tell the young master what you've seen. Go on, Jemma."

Thorn knew the type. Old before her time. There were plenty of women like that in Stour. Worked all day and night, and pushed out babies as often as lambing season. Some would make it, some wouldn't. She crunched her apron in her thin fingers. "Begging your pardon, sir, but what I saw was real."

"Saw what?"

"My old dad, he died last month. Caught a cold, and it turned his lungs to water. Nothing we could do."

"I'm sorry." He didn't know where this was going, but the woman was becoming more frantic. Something had her scared. *Really* scared.

"We buried him out there." She pointed to the field. "Washed him, put him in his bedsheet and a fine coffin. Oak, it was. I wanted to send him off in his best suit and with his tools, but times are hard, young master. We . . . we kept his boots. Them was new. But we did right by my dad. Flowers every week. I sweep his grave clean and everything. Then why's it happened?"

"What's happened?"

"He's come back, sir," Jemma sobbed. "He's come back."

TWENTY-FIVE

Anything unusual. That's what Tyburn had said.

Now, standing amid six upturned graves, Thorn reckoned this counted as *very* unusual.

Thorn, Wayland, five of his men, and some of the villagers had marched out to the field where the more recent dead were buried.

"Could be animals," said Wayland, gazing at the broken earth. "Or grave robbers. That's always been a problem in Gehenna."

"Why would anyone want to rob these graves?" Thorn asked. The soil had been upturned recently. Thorn couldn't be sure whether with a shovel or with bare hands.

"Look at those big tombs," said Wayland. "In the past, people were buried in their best clothes and with their possessions. A warrior would have his armor and sword. A farmer, his tools. Women would have plates and cutlery, yarn and knitting needles. Even a piece of jewelry or two."

Now it made more sense. Swords were expensive. Farmers were always needing new tools, and pottery often broke. You could just come out here and dig up whatever you wanted. In any other country, these things would have been passed down through the family. It seemed to him a waste to leave them in the earth.

Jemma sobbed on Valen's shoulder, and the other relatives looked at their family graves anxiously, more than a little afraid.

Thorn spoke to Jemma. "What did you see, exactly?"

The woman wiped her nose and pointed to the field between them and the village. "I came out to check on the cows. Then I saw him. My dad. Standing out in the field. It was a full moon, clear as day. It was him."

"When?"

"Two nights past."

"And these other graves?"

"We thought it was wolves," said Wayland. "They come sniffing and pawing at the graves in winter."

"Wasn't wolves," said Thorn. That was for sure. He knew wolf tracks and there weren't any here.

The captain looked down at the broken earth. "Get shovels."

It didn't take long. The ground was damp and already loose. They dug, and all the while Thorn kept an eye on the east. Those rain clouds were getting closer.

A shovel struck wood, and the work turned to hands brushing dirt from Jemma's father's coffin lid.

A long crack ran from head to foot, and the bare wood was splintered.

"Move those lanterns closer," said Wayland.

Everyone leaned over the edge as the captain jumped down into the pit. He grunted as he shifted the coffin lid.

Jemma gasped.

The coffin was empty except for a muddy shroud. Things were getting more unusual by the second.

Wayland clambered out and brushed off the worst of the dirt. "Worth digging the other five up?"

"They'll be just as empty," said Valen.

Could it really be true? Had the dead walked? Lily said such power didn't exist anymore, but Thorn was finding it hard to come up with any other reason the coffin might be empty. He picked up the lantern and roamed around. Plenty of footprints, all on top of one another. Then he spotted something. "You said you kept his boots?"

Jemma sniffed. "Yes, young master. Those weren't even a year old and still fit our Henry."

"What job did your dad do?" Thorn crouched down and examined the damp earth.

"Mason. He helped build the west wall of the kitchens at Castle Gloom. Lord Shadow said they was the—"

"He ever drop a stone on his foot?" said Thorn. "Say, on his left one?"

"Why, yes, he did, young master. Lost his big toe."

Thorn called Wayland over and pointed at the patch of earth in the lantern light. At the footprint he'd found. "There's only four toe prints on this left foot."

Wayland scowled. "They're heading off to those woods."

Thorn nodded.

Wayland's hand tightened around his sword hilt. "At times like these, the sensible thing would be to wait until daylight."

Thorn really wanted to agree. Empty graves. Footprints of dead men. He glanced up at the sky. The clouds were fat and black. "There'll be a downpour in an hour. Whatever prints we have now will be washed away. How big's the woods?"

"Big."

Thorn peered into the black wall of trees. He had no choice. "Then we'd better go find Jemma's dad right now."

TWENTY-SIX

Wayland handed Thorn a sword as they reached the edge of the woods. "You know how to handle one of these?"

It wasn't a proper knight's weapon, the blade little more than a foot long. Thorn did a practice swing. It felt clumsy. "Not really. Swordsmanship is for the older squires."

"It's simple. Just push that end"—he tapped the tip—"into your enemy as hard as you can. Repeat until they stop moving." He signaled to his men. "Spread out, but stay within sight!" The men raised their lanterns in acknowledgement and, with swords at the ready, went in.

This was worse than that wolf hunt he and his dad had gone on last lambing season. The local farmer had put a bounty on the wolf that killed half his flock, and Thorn's dad had gone after it.

But you can second-guess a wolf.

Thorn tightened his grip on his sword and followed Wayland.

More footprints joined up with the mason's, another five pairs. They dragged and stumbled and hadn't tried to cover their tracks.

The drizzle got heavier. Large raindrops fell and splashed upon the leaves, and soon rivulets of muddy water were running between their feet.

For the first time in his life, Thorn felt uneasy in the woods. It didn't smell right. Even the sounds were wrong. He glanced at Wayland. The captain's jaw was rock hard with tension.

Thorn stumbled over a twisted root and a branch slapped his face. What was he doing? Dad would be furious, him trampling around a wood like a city-born lummox!

Wayland seized his shoulder.

A figure stood among the trees, not more than ten yards away.

Wayland took the lantern from Thorn and stepped closer. "Identify yourself!"

Thorn's lips were parchment dry, yet his hands were sweaty. He stayed where he was. It was dark and the rain fell, but his hearing sharpened and he could identify more smells now.

Rain. Damp earth. Rotting wood and moldy leaves and the perfume of burning lantern oil.

"Didn't you hear me?" said Wayland. "Identify yourself!"

The man moved. He seemed to glide through the net of twigs and birch trees as if it was broad daylight. His steps were firm and sure. His clothing was well made and practical. A leather tunic, a heavy wool coat, thick breeches, and good waxed boots.

Wayland raised the lantern higher. "This is your last—"

Scars covered the man's face. Thick stitches crisscrossed deep grooves in his broken skin. The mouth was a twisted slash, its edges sewn up badly so it rose to one ear.

His eyes were two empty holes.

Wayland gasped and swung his sword at him.

The scarred man grabbed it. The shining steel began to rust, and in seconds, it crumbled to nothing.

Shouts burst out from the surrounding darkness. In the spots of lantern light farther along, Thorn glimpsed the soldiers fighting with strange, white-limbed creatures.

A foul, dead stench filled the air.

Leaves rustled and another figure, crooked-limbed and pale, pushed through the foliage toward him. This creature's legs moved stiffly, and his head was bent at an odd angle. His eyes were covered in gray film, his mouth hung stupid and slack. He turned toward Thorn and hissed with quiet fury.

"Get back, boy!" shouted Wayland. "Get back! It's a zombie!"

The scarred man was still there, but instead of attacking, he folded his arms and watched.

Wayland crashed the lantern down on the zombie's head, shattering its skull. The creature merely snarled, then grabbed hold of Wayland and beat his head against a tree trunk. Wayland moaned and slumped to the ground.

Then the zombie turned his sights on Thorn again. Thorn heard screams and cries from afar. The other soldiers were busy with their own zombies.

Thorn shook from head to toe. His heart raced. He'd hunted wolves. Tracked bears. Even chased down a wild boar, but nothing, *nothing* came close to the terror he felt now. He couldn't take his eyes from it and every part of him wanted to run, but he stood frozen; fear had robbed his legs of all movement.

Thorn stuck his sword out in front of him. "Stay back."

The scarred man chuckled but did not move from his spot.

Oil spilled from Wayland's lantern, burned on the leaves, and flames splashed onto the zombie's arm, but the creature ignored them. His beard crinkled and smoked.

Worms had been at him. They writhed within tears in his flesh and were big, fat, and white from good feeding on the dead meat. Where the skin was missing, Thorn stared at the exposed muscles, still moving, active though the heart was cold and unbeating.

Thorn gritted his teeth. He tightened his grip on his sword hilt, using both hands to hold it steady. Run or fight, that's what it came down to. And it was too late to run.

Then Thorn noticed that the zombie was barefoot. And he had only four toes on his left foot.

"You must be Jemma's dad," said Thorn. "She's real upset."

If he'd thought that mentioning Jemma's name might spark some faded memory, Thorn was sorely disappointed. The zombie stomped closer, getting faster, and with a hungry red fire glowing in his eyes. He reached out with his dirty, broken nails, opened his mouth, and let out a ragged scream.

Thorn thrust the sword in.

The steel went in straight and true, burying itself up to the hilt in the zombie's chest.

The undead thing merely swung its arm and swatted Thorn off his feet.

His head swam. Blinking away tears, he could only look up, dizzy and helpless, as the zombie, sword still jutting from his chest, reached down. He wrapped its bony figures around Thorn's neck and *squeezed.*

Thorn fought. He kicked and punched as his breath hissed out between clenched teeth. He stared at the deep, evil eyes of the undead thing and felt its stinking, cold breath on his face. Blood pounded behind Thorn's forehead.

His chest burned as the air left it. The zombie lifted him so that Thorn dangled, his toes barely touching the ground. How could the zombie be so strong? Thorn grabbed the sword hilt and twisted it in deeper. It made no difference. Out of the corner of his eye, he watched the scarred man, saw the interest he took in the zombie's work. He nodded with approval as Thorn's life began to leave him.

Desperately, Thorn dug his nails into the zombie's face. Skin flaked off and old, thick black blood oozed from the gashes.

Darkness fell as Thorn's senses abandoned him. He couldn't breathe.

I'm gonna die. . . .

Thorn clenched his fist for one last punch. His vision was clouding over, but he concentrated on tightening his fingers and putting the last of his strength into one final blow. Slowly, arms aching, he raised his fist. . . .

It didn't land, but something else did.

The zombie was ripped away from Thorn.

Thorn dropped to his knees, gasping. Air, clean and sharp, raced down his throat.

Hades pinned the zombie facedown on the ground. The undead thrashed its arms, but Hades's claws were deep in its back.

Hades sniffed his prey.

"Don't . . . don't just play with it. . . ." Thorn rasped, the inside of his throat feeling as if it had been scoured with sandpaper.

Hades snapped his jaws over the zombie's head and tore it clean off.

The body went limp.

Hades spat the head out.

"So there *are* things you won't eat." Thorn crawled to his feet, but it was hard work. He was nearly dead with exhaustion and every limb trembled.

The scarred man stared at Thorn and the monster beside him. He flexed his fingers.

"Try it," whispered Thorn, his throat too painful for anything louder. "Hades is still hungry. Aren't you, boy?"

Hades hissed in agreement.

The scarred man held out his arms and began *peeling* the shadows around him as though he was collecting blackberries. He pinched them from branches and off the ground, gathering them about him in a ribbon.

He spun the blackness around him. His limbs disappeared, his body and, last of all, his hideous, scarred face.

And then he was gone, vanished into the shadows.

Thorn hugged the bat. He could barely stand and hung on the bat's neck, burying his fingers in deep. Hades didn't seem bothered. He lowered his wings, enclosing Thorn in their folds. Both hearts, of monster and boy, beat together.

Thorn pressed his face into the beast's wet, smelly fur. "Good boy, Hades. Good boy."

TWENTY-SEVEN

"Tell me about the scarred man," said Tyburn. "Again."

Lily watched Thorn as he tried to explain, for the umpteenth time, what had happened at Graven the day before. The poor boy could barely stand, and the purple bruises around his neck looked horrible.

When she'd seen him come into the study, all battered and bruised, she'd almost jumped up to hug him, but she'd forced herself to stay seated at her desk. She was Lady Shadow, and such things weren't allowed, especially with Tyburn and her uncle present.

It was hard being this Lady Shadow.

Zombies. They had zombies in Gehenna. She wasn't sure if she was excited or scared. Probably both.

"It was dark," replied Thorn, sounding more than weary. "The flesh, I mean. Really deformed. I couldn't see his eyes. I'm not sure he had any. There were just holes. And the scars were deeper than just into the flesh. It looked like they went into the bone."

Lily spoke. "And what happened to the zombies?"

"When the scarred man disappeared, they just fell down. Proper dead this time," said Thorn. "Wayland ordered 'em all burned."

"Then Wayland did right," said Tyburn. "If they were undead, it's the only way to make sure they won't come back."

"If?" Pan cut in. "How can we have zombies? Just think it through. Iblis tried to raise one and failed. The effort almost broke him; he was comatose for a week."

"What about our Immortals? And old One-Eyed Ron?" said Lily. "They were all zombies."

"And all created by your great-great-grandfather," answered Uncle Pan. "Since then, we've only had the power to maintain them, not raise any new ones. Now you're talking about six. Six! All up and dancing the jig in some field!"

He may have been drunk—as usual—but Pan had a point. Bringing someone back from the dead was the greatest necromancy there was.

Then how come I was able to do it?

Okay, it was the ghost of Custard, and it had only lasted for a few seconds, but she'd done it.

A zombie was on another whole level, though. That wasn't just summoning a spirit—it was bringing back life itself. A feeble half-life, sure, but life nevertheless.

"No, there is a simpler explanation. One that doesn't require any magic." Pan leaned back in his chair, arms crossed over his fat belly. "These villagers fell ill. They weren't dead, but in comas. They were buried accidently, then woke up and dug themselves out. It happens on occasion."

Lily looked over at Thorn. "Is it possible that's what you really saw?"

"No, it ain't." The reply was firm and definite.

"What do you think, Tyburn?"

"Captain Wayland is a reliable man," said Tyburn. "And young Thorn here has proven himself to be equally so. I've had letters from other villages and towns within Gehenna, all referring to disturbed graves. I assumed they were robberies, the sort we get from time to time. But given what young Thorn has told us, I must conclude that we have a necromancer in our midst, and a very powerful one."

Pan muttered under his breath.

Tyburn addressed Thorn. "Do you remember *anything* more about the scarred man? Think, boy. How tall was he?"

"Kinda average, I suppose." He glanced at Pan. "About your height, m'lord. And he was well-dressed, like a noble."

"Are you sure?" asked Tyburn.

"About them things, yeah, I am," said Thorn. "He just stood there, watching me die. It was like he wanted to see if the zombie could kill me."

"I want this kept to ourselves until we know more," said Pan. "The last thing we need is fairy tales spreading about necromancers and people crawling out of graves."

"Think this might scare people?" asked Thorn.

"This is Gehenna," said Lily. "It'll probably get them all excited. The next thing they'll be expecting is this unknown necromancer to raise an undead army and head off to conquer Lumina."

Thorn's laugh came out like a croak. "Yeah, I forgot. Other people's nightmares are your bedtime stories."

Lily smiled at him, happy that Thorn was sounding like his usual self again. "How's Hades doing?"

Uncle Pan grimaced. "That monster ate one of the horses."

"He'd flown a long way. He was hungry," said Thorn defensively. "He saved my life."

Uncle Pan glowered. "That beast is a menace. We should get rid of him before he does some real harm."

"No," said Lily. "We'll arrange regular meals so he doesn't gobble up a stable boy by accident."

"The bat is valuable," said Tyburn. "I have plans for him."

As he spoke his gaze fell on Thorn, and Lily wondered what plans her executioner had for him.

Pan wandered to the side table and emptied the carafe into his goblet. "The Lumineans know something is going on. The duke has left Lord

Argent in charge, and I'm dining with him tonight. What shall I tell him?"

"Nothing," Tyburn replied.

"They are our allies, Tyburn. Soon to be family. This is a noble of Lumina we're talking about, not some village peasant."

Lily interrupted. "Tell him one of your adventures, Uncle. About your first expedition into the Shardlands. The one with the wyvern. Thirty feet long, wasn't it?"

Pan puffed up his chest. "Fifty, at least. With enough poison in its spike to kill a herd of elephants." He jagged his finger forward. "Killed it with a single lunge straight into its black heart."

Good. That tale would keep Pan, and Lord Argent, busy for hours.

"Anything else?" Lily asked. She wanted to get this meeting over as quickly as possible. Tyburn wasn't the only one who had plans. . . .

Tyburn grimaced. "With the Halloween Ball only a week away and the fair on Devil's Knoll, we have thousands of people camped around Castle Gloom. We are receiving dozens of deliveries every day, and there aren't enough guards to man all the gates. And there have been fights. . . ."

"Fights? Between who?" Lily asked.

"The Solars and our people. There is plenty of distrust between the Gehennish and Lumineans. That's to be expected after so many centuries of war. The duke has many of his paladins here, so Baron Sable summoned his three sons and they brought their troops with them. The situation is volatile." Tyburn looked at her. "It might help for you to speak with Baron Sable."

"Me?" she blurted involuntarily. It wasn't that long ago that Lily used to ride on Sable's back and have pillow jousts with his youngest son, Caliban.

He'll listen because I'm Lady Shadow.

She recovered quickly. "Yes, I will. And what about this poisoner? Any closer to catching him?"

Tyburn's gaze narrowed. "Yes. The border guards are on alert; no suspect has left Gehenna. His head will be mounted upon Lamentation Hill soon enough, m'lady."

Chill fingers caressed Lily's heart. Tyburn had never failed House Shadow. "Let's hope it's sooner rather than later."

Tyburn nodded. "Meanwhile, you must remain here, in Castle Gloom, m'lady."

Lily's chill turned to fury. "But I was planning to go to the Halloween fair! It's just opened, and I always go!" She'd heard the maids talking about it, and she'd been cooped up in Gloom long enough.

"We have not yet discovered who tried to poison you," Pan continued. "The fair would be a perfect opportunity for a second, more direct attack. There are plenty of strangers, noise, and tents, too many places an assassin may lurk. Tyburn's right, Lily. You must stay in your quarters."

"But it's at Devil's Knoll! That's not even a mile from the gates!"

"I wouldn't care if it was only an inch from the gates. You are not stepping outside Castle Gloom. Do I make myself clear?"

"But—"

"*No*, Lily. Just this once, will you do as you are told!"

She glowered.

Pan softened. "There is no reason you cannot have company, of course. I will send for Rose."

"And K'leef," Lily added.

Pan didn't look happy. "Very well, I will—"

"And Thorn stays. He's amusing."

Pan scowled. But what could he do? Thorn was a hero right now. He'd beaten Gabriel, tamed Hades, and fought a zombie. Lily knew that her uncle couldn't refuse without sounding utterly ungrateful. His reply crawled out through his gritted teeth. "Very well. The stable boy also."

Pan stormed off. Tyburn lingered, nodded to Thorn, then he too departed.

TWENTY-EIGHT

Thorn threw himself onto the sofa. "Phew! I thought they'd never leave."

Lily stared at the door. She wanted to march straight through it, out Skeleton Gate, and off to Devil's Knoll. She should do it.

How far would she get before she was stopped?

Not far at all. She'd be lucky to make it to the end of the corridor.

What was the point of being Lady Shadow, ruler of Gehenna, if she wasn't even able to go to the fair? She bet no one would dare prevent Duke Solar from going.

Lily perched on a chair near the sofa and said to Thorn, "I think Tyburn likes you."

"Does he? It's difficult to tell with him." He yawned as he stretched out over the cushions. He rubbed his neck. "All this talk's starting to hurt. It's like I've swallowed rocks."

"I'm glad you're safe." She was, and she hoped he knew that. "When I heard what had happened, I was . . . worried."

He looked at her, his green eyes sparkling with mischief. "Really? How worried?"

"Not that worried."

"Did you tear up, Princess? A little? Come on, you can tell me."

"You are impossible." She flicked his ear. "You really saw a zombie? We used to have hundreds around the castle, once upon a time. The last one was Ron, but he finally fell apart when I was seven. Father was very upset. Ron had practically raised him."

There were plenty of portraits of Ron around the castle. He'd served the family for four generations. In the early ones, he almost passed for a living person, but as time progressed, he got more decayed and bits fell off. In the last portrait, painted in her grandfather's time, his skull was visible through his patched skin, one eye socket was empty, and the other oozing yellow pus. His right ear was missing, and his jaw was held in place by wire. Her father was in that last painting, a young black-haired boy sitting on the zombie's bony knee.

K'leef and Rose entered. When K'leef spotted Thorn lying on the sofa, he asked, "What's going on?"

Thorn sank deeper into the cushions with a groan. "Lady Shadow's been looking after me. I've been very heroic, in case you hadn't heard." He coughed feebly. "Could you get me a glass of water?"

"Get it yourself," snapped Lily.

K'leef's gaze went from Thorn to her and back. He scowled, and Thorn grinned.

I don't believe it. He's jealous of Thorn.

K'leef flexed his fingers. "It's a little too dark in here." He snapped them, and the candles along the table flared to life. "There, that's better." He grinned, and Thorn scowled.

Lily tried not to laugh. Boys . . .

Rose hurried over. "So it's true? There are zombies in Graven?"

Lily scowled. "How do you know?"

"Oh, the steward was listening at the keyhole."

"Does that happen a lot? Servants listening at keyholes?"

Rose looked surprised at her question. "Er . . . all the time? How else are we to know what's going on? No one actually *tells* us anything."

Thorn struggled to sit up, moaning all the while. "No, don't help me. I can manage, honestly. So"—he looked around at them—"who wants to hear about how I faced a creature from the very pits of the underworld?"

"Me," said Rose, dragging a chair over. "Tell me everything."

Thorn arched an eyebrow. "K'leef?"

K'leef tried, but failed, to control his smile. He took a cushion and sat cross-legged on the floor. "I suppose."

Thorn repeated the story, though it wasn't quite the same as the one he'd told Tyburn and Pan. This new version had a lot more zombies in it and Thorn fighting them on a cliff top with the sea lashing the rocks below and the ground crumbling away under his heels. Which was odd, since Graven was a hundred miles from the sea.

Rose stared at him. "That is really—"

"Unbelievable," said K'leef.

Thorn drew an X over his chest. "Every word of it is true. Cross my heart and hope to die."

"And be raised as some sort of undead monster, given what's going on," said Lily. "I think you'd make a great ghoul."

Thorn frowned at her. "You really are a very, *very* strange girl."

"So, how many of them did you destroy?" asked K'leef.

"Six, at least."

Lily smirked. "Are you sure it wasn't more like ten?"

"Yes, it probably was. I was so busy hacking off limbs and heads and such that I couldn't tell which body part belonged to which zombie. Easily twelve, and it would have been a lot more if I'd had my bow and arrow. An arrow in each eye socket, and it would have been job done."

Now *that* Lily could believe. "How *did* you learn to shoot so well?"

Thorn shrugged. "Dad taught me."

"They teach the squires, too, but none of them can put an arrow down a gargoyle's gullet," said Rose.

"It ain't the same. The squires practice in the courtyard, where everything is neat and tidy. When it's dry and not too windy. That ain't real practice." Thorn rubbed his thumb. "Dad had me shoot out in the woods day and night, wet or dry, whether the air was still or the trees were shaking. Try shooting when you're so hungry your belly's eating itself and missing means starving some more. That's how you learn to make each shot count."

"I thought you said your father was a woodcutter." Lily met his gaze, and Thorn looked sheepish. "I could be wrong, but one doesn't usually hunt trees, correct?"

"I don't want to talk about it."

K'leef joined in. "Hmm, what might one be doing in the forest with a bow and arrows?"

"Shut up, K'leef," said Thorn. "I mean it."

"You're poachers," said Lily. "You and your father."

Lily pretended to shoot Rose, who proceeded to die an extravagant death, collapsing back onto her chair with lots of choking, gagging, and gurgling.

Thorn glared at Lily.

She stopped. Why was he so upset? "We're just having fun, Thorn."

"It was all my fault," he muttered.

"What happened?" Lily asked, suddenly serious.

"My dad *is* a woodcutter, that part is true," said Thorn. He touched the acorn amulet around his neck. "But selling logs is hard work and don't always put enough food on the table. Dad taught me how to hunt, how to track and catch game. Mainly small animals, like rabbits and hares. They're just forest vermin, nobody misses 'em." He shook his head. "But times were hard, so I hunted something bigger. A deer."

"But deer are the property of the local lord," said Lily. "It's illegal to—"

"I know that, but what else could I do? I snuck out one morning before anyone else was up. There was a watering hole, and the deer come down to it before dawn. One shot was all it took. The deer didn't feel a thing."

"Then what?" asked Lily, leaning closer.

"I got caught."

Lily felt Thorn's pain. Losing a few animals didn't bother her much, but she knew of nobles who guarded their hunting rights fiercely, with terrible violence against any poachers. Hands were cut off, and worse.

"Local soldiers kicked down our door and found the carcass. Dad told 'em that he did it." Thorn choked in a sob. "I was a coward. I should have told 'em the truth, but I didn't. I let Dad take the blame. They whipped him so bad he could barely walk, right in the village square. Then they threw a rope over a tree branch."

No one spoke, dreading what was coming next.

"They'd caught him poaching years ago and punished him for that, punished him bad," said Thorn. "This time they was gonna hang him, and no one did nothing. Everyone was too scared. Including me. I couldn't save my own dad."

That hit Lily hard. It was the same dreadful sense of failure she felt.

Save my own dad.

Thorn clenched his fists. "Dad grabbed a sword off one of the soldiers. He fought and took a horse and rode away. Once he was in the forest, no one was going to find him."

"So he escaped?" asked Lily. "That's good, isn't it?"

Thorn's tear-streaked face now shone with pride. "They set the dogs after him, but we're Herne's folk. We know all the tricks of the forest. If my dad don't want to be found, then he ain't gonna be found. Not by men, not by dogs, not by nothing. Our local lord declared him a wolf's head."

K'leef sat up. "Wolf's head? What's that?"

"An outlaw—it means anyone can kill him for a reward. He's got no hiding place, can't trust no neighbor. It brings in men who hunt others for reward," explained Thorn. "Dad snuck back a week later, late when everyone was asleep. He spoke to Mom, I listened from my bed. He told her he was gonna do some soldiering. Said there was always work for good archers and you got paid in gold, not coppers."

That was true. Learning to shoot accurately took years of practice. Castle Gloom employed archers, and their wages were double those of the men-at-arms. In wartime, the best could make small fortunes.

"He said Gehenna and Lumina were always at each other's throats, so he'd get work with one side or another. Then he'd come back with gold in his pocket and take us all far away. Start again with a farm or tavern or something. I ran down and asked to go with him, but Dad wouldn't have it. He wanted me to stay and look after our family. He took his bow and ax and promised he'd be back before planting season. But he wasn't. He didn't come back by harvest, neither." Thorn let out a bitter laugh. "Then we heard you and Lumina had made peace. That got us worried. Why wasn't Dad back, then? So I went looking for him. To make things right. I thought I'd only be gone a few weeks." Thorn's face fell. "You know the rest. The slavers got me, and now I'm here."

"I wish you'd told me all this earlier," said Lily.

"I should never have left. It was my job to look after my mom and my brothers and sisters. My duty, y'know?"

Yes, she did. Lily knew all about duty.

His gaze dropped to the floor. "I'm a big, stupid failure."

K'leef got up and sat down beside Thorn. He didn't speak, just sat with him.

It didn't matter that one had been brought up in a palace and the other in a hut. They were two boys a long way from home.

She went to her dressing table and took out her jewelry box. She held it out to Thorn. "Here. Have it. Go to Port Charon and buy yourself passage back home."

"No. Thanks, but I can't. We have a deal." He nudged K'leef. "I think I've caught something from you: honor."

K'leef laughed. "Careful it doesn't ruin your life. My father says honor is like a weed. Once you've got it, you can't get rid of it."

"He sounds like my grandpa." Thorn wiped his face, and he was back, cocky and sure of himself. He stood up in front of Lily. "I help you track down your poisoner, and then you pay me. Not before."

Lily nodded. "I've got an idea that'll cheer you up. Let's go to the fair."

"What about everything your uncle just said?" asked Thorn. "About the poisoner still being on the loose?"

"That's why I'm going in disguise." Lily pulled Rose from her chair. "I'll need your clothes."

Rose frowned. "We're not swapping clothes just so you can sneak out."

"We used to do it all the time."

"And I always got into trouble." Rose crossed her arms. "The answer is no."

Lily wandered over to her wardrobe. "What are you wearing to the Halloween Ball? It's not far away."

"This." Rose scowled down at the plain black shift she was wearing. "Mary has me working in the kitchens on Halloween. There'll be no ball for me."

"I'll make sure you have the evening off." Lily selected one of her own dresses and fanned it out in front of Rose. "Wouldn't you rather wear this and go dancing with Fynn? I could arrange it. Mary doesn't rule Castle Gloom, even if she acts like she does."

Rose frowned, not quite convinced. But Lily could see the desire in her friend's gaze as it fell upon the rippling silk. Lily brushed her fingers over the sleeves. "Why don't you try it on? Just to see if it fits?"

Rose grabbed the dress and ran behind the privacy screen.

"And you two," said Lily, pointing to the boys, "can turn around and face the wall."

A few minutes later, Rose was in a dress of elegant black silk and velvet with pearls and silver on the collars and cuffs.

Thorn stared. "By the Six, you look . . . wonderful."

Rose curtseyed. "Thank you, Sir Thorn."

"What about me?" asked Lily, standing beside her and dressed in Rose's outfit, faded by wear and tear. She spread out her arms. "Well?"

K'leef frowned. "You look like a noble wearing a maid's dress, but it'll be dark so you might get away with it."

"We could mess up your hair," added Thorn. "Snip off a few bits to make it more uneven."

Lily stepped away from him. "You are not touching my hair."

K'leef pointed at the door. "What difference does this make? Your uncle's put two guards at the end of the corridor. We're not going anywhere."

Lily grinned. "Show them, Rose."

Rose swept over to the wall and lifted off a full-length portrait of old Jamaz Shadow. "Ta-da," she declared.

K'leef frowned. "It's a wall. How does that help, exactly?"

Rose touched the top right corner of one of the stones in the revealed wall.

Dust motes filled the air as the wall shuddered. Old gears, hidden in the masonry, creaked to life, and a whole section, five feet in height and almost as wide, slid back. Beyond was an opening, framed by cobwebs and carpeted in dust. A red-eyed rat squeaked in surprise and scurried off.

"A tunnel. Very clever." K'leef peered in. "And this takes us where?"

Lily took up a candelabra. "To the northern passageway. From there, it's a short walk to Skeleton Gate."

"Are there many of these in Castle Gloom?" asked K'leef.

"Hidden passageways. Air vents. Ways in and out," said Lily. "No one knows how many, and half of them are closed off now. I used to explore them with Dante."

"Mary would be furious," said Rose.

Thorn was already standing in the tunnel. "What are we waiting for?"

"I never realized this dress was so tight," said Rose, straining within her bone-framed corset. "How do you breathe?"

"As little as possible," said Lily.

Rose turned in front of the full-length mirror, admiring herself from all angles. "Just wait till Fynn sees me in this."

"You'd better stay here tonight," said Lily. "If anyone sees you strolling about in my clothes, they may start wondering who's wearing yours."

"What?" Rose stopped twirling. "You mean I'm stuck here—"

"Sorry. But look at it this way, why spoil the surprise by showing Fynn the dress tonight? Think how amazed he'll be when he sees you in it at the Halloween Ball."

"I suppose. . . ."

"He'll probably want to marry you right there and then. In the meantime, try to enjoy your time off. . . ." Lily said with a guilty smile.

Rose frowned and plopped down on her chair. "You owe me, Lily."

"I know." Lily took an apple from the fruit bowl on her way into the passage. This was going to be fun.

TWENTY-NINE

No one looked at Lily. No one paused and bowed or doffed their caps as she went past, K'leef on one side and Thorn on the other. The guards didn't give her a second glance as she strolled through Skeleton Gate along with a dozen or so servants having their evening off to go explore the delights of the fair. Black bunting hung between the gates, and a group of squires were painting giant skeletons and swooping ghosts on the inner walls. Others were busy washing the weathered statues of some of Gehenna's ancient rulers.

"What are they doing that for?" asked Thorn.

"Castle Gloom needs to look its best for the Halloween Ball." She finished her apple as she crossed the bridge and tossed the core into the moat. "Halloween is our biggest holiday of the year. There'll be guests from all over Gehenna, villagers as well as nobles. Duke Solar's even invited some of his relatives from Lumina."

"They'll be your relatives soon," said Thorn.

"Say that again, Thorn, and I'll have words with Tyburn."

"Look up there," said K'leef, his gaze on the battlements. "It seems the Solars are getting settled in."

The black banners were gone. Instead, hanging from every flag post were the white-and-gold flags of House Solar.

Lily gritted her teeth. How dare they? This was *her* home. She would order Baron Sable to pull each and every one of them down.

A group of stable boys barged along, wearing masks of skulls, ghouls, vampires, and hideous jesters. They were laughing and pushing each other, eager to get to the fair. They boasted about the games they'd win, and discussed the shows and tricksters and magical animals at the circus. And the girls of the roaming folk.

They were different than usual. Relaxed. Unafraid. Looking around excitedly instead of gazing at the ground.

They are on their guard when they see me. Everyone is.

It wasn't fear, not exactly. But the Shadow name had power. It created an invisible shield between her and everyone else.

No wonder she'd been so lonely. Whenever she'd played games with the servants, she'd won. Always.

Eventually she'd realized that they lost on purpose. No one was *that* good.

Devil's Knoll reared up ahead. Even from here, she could hear the music. A grand tent hunkered in the center of dozens of smaller ones, like multicolored toadstools circling a tree stump. Flames shot in the air, and sparkling fireworks burst among the stars beginning to peek through the curtain of night.

"Hurry up!" said Thorn. "We're missing all the good stuff."

"Shall we just explore a little?" asked K'leef.

"Fine by me." Lily headed to a ring of brightly painted wagons. Clotheslines crisscrossed the space between the wagons, creating a flapping wall of color.

The men wore baggy, striped pantaloons and embroidered waistcoats, with bandanas around their dark hair. Gold dangled from their ears and shone in their teeth. The women jingled as they walked, wearing ankle bells and skirts decorated with hundreds of coins. Rings and necklaces sparkled in the torchlight.

This was the best thing about the fair, seeing all the roaming folk. They were a tribe of all kingdoms. She saw women of the far south, skins so dark and shiny they looked as if they'd been carved from jet. There were men with feathered cloaks from beyond the Eagle Mountains, and even an old man with webbed hands and a suit covered in fishlike tin scales, honoring some House Coral ancestor.

Lily had never been beyond the borders of Gehenna, so it was thrilling to mingle with people who had been to all corners of the New Kingdoms and hear all their strange and beautiful accents.

K'leef pointed over to a line of wagons. "I want to see that."

The big wagon in front had a dragon painted on it. A huge red beast with flames pouring out of its mouth and smoke coming from its nostrils as it glided over a green landscape dotted with tents and prancing animals. Also included were images of a unicorn, a manticore, and a massive three-headed dog. Across the top of this epic mural was a crudely painted scroll. Lily read it out loud.

"Maximilian's Marvelous Magical Menagerie."

"Menage-what?" said Thorn.

"Menagerie. It's a posh name for a zoo." She looked at the name. Maximilian. Why did it ring a bell?

Thorn frowned. "And you think this Max has a dragon?"

"That's what it says." Lily gazed along the row of wagons. "Maybe a small one?"

"Greetings!"

Lily jumped as a man stepped out from behind the nearest wagon. He performed an extravagant bow with three flourishes of his long-feathered cap. "Maximilian Milo at your service. Welcome, welcome to my humble yet tastefully sublime circus." He looked them up and down. "Ah, from Castle Gloom I see. Excellent!" He swept his arms wide. "You'll find a visit both entertaining and educational. And only five coppers each!"

"Five?" exclaimed Thorn. "Forget it. For five I don't want to just see a dragon, I want to ride it."

The man stood up straight. He was thin and tall and, though youngish, had already lost much of his hair. His wispy red locks were combed across his bald pate but had the unfortunate tendency to fall over his face. He pushed a few long strands aside. "Hmm. I tell you what: it's early, so I'll make you a deal. Because I like your faces." He gestured to Thorn. "Though yours, not so much. Six, for all three. Nonrefundable."

Lily grimaced and held her hand out to Thorn. "Can you lend me some money?"

"You didn't bring any?"

"I never carry money. I don't need to. Everything's just given to me." Lily saw the disapproving look in Thorn's eye. "Remember, I do actually own everything in Gehenna."

K'leef cleared his throat. "Uh, Thorn . . ."

Thorn frowned. "What, you ain't got none, neither? How about them rings of yours? They'll be worth a few sovereigns each."

"First, I'm not wearing any rings—those were all just for show when I arrived here," said K'leef, waggling his bare fingers. "And second, those rings are family heirlooms. I would never sell them. I'd rather starve. It's a matter of—"

"*Honor.* I know. I just don't believe it," Thorn grumbled. But he handed over his silver crown. "I want change for that."

Max pocketed it with a broad grin and gave Thorn his fourteen pennies. Which Thorn double-checked.

"Come, my friends, come!" Max lifted the curtain suspended between two wagons. "Prepare to be amazed and see creatures so rare, so marvelous, that your lives will never be the same again. I, Maximilian Milo, have traveled into the very depths of the Shardlands to capture some of these beasts. Explored places no civilized man has even been and lived among cannibal tribes who now, if I may be so immodest, worship me as their god!" He took a few steps ahead. "Maggie, we've got some guests!"

Cages and pens and wagons lay in a messy series of rows among tents and campfires. A girl a few years younger than Lily ran up to Max. She had the same skinny build and her hair was a pale dirty blond. Her patchwork dress was enlivened by a coin-studded belt. She made a curtsey. "Hello, fair visitors. Prepare yourselves for an . . . an . . ."

"Amazing experience?" prompted Max.

"Yes. And everything else, too."

Max led them to the first animal. "Behold, the Pegasus!"

Lily looked at the animal. It was a young foal. A good beast, light gray with white socks, but something was not quite right about it. "Pegasus, right?"

"Indeed. A Pegasus."

"It doesn't have any wings."

Max nodded thoughtfully. "Well spotted. That's because it's young. The wings haven't grown in yet. Come back next year, maybe two, and then you'll see a beautiful pair, dozens of feet long. Honestly."

Thorn muttered something as they moved on toward the cages.

Max put his finger to his lip. "Now, be careful. This next creature is one of the most feared predators of the underworld. I was a personal friend to the last Lord Shadow, may the Six Princes guard his soul, and when we were young men full of hot blood and a lust for adventure, we took a journey into the Twilight. To the very gates of the lands of the dead."

"Really?" said Lily. "How come my father never—"

Thorn clamped his hand over her mouth. "Never visited you before? That's what she was about to say."

Max looked hard at her. "And who's her father?"

"Oh, the privy cleaner."

Privy cleaner? Lily was speechless. How dare he? A privy cleaner!

Thorn glared at her. "Yes. He's a privy cleaner, and you're just his daughter and a servant like me, aren't you?"

Lily nodded slowly. She'd get Thorn back for that later.

There was a growl from within the dark cage. A large lump of brown shifted.

Max stepped back. "Not too near, mind! I don't want you losing a hand or anything! Not suitable for children under five!"

Maggie stepped between them. "Behold, the utterly fero . . . fero . . ."

"Ferocious," finished Max.

"Behold that word wot my dad said and the unique and one and only single-headed Cerberus!"

A huge wolfish dog got up off its bed of hay and sniffed the bars.

"Single-headed?" snapped Thorn. "I thought Cerberus had . . . more?"

"You're referring to the *common* three-headed Cerberus. Every zoo from here to Silver Sea has one of those," said Max. "This is the extraordinarily rare single-headed version."

The dog continued its lazy search for a treat.

K'leef pointed to another animal farther along. "And what's that? A hornless unicorn?"

Max shook his head. "Don't be daft. That's just a donkey."

"I want my money back," said Thorn.

THIRTY

Thorn huffed loudly. "Come on, let's go. Anything's better than this rubbish."

"I'll be staying around here for a while," said Lily. "They've got fortune-tellers, music, and stories. It'll be fun."

"But Wade told me there's an archery stall. If you score three bull's-eyes, you win a whole cake." Thorn grinned. "I could get us a few each."

Lily could see the longing in his eyes. "Go ahead. I'll be fine. I am in disguise, remember?"

"I'll stay with her, Thorn," said K'leef. "Some of these roaming folk would have come up from the Sultanate. They'll have news from home."

Thorn nudged him. "And maybe they could help you sneak back south, right?"

"I am a son of House Djinn. We do not sneak off anywhere. It's a matter of—"

"By the Six, we know," interrupted Thorn. "You two stick together, all right?"

Lily gave him a push. "Just leave."

And with that Thorn ran off to explore the rest of the fair.

K'leef and Lily went around the animals once more. K'leef took an apple from his cloak pocket and fed it to the foal. "This is a good colt."

One of the roaming folk wandered over with a small sack of oats. He nodded at them and tipped the oats into a bucket. The colt started eating, his ears twitching with enthusiasm.

"This is a fire breed, isn't it?" asked K'leef.

The roaming man stroked the foal's neck. "From the desert of the Sultanate. As fast as falcons, or so they say."

K'leef's smile was the deepest and brightest Lily had ever seen. It was as if he'd not been truly happy until this moment. "They are indeed. Such an animal doesn't need wings to be magical."

They moved to the next cage, the one containing the "Cerberus." "You hungry, boy?" The dog drooled as the man showed it a gristly bone. Lily noticed that the first two fingers of the man's left hand were missing. Had his pet snapped those off?

The man unlocked the cage and took hold of the dog's collar. "Come and get it."

The beast snarled as it saw Lily, peeling back its black lips and revealing a row of long, dagger-tipped fangs.

The roaming man whistled, a sound as sharp as an arrow. The dog twitched his ears, then sank down on his haunches. The man scratched under its slobbery chin. "He's just scared of you, m'lady."

"I'm not a lady, I'm just . . . erm, the privy cleaner's daughter."

"If you say so, miss." His green eyes narrowed, and Lily wasn't sure he believed her.

"Why is he scared of me?" That sounded . . . unlikely.

"You're from Castle Gloom," the gypsy continued. "You've got the wrong smell."

"What smell is that?"

"You smell of stones and bones, miss." The roaming man met her gaze. "Lifeless things."

Did he know who she was? She lowered her gaze. "Is that . . . safe?" The dog looked a lot bigger now that he was out of the cage.

The man shook the dog's cheeks, and the big beast rolled over. Lily laughed. Custard used to do the same.

K'leef seemed fascinated by the dog. After a nod from the roaming man, he too stroked the animal's brown fur. The beast gave a rumble of pleasure.

Lily decided to leave them and wandered toward the fire.

Maggie stirred the embers to bring more life to the flames as Max stuffed a thick wad of tobacco into his pipe. "Should never have gone into the monster business. Total mug's game."

"But you don't have any monsters," said Lily.

Max picked up a burning twig and lit the pipe. "Not now I don't, not now." He flapped his hand in the air. "The Pegasus flew off the first week. How was I to know you have to clip its wings every month?"

"What about the three-headed dog? Did you have one of those?"

Max sighed deeply. "He ate the hydra. How that serpent got out of the cage I'll never know, but you wouldn't believe the noise the two of them made. By the time I got there, the hydra was half gobbled up. I tell you, it's not a sight you forget. I tried to get the dog off, but it was no good. Stupid mutt got food poisoning and was dead by morning."

"That's a shame. Couldn't you get any more?"

"How? Take a trip to the Shardlands? Not likely." Max glanced at her. "From the castle, aren't you?"

"Yes."

"Do you know the earl? Is he around?"

"Pandemonium Shadow?" Lily lowered her head. "I've seen him. Why?"

"I've some business to discuss with him."

"What sort of business?" Why would her uncle be dealing with this man?

Max winked. "See that chest over there?"

"Yes."

He dragged it over and kicked the lid open. "What do you think?"

Cheap trinkets. Some bracelets. A couple of nice necklaces and pendants. A few masks probably from earlier masquerades, some of them just broken pieces. Nothing special. "Not a lot, to be honest."

"Exactly, exactly. Sold a box just like this to the earl last year for . . . guess how much."

"Ten crowns?" Even that was being way too generous.

"A hundred. *Sovereigns.*" Max laughed. "Just junk I got off a Shardland nomad. Told him they were magical. That's how I bought the menagerie in the first place."

Now Lily knew why the name Maximilian Milo had sounded familiar. Pan and Father had had a big argument over that box. About all the money Pan had wasted on rubbish.

Max looked into the fire, and his eyes were gold with the flame light. "He's desperate for magic. This box here'll fetch me another hundred at *least.* And you know what they say about a fool and his gold. Well, that goes double for Pan Shadow."

"Do you always gossip like this?" asked Lily, feeling bile rise in her throat.

"I don't mean any harm, girl." Max gestured with his cup. "Everyone knows the old earl isn't the man he used to be. He likes his drink, if you know what I mean."

"Stop talking about him like that! He's sick!"

"Sure he is. It's called a hangover."

"Shut your mouth! Don't you dare talk about him like that!" Lily kicked the fire and stormed off.

She should tell Max exactly who she was. Tell him and get some guards to punish him.

For what? For telling the truth?

"What's going on?" K'leef had run over. "Lily, are you all right?"

Lily glared back at the menagerie. "That Max is an idiot and he doesn't know anything. He called Uncle Pan a drunken fool."

K'leef stopped. "So?"

She pushed K'leef. "That's what you think, too, isn't it?"

"That's what everyone thinks, Lily." He reached for her but she pulled back. "He's a laughingstock from here to the Coral Isles. If he had any honor, he would—"

"Will you shut up about your stupid honor!" She didn't want to hear any more. Tears blurred her eyes as she turned and ran.

"Lily!"

She kept going, stumbling away from the fair. She had to get away from them all.

Uncle Pan *was* a drunken fool. He'd wasted fortunes on wild schemes all his life. Fake treasure was just a part of it. He always claimed that sooner or later he'd find something, something magical from the time of the Six Princes, but he never did.

Eventually she stopped, beyond the edge of the fair. She saw a line of trees up ahead, and beyond them, an empty road.

What if she kept walking?

What if I just left and never looked back?

It seemed like the answer to all her problems. No Gabriel. No responsibilities. No rules anymore.

A life of total freedom. Who wouldn't want that?

But to abandon Castle Gloom?

She might as well cut out her own heart. She'd never leave her home. Her blood was the blackest of all. Others saw cold dark stone, but they hadn't heard the laughter that echoed in its halls during feast days. They saw grim gargoyles, but they'd never spent their summers climbing them. The view from the tower roofs was breathtaking. On a clear day, you could see all the way to the Three Princes, the highest peaks in the country.

Lily would never move out of Castle Gloom. Somehow, she had to outwit the Solars.

She lifted the hem of her skirt out of the mud and started marching along a line of trees toward the big tent. A cluster of bats swooped overhead and disappeared among the branches.

A twig snapped. Lily stopped and peered into the brush. "Who's there?" she asked the darkness.

Probably some village child dressed as a ghost and waiting to jump out and scare her. Still, she didn't like it. "This isn't funny, you know!"

The wind blew through the trees, and the leaves rustled in alarm.

Lily picked up a stone. "I'm warning you!"

How had she ended up here? Castle Gloom suddenly seemed miles away. And how could she have wandered off without K'leef?

The hairs on the back of her neck rose, and a chill crept up her spine. Her breath struggled as her chest tightened with fear.

Someone, something, was here with her.

She gripped the stone harder. But what good would it do? She didn't know how to fight.

Lily forced herself to turn and face whatever it was that stood behind her. Nothing.

It must have been a fox, hunting through the undergrowth.

She laughed. How embarrassing. A Shadow frightened of her shadow.

The hand clamped over her mouth before she could scream.

THIRTY-ONE

Thorn found a body lying outstretched in front of him, behind the beer stall.

Earl Pan Shadow still clutched his mug. He was snoring. His breath rattled in his throat and made its way out, laboriously, through the nostrils. It did not sound good. It smelled worse.

Thorn nudged him. "M'lord?"

Lily's uncle woke with a snort. His eyes peeled open and, bloodshot in the worst way, tried to focus. "Thorn?"

Thorn helped him up. "I think you need your bed, m'lord."

Earl Pandemonium Shadow groaned as he stood. "My bed?"

"Yes. Your bed." Thorn wasn't in the mood to be looking after the castle drunk. He spotted something on the ground. "You dropped this, m'lord."

It was an obsidian mask. Old and cracked. Why did the earl wear something like this? But then, looking at the earl, Thorn realized it suited him. A broken mask for a broken man.

Pan took it back and carefully put it into his tunic. "I can't enjoy the party without this."

Thorn wondered how many other nobles were at the fair with masks protecting their true identities.

Pan flipped him a coin. A silver crown. "Let's just keep this between the two of us. I don't want Lily worrying."

"Of course you don't."

The earl burped loudly and staggered off, roughly in the direction of Castle Gloom.

Thorn explored the fair for a good few hours. The rest of it was way better than that stupid zoo. He nibbled at the cake he'd won at the archery stall.

Almost everyone wore masks. Stalls sold all types, made of papier-mâché, of stiffened silk, or carved wood and beaten metal. Skull faces were popular, closely followed by vampires and ghosts. Singers wrapped in shrouds sang haunting laments. Village children were constantly jumping out from behind their wagons, shouting and howling like banshees.

Is this how you beat your fear of death? By celebrating it?

He spotted Gabriel and a bunch of his cronies. They were the last thing he needed tonight. He hid behind a tent before they saw him.

A group of musicians sat around an upturned barrel loaded with wine and plates and discarded masks. They wore outfits of rainbow colors and played flutes, harps, and lutes. The man leading them looked more ragged than the rest, his costume a threadbare motley, his eyes closed and lost in the dream of the tune.

Hold on . . .

"Merrick?"

The man's eyelids flickered. Then widened.

Merrick the minstrel leaped to his bandy legs. "My young Thorn!" He grabbed hold of his hands and danced a sharp-kneed jig. "It's grand to see you!"

Thorn forced him to stop. "What are you doing here?"

"What am I doing? Earning an honest wage, young boy. An honest wage. There's money to be made, at the fair and at the ball. I'm hoping to have my merry band of players invited to perform within the castle. Did I not tell you that I once—"

"Yeah, I'm sure you did."

Merrick dropped his arm across Thorn's shoulders and pulled him tight. "Are you enjoying the fair? Is it not splendid?"

"Better than the fairs we have in Stour, that's for sure. All we have is pig jousting."

"Pig jousting?"

"It's funny the first time you see it." He broke off a piece of his cake and handed it over.

Merrick gratefully accepted it and swallowed it in two bites. Then he picked up a devilish mask and covered his face. "What do you think? Will this do for the Halloween Ball?"

"Nice horns."

"It's a bit faded, but with a bit of paint, it'll be as good as new. We must look our very best. Will you be there?"

"I ain't really thought about it."

"Get yourself a mask. I will provide a costume." Merrick gestured back toward the stalls. "The merchant in the blue tent will sell you some bits of old broken masks for a penny. Glue them together, and it would be most horrific."

"I suppose."

"Let me have a good look at you." Merrick stepped back and nodded thoughtfully. "You've added some meat to your bones. Tyburn is treating you well, then?"

"Well enough." Thorn looked past Merrick. The mention of the executioner made him think he should find the others and get back to the castle. "Nice to see you, Merrick. I—"

"What's the hurry, boy? Join us for a song. Who knows? You could even pick up a coin or two yourself. I've been to fairs before, but never one quite so crowded. But I suppose it's to be expected. What with all the rumors."

"What rumors?"

"About the dead rising from their graves." Merrick clapped. "Can you believe it? Zombies, back in Gehenna!"

Thorn stared at the minstrel. "No. They're not true. Er, who told you that?"

Merrick's eyes shone. "It *is* true—I can see it in your face. You're not a good liar, Thorn. I've just spoken to a man fresh from Graven. He told me of zombies seen just the other night. And of a boy on a giant bat." He paused, assessing Thorn again. "Why do I suddenly think that boy was you?"

How could that story have spread here already? Thorn had only left Graven this morning!

Merrick continued, leaning in conspiratorially. "There's been ghosts seen at Witch's Grove, and the graveyard at Gallowtree is empty. A man told me his cousin saw the dead dancing in the moonlight. These tales have been floating about for almost a year, but they've increased most recently." He looked around and whispered, "Some mention a scarred man, a necromancer behind all these strange events. Do you know who he is? Most people think it's Lord Iblis, back from the dead."

"What?"

Merrick frowned. "Iblis Shadow *was* a powerful sorcerer. If anyone could come back across the Twilight, it would be him. I bet he's more powerful in death than he ever was in life."

Thorn cursed. "Listen, I don't want no talk about Lord Shadow being back. First, it ain't true, and second, think how Lily would feel, people talking about her dad like that?"

"Lily, is it? My, you have come far in the world since I saw you last." Merrick grabbed Thorn's arm. "Could you perhaps arrange an introduction? To Lady Shadow, I mean? Or better yet, to Duke Solar! Oh, he is the most generous patron to musicians!"

Thorn pulled himself free. "Good-bye, Merrick. Go back to your dreadful singing and leave off with the gossip."

"Thorn, don't be like that." He nudged him. "We could split the payment."

"*Good-bye*, Merrick."

Thorn trotted back under the stars. He hadn't gone far when he saw crowds gathered along the edge of the castle moat, halfway between Skeleton Gate and Troll Gate.

Some women were screaming, and others were crying.

Soldiers, both Shadow and Solar, leaned over the battlements, pointing down at the crowd. Lanterns spilled out of the gates and lined up along the moat's edge.

Fear rose in his chest.

The ground was uneven and it was dark, but Thorn ran, stumbling, tripping, but not slowing. He was panting, but it wasn't just breathlessness.

A maid kneeled in the earth, sobbing. Others stumbled about, too dazed to speak.

Thorn skidded to a halt. "What's going on?"

The maid shook her head. "She's dead. She's dead! They killed her. . . ."

Thorn's heart almost stopped. "Who?"

"They wanted her dead, and they finally did it." The maid closed her eyes, but it didn't stop the tears. "They've killed Lady Shadow."

THIRTY-TWO

"**O**utta my way!" Thorn shoved through servants and soldiers, all milling about, not understanding what was happening. "Outta the way!"

People crowded along the edge of the moat. Two guards were in the water, lifting out a body. Another pair helped carry it onto the bank.

"Get outta the way!"

The body lay soaked through, covered in mud, her face obscured by her tangled hair and weeds.

"No, Lily . . ." whispered Thorn. He looked up at the guard. "Please, she's my friend."

The guard nodded and allowed Thorn closer. He sank down beside her, suddenly feeble.

K'leef pushed his way through. He gasped when he saw the body. "She ran off without me," he said, his voice cracking. "I looked and I looked . . ."

"You should have been with her!"

How long had she been in the mud? A boot was missing. Her clothes must have dragged her down.

Lily . . .

Thorn reached over to her face. His fingers trembled, but he couldn't let her lie here like this. He gently pulled her hair back and wiped the mud away.

It wasn't Lily.

Air stuck in his throat; he was too shocked to breathe.

"That's not Lady Shadow," said an onlooker. "That's her maid Rose."

They'd swapped clothes. Thorn had been there when it happened.

Rose's lips were blue, her face a cold, sickly white, her eyes—thankfully—closed.

"What's she doing wearing the mistress's clothes?" The servants gathered closer.

One of the older maids sighed. "They used to do it when they were younger. Lily . . . I mean, Lady Shadow would dress up in Rose's clothes and go make mischief, fighting the squires, and sneaking out of the castle. It used to drive Mary insane."

Mischief. They'd only intended to have fun at the fair, but now look. Thorn sat beside the dead girl. This was his fault. He'd encouraged it.

"Did she fall in?" asked someone else. "It's tricky around the edge here."

"What's that?"

Something was held in her right fist. A strip of cloth.

Thorn drew it out.

A strip of white lace. "I've seen this before," he said.

Did Rose fight back? Did she claw at her attacker as she was pushed into the water? Grab him and tear this off him?

"Who else wears white?" said one of the guards. "It's one of them Solars. They killed her. As plain as day."

Thorn stood up, the lace still in his hand. "Gabriel."

The duke's son and his squires reached the front of the crowd. Gabriel saw Rose and his lip curled in distaste.

Thorn tightened his grip on the cloth. What more proof did he need?

"You killed her," said Thorn.

Dark threats hissed in the air.

"How dare you accuse me?" Gabriel and his squires huddled together, sensing the mood of the people around them. "Step—step back," said Gabriel. "Do you know who I am?"

"A coward and a killer!" someone shouted.

"I did not kill anyone!" Gabriel shrieked.

The mob drew closer. Men bent down to pick up stones, and a few tapped heavy cudgels in their meaty hands. Rose had been part of their family. She'd grown up in the castle. Her blood was black, just like theirs.

"Look—look," said Gabriel, his voice rising in pitch with fear. He stared toward the nearest guards. "There are rules, laws. Laws of hospitality. I am a guest of Castle Gloom. I cannot be harmed within its walls."

The guard drew his sword. "You're not within its walls, m'lord."

Thorn hated Gabriel. The boy was all that was wrong with the world. But his hate was nothing compared to the Shadows' resentment of the Solars. The countries had been at war for centuries. The Solars had taken over vast chunks of Gehenna and were now, with the marriage to Lily, about to take over the rest. The people would be slaves to the white flag.

They wanted revenge.

K'leef came up in front of him and put his hand on his chest. "No, Thorn."

"Get out of my way, K'leef."

The Sultanate boy's dark eyes hardened. "Do not do this. If Gabriel is guilty, then we'll do it properly, according to the law."

"The law doesn't count for people like him." Thorn pushed K'leef, who tried to move forward, but one of the Gehennish held him back.

"Don't be a fool, Thorn!" K'leef shouted.

Thorn wasn't listening. Gabriel was going to pay for his crime right now.

"Stand back!" Gabriel screamed. "Get back, or I will use my magic on you!" He raised his arms. "This is your last warning!"

The mob came closer.

"I'm warning you!" Gabriel threw out his arms. "Stay back or else!" His face went red and he trembled. "It's . . . coming . . ."

Lights flickered on his fingertips. Small fairy lights that shone and faded like sparkles off a firework. Just not as impressive.

Gabriel gritted his teeth.

The sparkles became a dazzling fountain of light.

It was pretty for about five seconds.

Thorn shook his head. Typical Gabriel. Pathetic.

"We don't want trouble," said one of the Solar squires.

Thorn pointed at Gabriel. "We just want him."

Would the squires side with Gabriel? There were six of them. Maybe enough to almost even the odds.

The squires looked at each other and then stepped back, abandoning the duke's son. He stared around, terrified. "You . . . you can't leave me!"

"Why ain't I surprised?" Thorn grabbed Gabriel and shoved him to his knees. "Any last words?"

The boy sobbed. "You can't do this. . . ."

"I can." It was the plain truth.

He knew Gabriel had done it. Either killed Rose on purpose or by accident, sneaking up and shoving her in the moat and letting the thick weeds and her heavy dress do the rest. Rose, who'd done nothing to anybody.

"You tried to poison Lily," said Thorn. "You messed that up, so you had another go and drowned her. And just like with the poisoning, you got the wrong victim."

"Poison her? No, I didn't! You have to believe me!" Gabriel tried to beat off the hands holding him. "I didn't do anything!"

"You're lying. Rose saw you put something in Lily's cup that night of the feast."

"It was spittle! I spat in her cup! That's all." He looked around, his face white with terror. "She insulted me. In front of everyone. In front of my father. She snubbed me when she danced with . . . him!" Gabriel stabbed his finger out at K'leef. "He's our prisoner! So I spat in her cup to teach her a lesson. That's all. Please, I'm telling the truth."

Gabriel's confession smacked Thorn in the face.

He held the strip of silk before Gabriel's eyes. "And this?"

"That's off my old suit. The one I was wearing when you dropped me in that horse dung. I threw it away right after! Someone must have gathered it up. Please, you have to believe me!"

He's telling the truth. He's too scared to lie.

"Get up," said Thorn. "Get up and run."

Gabriel remained on his knees, shaking. "What are you going to do to me?"

Thorn grabbed his collar and lifted him to his feet. "I said run."

Gabriel wiped his nose and looked at the gathering. "You'll pay for this." He turned around and ran back across the bridge. A few stones and clods of earth were thrown at him halfheartedly, but none hit.

The man holding K'leef let him go. K'leef scowled, then joined Thorn. "You did the right thing."

"Then why do I feel so bad?"

One of the servants shoved Thorn angrily. "You should have let us have him. He deserves it. Look what he did to Rose."

K'leef stepped between them. "Don't you realize that Thorn just saved your lives? If anything had happened to a single blond hair on Gabriel's head, the duke would've had you all dangling on ropes by dawn. Now get back to your homes before you make things worse."

"What about Rose?"

K'leef took off his coat and laid it over her. "We'll look after Rose."

THIRTY-THREE

I t was Tyburn's hand that had covered Lily's mouth. He had tracked her down at the fair and brought her home through an underground tunnel she had never seen before. He had put two guards on the door to her rooms and given her a strict warning not to leave again. Then he had headed back out to try and restore some semblance of order.

Tyburn knows the secret ways in and out of Gloom. What other secrets is he keeping?

Now Lily sat in her chambers, a bar of chocolate on her lap. She had planned to give it to Rose as a thank-you present for helping her escape tonight.

Rose is dead because of me.

Why had Rose gone out there?

Because she had wanted to show Fynn how fine she looked, wearing that dress. Like a princess.

In the corner of the chamber was the Mantle of Sorrows, hanging from a stone mannequin. It was not made of any mortal cloth, but woven out of misery and guilt. Every ounce of suffering, every poor mistake, every wrong judgment made by the ruler of House Shadow added to its length and weight.

How heavy would Rose's death be?

Mary entered. She said nothing and did not look at Lily. She walked to the table, took a taper from her apron, and lit more candles.

"I want it dark," said Lily.

"That won't make it better, my love."

"Nothing should make it better." Lily fought the urge to cry, but all she could feel was this wave, a huge overwhelming wave of sadness rising from deep inside. She couldn't give in—if she did, she'd drown. "What have I done, Mary?"

"You, Lily? You've done nothing."

"But I made Rose wear my clothes. The killer thought she was me." Horrible thoughts tumbled around in her head. She hadn't saved her family, and she hadn't saved her dog, and she hadn't saved Rose. She'd failed them all. "I'm so useless."

"Don't say that, Lily. You're just—"

"I am! I've never done anything good, ever! Not since I was born. Just a useless girl with no purpose but to marry the village idiot. My parents gave everything to Dante because he was everything they wanted. They never needed me, and they never wanted me."

"Of course they did. They loved you just as much as they loved Dante."

"Then why did they leave me?"

Mary said nothing but opened up her arms.

Lily pressed herself against her old nanny, clutching onto her desperately.

There was Mary's heartbeat. Strong, solid, and constant, as it had always been.

"The Solars killed her," said Lily. "I know they did."

"Hush now. Don't fret about that," said Mary. She brushed her fingers through Lily's hair. "Hush, child."

How could Mary's heart be so steady? The Solars had robbed her of more than most: her only children. Mary's two boys had helped Lily climb trees to get apples, had brought her cakes steaming hot from the kitchen. Lily remembered the day when Mary had waved them off to war, all crying and smiling and proud.

Then, not much later, Mary had watched Old Colm lead a cart back through the gates with them both lying pale and gashed by sword and spear.

How could her heart still beat at all?

Lily looked at the face that she knew almost as well as her own. There were wrinkles, and there was silver hair, and her eyes were not as bright as they'd once been. Yet it was the face Lily had kissed more than any other. "Never leave me, Mary."

Mary stroked her cheek. "As if I ever would."

A fist banged on the door.

"Lily!"

"It's Uncle Pan." Lily wiped her face. "Let him in."

Pan barged in and stared at her. "Lily, thank the Six you're safe. I heard something . . . terrible." Pan's hair was a tangle of greasy gray rat tails that hung twisted over his equally gray face. Wine stained his shirt, and his trousers were undone, exposing the pasty white flesh of his bulging midriff.

Lily was appalled and disgusted. This was her uncle? It was as if she was seeing him for the first time.

When had things gotten so bad?

"Where have you been?" snapped Mary.

Pan wore a mask—or rather, had pushed it up onto his forehead. He took it off and fiddled it with it nervously. "I had some business at the fair."

"Buying more junk from con men, Uncle?" said Lily. "How much did you give him this time?"

He'd gone disguised, wearing that mask, perhaps hoping no one would know what a fool he was. Lily grabbed it from him.

"Lily!"

She looked at it. It was hideous, a piece of rubbish. Maybe it had been elegant once, but it had obviously been broken and poorly repaired. There were pieces missing, and the joints hadn't been glued properly.

"I could buy you something better, Uncle," she said more gently. "You only need to ask."

He snatched it back. "I do not need my niece to look after me!"

Why is he so angry? Can't he see I just want to help him?

Tyburn entered and stared at all three of them. Lily wiping her tears away, Pan glowering, and Mary adjusting some cushions.

"We need to move Lady Shadow," said Tyburn, breaking the awful silence. "Her apartments have too many ways in and out."

Mary spoke. "Baron Sable's castle is a day's ride. We'll take her there."

"I am not leaving Castle Gloom."

"Lily, be sensible."

"I'm staying."

Tyburn looked at Mary. "Put Lady Shadow in the Needle."

"But that's a prison!" Lily protested.

"And probably the safest place in the castle," replied Tyburn. "You will remain there until we find this assassin."

Lily sank into her chair. Her oldest friend was dead, she was moving to a prison, and in seven days she would have to leave Castle Gloom, forever.

"What am I supposed to *do*?" Lily asked the moment Tyburn and Pan had left.

Mary opened the first wardrobe and took out three dresses. "Stay out of trouble."

"And Thorn," added Lily. "How come Thorn can help, but I can't?"

"It seems that boy has unique skills suited to this line of work."

"I have skills, too."

"Yes, but I'm not sure how much use embroidery will be right now."

Mary rubbed her forehead. She always did that when she felt a headache coming on. "Until we know who killed poor Rose, you're in danger. We can't have you wandering around the castle on your own."

"And the poison," said Lily. "The person who killed Rose poisoned Custard, too."

Mary frowned. "Hmm . . . I suppose. Well, if that's all, I think you need to rest. It's been a terrible day, and I've still got to arrange your move to the Needle."

"For how long? I'm going to hate it there."

"Until it's over, Lily."

Lily stopped. There *was* something she could do instead of just sitting locked up in a tower. Something frightening.

"Where is Rose's body?" she asked as innocently as possible.

Mary sighed. "In the chapel. Her parents will collect her soon and take her home for burial."

"Castle Gloom was her home. I . . . I want to pay my respects."

Mary didn't look like she believed her. She knew Lily was up to something but couldn't figure out what. "That's good and right," said Mary, warily. "But can't it wait until morning?"

"No, it really can't."

"Then take the guards with you. I don't want you roaming the corridors alone."

"I'll take K'leef and Thorn."

Mary scowled, but Lily insisted. "Tyburn trusts Thorn to look after me, and K'leef's a sorcerer."

"Hmm. All right. Pay your respects, then. But be quick."

Lily kissed her nanny's cheek. "Thank you, Mary."

It wasn't just Thorn who had unique skills.

I have unique skills, too, Mary. Skills you wouldn't believe. It's time I used them. It's time I spoke to the dead.

THIRTY-FOUR

"We used to be able to summon ghosts with a click of our fingers," said Lily as she, Thorn, and K'leef made their way to the chapel. "But over the centuries, the magic's faded, not just for us, but for all the Great Houses."

"Contacting the dead is a huge, dangerous step, Lily," said K'leef.

"I've got to do it."

"The princess is right. We need to know who killed Rose and make him pay." Thorn replied grimly.

She would find out the truth. Was it this sixth brigand, as Tyburn suspected, trying to finish the job? She might speak to Rose, tell her how sorry she was and see if there was anything more she could do, like help Rose's family. They were all good reasons.

And also to prove that she could.

Why stop at Custard? Surely it was her job, her *duty*, to use her magic to help her people? Father had won great battles with his magic. And Lily was—wanted to be—her father's daughter.

"Have you forgotten the penalty?" said K'leef. "They'll burn you at the stake for this."

"Only if I get caught." She looked back at them. "If you've changed your minds about this, you can go back. It's all right."

Thorn touched her arm. "Rose was our friend, too."

K'leef nodded. "It is the duty of a noble to uphold the law. The killer cannot be allowed to get away with this."

"Thank you." She meant it. Lily knew she wouldn't be able to carry on if Thorn and K'leef weren't here with her.

They turned the corner toward the chapel. Tall candles lit the corridor leading to it, and there were fresh flowers laid at the door. "Just imagine if I could summon undead armies, like Astaroth Shadow. That would be *amazing*."

"You said Astaroth was pure evil," reminded Thorn. "You really want to be like him?"

"I'd be a *good* necromancer."

"Do you know how wrong you sound?"

K'leef waved small flames over his fingertips. "Not that it matters. That level of power no longer exists."

"The age of sorcery is coming to an end," said Lily. "Soon we'll all be just like you, Thorn."

"There ain't no one else like me."

"It's the age of steel now," said K'leef. "The future will be decided by men like Tyburn."

Lily touched the bronze door handle, forged in the shape of a skeletal hand. This was it. She opened the chapel door.

Three maids all jumped up. They'd been praying. Iris brushed the tears from her eyes. "M'lady, we weren't expecting you."

Clare and Dot were with her. Rose's friends.

Rose lay upon a stone slab, surrounded by fresh flowers, hundreds and hundreds, their scents filling the room with thick perfume. Roses, lilies, tulips, daffodils, and snowdrops. All black.

Rose wore her best dress. As dark as midnight and not coarse wool or rough linen, but fine crushed velvet with sleeves made of silk, the skirts layered satin and the collar fur. Her boots shone in the candlelight, and the buttons on her dress were silver, sparkling and newly polished. There was a necklace of small black pearls around her neck and onyx rings on her white fingers. She clutched a bouquet of black roses, tied in place with ribbon.

Death's bride. That was how it was done in Gehenna. You crossed from the lands of the living to the dead in all your finery.

Lily looked at the three girls. They must have prepared all this. Washed the body and perfumed it and dressed her and arranged all the flowers. "She looks beautiful. Rose would be pleased."

Dot sniffed. "Thank you, m'lady."

It didn't seem right, telling them what Rose might think. They all knew Rose better than she did. Lily took off her wrought silver bracelet and put it on Rose's wrist. It was customary to give the dead gifts for their journey.

The maids left, and Thorn closed the door behind them.

Should she do it? She didn't feel so sure now, standing beside Rose.

She looks so peaceful. Should I just leave her be?

But what about her killer? Were they just going to let him get away with it?

No. Rose belonged to Castle Gloom. We look after our own.

Lily closed her eyes and concentrated. This wasn't like being in the Shadow Library; it felt different.

Things came here to be laid to rest. They did not want to be disturbed.

Lily held Rose's hand. It was cold but soft.

A new, unpleasant smell brushed Lily's nostrils. It was damp and thick with soil—strange, odorous, rotting. Moldy. There was nothing in this chamber that smelled like that.

She winced as she felt, imagined, a blow to the back of her head. She swayed, and Thorn held her until she steadied herself.

Lily's chest tightened. Her breath fought against her. She felt long weeds clinging to her legs and wet leaves sticking to her face and arms.

Tighter and tighter the plants within the moat entwined her, holding her down.

Water rushed about her. Bubbles of air spilled from her mouth.

She wants to reach the surface; she can see the moon shimmering just beyond her fingertips. But her dress weighs her down and the more she kicks, the more the weeds tangle her legs. She grabs for the side of the bank, but her fingers slip.

Her head aches from when she was struck from behind, moments before she was pushed into the moat.

There is a person standing on the edge. His face is broken by the rippling surface of the water. No, it's not the ripples that break his face, but deep scars. He watches from eyes that are two black holes.

The man reaches and holds out a strip of white cloth. Rose grabs it and hope fills her heart. He will help pull her up.

Instead he slowly begins to let the cloth slip.

No! Rose clutches the material even tighter.

The man lets go.

Lily's throat seized up. An invisible weight crushed her lungs.

The moonlight fades away. . . . It is growing murky dark all around her.

Only her fingertips catch the moonlight as she tries, in vain, to reach for the surface. It spreads a rippling pattern over her, a shroud of pale light.

Then Rose sinks into darkness. Her last thought is that now Fynn won't see her in this beautiful dress.

Lily opened her eyes, gasping for air. She was blind with tears. "Oh, Rose, I'm so sorry."

Thorn put his arms around her. "What happened?"

Lily heaved, trying to breathe deeper. She wasn't getting enough air. "I was there, Thorn. I felt what she felt."

K'leef knelt down in front of her. "Did you see who did it?"

Lily still clenched Rose's hand. She shouldn't have done it, delved into Rose's last moments. Was that all her spirit could remember, the awful death? That was too horrible. Rose should go to the lands of the dead with only sweet memories.

"Lily, did you see?" asked K'leef, his eyes dark with worry.

"Yes," Lily gasped. "It was the scarred man."

THIRTY-FIVE

Who was the scarred man?

The question ticked over and over in Thorn's head throughout the next few days. Was he working for this sixth brigand, or was he an entirely different enemy? Thorn tried to see Lily, between his errands and training, but Mary guarded the door into the Needle and shoved him off. For a small woman, she could be very forceful.

Lady Shadow needed her rest, that's what Mary had told him.

Who was the scarred man?

Thorn rubbed his aching head.

Face it, you ain't got a clue.

He wasn't smart like Lily or K'leef. He had no book learning and no magic, and the answer to this question needed plenty of both.

Thorn yawned. With Halloween only around the corner, more and more guests were arriving, and he hadn't stopped since sunup. The stables were overflowing, and every lord and his squire wanted hot food and cold drinks, baths and clean bedding, and all of it immediately. His arms ached from lugging sacks of oats, and his feet were sore from running up and down countless steps and along miles of corridor. He was the lowest of the low, which meant that *everyone* ordered him around. Body and brain were exhausted. He just wanted his bed.

And maybe if he hadn't been so tired he would have been ready for the ambush.

An icy breeze touched his neck. A torch flame flickered and, briefly, a shadow loomed over him. And then it was too late.

Something grabbed his shoulders, its strength incredible, and then the ground fell away.

"Hades!" Thorn yelled. "Put me down right now!"

The giant bat snarled as he soared upward with Thorn dangling under him, trapped in his claws.

"Put me down! I'm not in the mood!"

Hades ignored him. Higher and higher they rose, the giant bat gathering speed amid his entourage of lesser bats. More and more flocked about him, their king.

Hades threw back his head and shrieked. He flipped over and wove between a pair of tottering chimney stacks, the brickwork skimming past Thorn's nose.

"No! I'm not enjoying it!"

But, clearly, Hades was. A lot.

Swinging from his claws was not the same as riding on his back. Thorn's stomach tossed and rolled in wholly bad ways. "I think I'm gonna puke."

Hades hissed.

"Really, I am!"

Hades spun upward, twisting in tight corkscrews, and Thorn clamped his eyes shut as the world became a belly-flip-flopping blur.

Thorn gulped. "It's coming up...."

Hades dropped him.

Thorn didn't have time to scream before he hit cold, damp stone.

Shouldn't that fall have taken longer? And hurt a lot more?

He opened his eyes. "Oh, very funny."

He was on the roof of a tower. The highest tower in Castle Gloom. The Needle.

Hades settled himself down beside Thorn, who looked over the edge and instantly regretted it. People milled in the courtyard far below, ant-sized.

"You really shouldn't be up here, Thorn."

Lily sat on a gargoyle, her skirts fluttering in the night wind, her head resting on the stone creature's brow.

"And I doubt you should be up here, either, Princess."

"I come here to think. Up here with Flint." She patted the gargoyle's cheek. "It's quiet, and we don't get disturbed. Usually."

"You want me to leave? It wasn't my idea to—"

She shook her head. "I'm not getting anywhere. My brain aches with it all. I'm due to marry a boy I loathe. I'm to leave my home to live with my enemies. Someone tried to poison me, and a few nights ago, my oldest friend was murdered. And I've got no one to help me."

"I'll help you. With anything. You know that, right?"

"Thanks, Thorn. I know I can count on you and K'leef, but . . ." She sighed. "I went down to the Shadow Gallery. The walls are filled with portraits of my family going back a long, long way. Could one of them be this scarred man? Come back from the grave, somehow?"

"If he is one of your relatives, why does he want you dead?"

"I'm not much, Thorn. I can't protect my people, and I'm about to hand over my kingdom to our enemies. I can imagine lots of reasons why another Shadow might want me dead." She turned and gazed out over the castle, toward Spindlewood and beyond. "I came up here the night they died."

No need to ask who "they" were. Lily was talking about her family.

"I waited and waited until the sun came up. I would have waited another whole day if Mary hadn't found me."

"I . . . I don't know what to say, Lily. I'm sorry."

"Even when they were dead and Tyburn brought their bodies home, I didn't really believe they could be gone. I kept on thinking it was a mistake and they'd come riding through the gates and it would be someone else all burned and unrecognizable. Isn't that evil of me? Wishing it was someone else's parents, someone else's brother, who was dead?"

"No, I'd call that normal. Who would choose grief?"

She looked at him intensely. Then she nodded slowly. "I remember the very moment I realized they were *never* coming back. It was Rose. She came in with breakfast and called me 'M'lady Shadow.' Until that morning she'd always called me Lily."

This brought to mind Rose's killer—the scarred man—again. "What about using more of your magic? Maybe you could learn something new."

"No more magic for me, Thorn." Her shoulders sank, and she looked utterly defeated. "What good has it done? Poor, poor Rose. I should have just left her alone. I thought I was so clever, so good. Now I realize why everyone fears the Shadows. The dead *should* be left in peace."

"That's not how I see it. You can do amazing things, Lily. Better than the other sorcerers. K'leef can light a candle with his magic, that's all. And Gabriel? Just a few sparkles. You can call on ghosts. That's without even trying. You saw who killed Rose. We need to find out who this scarred man is. If you did some more—"

"More what, Thorn? More sadness? More memories of people who wanted to live? You don't know what it feels like, the longing the dead have. How much they miss this world. They are empty, and their despair has no end. I won't go there again. And why can I do such magic? It scares me, Thorn. I don't feel in control." Lily's shoulders slumped. "Uncle Pan warned me about this the night he caught us in the library. This is why women aren't allowed to practice magic. It's too powerful."

"Maybe the answers are in them books in your library."

"Uncle Pan won't let me anywhere near there after what we did. It's best to forget it."

Thorn didn't like the way she was talking. This wasn't the Lily he knew. It sounded like she was giving up. "Why don't you come back onto the roof, where it's safer?"

She stood up on the gargoyle's horns. "I didn't expect you to be afraid of heights."

"Trees is different. The higher you go, the more branches there are between you and the ground. Here, all you've got is air. If we were meant to live this high, we'd have been born with feathers."

"That's one of your grandpa's idiotic sayings, isn't it?"

She faced him, hand on slanted hip, her hair all loose and wild and the moonlight turning her skin to the palest porcelain. Her eyes, her storm-gray eyes, were large, and Thorn couldn't take his gaze away from them. He blushed.

"Are you all right?" she asked.

Thorn cleared his throat. "You should wear trousers if you go climbing."

Lily hopped off the gargoyle onto the roof. "Ladies do not wear trousers."

He looked about him. "How did you get up here? I don't see no hatch, and I know there ain't no windows."

Lily replied with a sly smile. "Castle Gloom has many secrets, Thorn. Surely you know that by now."

"So here you are, trapped in the tower like some fairy-tale princess."

She curtseyed. "Are you here to rescue me?"

A wild, insane thought jumped into his head. "We could leave and never come back. You and me."

Lily's eyes widened with shock. She recovered quickly, turning away with a cough, but Thorn burned with embarrassment. He wanted to slap himself!

Who did he think he was? He was just a peasant boy, and she was, even if she didn't like the word, a princess. Peasants and princesses did not run away together. They couldn't; they lived in different worlds.

"I . . . I meant we could just get off the tower. Only if you want."

Hades twitched his ears and made an unpleasant noise in the back of his throat.

Thorn glared at him. "Oh, and what's wrong with that?" He pulled the beast's head down so they were face-to-face. "I don't care what you smell. She's Lady Shadow, and you've got to be more polite."

Hades drew back his lips, revealing his immense fangs. They looked longer than before. Thorn checked him over. Was Hades still *growing*?

"What have you got in mind?" asked Lily.

"How about a ride on Hades?"

The bat jerked back, indignant.

Thorn sighed at the monster. "Oh, is that what you think? Fair enough."

Lily frowned. "Can you really understand what he's saying? And what *is* he saying?"

Thorn sighed. "He's saying he won't do it. He says you smell . . . funny. But you know what I think? I think Hades can't carry us both. Because he's *old*."

Hades growled.

Thorn continued. "Old and weak and a bit past it. There's no way he's strong enough to carry *two* people; he can barely carry me. I'm sorry, Lily, but I've got to get Hades back to Murk Hall. He gets tired easily, what with him being two hundred years old and all. And his hearing's not what it used to be. I wouldn't want him crashing into a wall or nothing."

Hades thwacked Thorn. The beast glared at him.

"Really?" said Thorn. "Well, if you insist." Thorn grinned at Lily and patted Hades's back. "Up you hop."

Lily looked uneasy. "Are you sure about this?"

"You get up onto the shoulders. I'll sit behind you. If he gives you any trouble, just pull his ears. Hard."

Hades twitched his ears warily.

Lily got on and shuffled as far forward as she could. Thorn jumped on behind her and got up close.

He didn't know what Hades was complaining about. Lily smelled nice. Her hair flicked in his face. How could hair be so soft?

"Sorry. Should I tie it up?"

"Er . . . no. It's fine." Thorn hadn't planned for this. Lily could hold on to Hades's fur, but he couldn't reach from behind her.

"Put your hands around my waist, Thorn."

"No, I'm fine. I'll just balance like this."

"Put them around my waist."

He did.

"Tighter."

"Um, okay." Then he leaned toward Hades's left ear. "No funny business. Fly smooth and straight."

Hades shuffled to the side of the Needle. And tipped himself off.

Wings folded, he dropped like a stone. The wind roared in Thorn's ears and Lily's hair covered his vision. He felt her tremble as their bodies pressed together. Was it fear or excitement?

The wings unfurled, and they swooped over the shouts of the soldiers in the courtyard. Horses neighed and reared up on their back legs.

Trailing behind like a fluttering cloak came thousands of bats.

Hades swept his wings in slow, easy beats. He gave himself space and glided gently.

Lily gasped, and she turned her head. She stared at Thorn, grinning, unable to speak.

Their faces were so close and lips inches apart—

Lily howled and faced front.

Thorn's heart raced, and it wasn't because of the thrill of flying.

"Look, Thorn! The Night Garden!"

"That's where we buried Custard, right?"

Hades swooped down and skimmed his claws over the tips of the trees. He swirled around and flapped above the large central pond, admiring his own reflection.

"You really do love yourself," muttered Thorn, nudging the bat with his heels.

Hades dipped his lower back, then bucked hard.

Thorn was thrown into the air, the wind whistling in his ears, along with a burst of laughter from Lily.

He splashed into the pond. It wasn't deep, so he scraped his backside on the gravel at the bottom.

Spluttering and pulling weeds out of his hair, Thorn scrambled to his feet, standing chest high in the water. Hades was scratching in the pebbles along the path, and Lily had dismounted and stood at the edge of the pond. She extended her hand while her shoulders shook with barely suppressed laughter. "Here, let me help you out."

"I can get out by myself!"

Stupid bat. Ugly bat. Evil bat.

Thorn coughed and spat out more pond water. He glared at Hades. "That's it. You're having hay with the mules."

Lily held up her hand. "Stop, Thorn. What's that?"

He looked around him.

A fish floated dead upon the water. Thorn picked it up. Green froth clung to its gills.

"There's another." Lily pointed to his right.

The whole pond reeked of dead fish. They bobbed on the ripples, their scales peeled off, their mouths and gills green.

Lily crouched down and took one out. She rubbed the green paste between her fingers and went pale. "This is life-bane. The same poison that killed Custard."

"What's it doing here?" Thorn looked at the dead fish in his hands. He quickly dropped it and wiped his hands. Then he started spitting. "I swallowed some of this water."

Lily frowned as she peered into the pond. "See that? Something glinting among those rocks. Just under the surface."

Thorn saw it. Something shiny and orange. He reached down and with some scrabbling felt a metal shape. He closed his hand around it and waded over to Lily.

"What is it?" Lily asked.

Both leaned over to look as Thorn unfurled his fingers.

It was a ring with a large amber stone. The stone was hinged, and underneath was a secret compartment. Lily picked up the ring and scraped her nail along the inner edge. "This is an old assassin's device. Poison hidden in a hollowed-out ring." She held up her finger, showing the green powder collected under her nail. "More life-bane."

"It can't be...." Only one person at Castle Gloom wore amber. Thorn had met him here, the night of the feast, the night Custard had died. "He said he was throwing *pebbles* into the pond, but he lied, didn't he? He was trying to get rid of this ring."

Lily stared at it. "When we danced, he said he didn't want me marrying Gabriel. He said it would be bad for his family if the Shadows and Solars made an alliance. I just didn't realize how far he'd go to stop it...."

They'd found the poisoner.

K'leef.

THIRTY-SIX

Thorn raced off, leaving Lily far behind. He needed to get to K'leef.
It wouldn't be long before Lily reported him, and after that, there'd be guards, there'd be Tyburn and Duke Solar, and it would be too late.

He needed to find out the truth.

The ring was K'leef's. No doubt about that. The ring was designed to hold poison. No doubt about that, either, and he knew, *he knew*, that K'leef had chucked it into the pond.

But K'leef, an assassin? He couldn't believe it.

He didn't want to believe it.

Thorn leaped up the steps to the Eclipse rooms two at a time. This time of night the castle should be deeply asleep, but he could already hear the sound of armored men shouting out in the courtyard. Doors slammed and boots hammered on the steps below, not far behind him.

He reached the top and spilled out into a small hall, bare except for a stout wooden and brass door. Thorn banged on it, hard. "K'leef! Open up! Right now!"

I have a minute, maybe two, before the others get here.

Thorn smashed his fist against the thick oak. "OPEN UP!"

He barged in the moment the bolt slid open. "We found the ring."

K'leef stood before him, blinking, mouth agape, dressed in a pair of baggy silken trousers and a hastily wrapped blanket. He twitched his head, trying to recover his wits. "What—what ring?"

"Don't treat me like an idiot, K'leef." Sitting there on the dressing table was a red lacquer box filled with amber rings. Small, large, dainty, chunky. All sorts. Thorn grabbed a handful and threw them at K'leef. "Which one of these has poison in it, K'leef?"

"I—I—"

Thorn slammed the door shut. The shouts of the guards echoed upward, getting louder by the second.

Thorn faced his friend. "Tell me the truth, K'leef. You don't have long. Did you try and poison Lily?"

"Of course not!"

"Then what happened? Quickly!"

K'leef looked anxious. "I have that poison—it's true. It was stored in my ring ages ago, as a powder. It's common in the Sultanate. You can use it against rivals and . . . on yourself."

"On yourself? Why?"

"To ensure you aren't taken alive. So you don't become a hostage. I should have taken it the second I was captured by the duke, but I didn't have the courage."

"Killing yourself doesn't sound courageous; it sounds stupid."

Thorn saw tears fall as K'leef continued. "I kept the ring in that box. I never wore it. Please believe me. I *never* wore it. But someone must have come into my room and found it. They must have used a few pinches of the poison, then returned the ring. When the puppy died, I knew it was life-bane. Don't you see? Someone's trying to set me up! I had to get rid of the ring! I was going to bury it in the Night Garden, but then I heard you and Lily coming, so I threw it in the pond." He looked at Thorn, eyes imploring. "It's the truth, Thorn. On my honor."

Thorn didn't know what to do, what to believe. He wanted to shake

K'leef, shout at him for being so stupid, for lying to them, his friends. But it wouldn't do any good now.

Thorn could track animals, he could hunt, and he could travel by the stars, but he had a hard time understanding politics—things like sabotage, treason, and assassination. These things didn't happen back in Stour. "Why would someone want to set you up for killing Lily?"

"To make us enemies. To make the Shadow family hate mine, House Djinn. Then, when Duke Solar next attacked my country, he'd have everyone from Gehenna beside him."

It made horrible sense. If Lily had died and the blame had fallen on the sultan's son, then Gehenna would have gladly joined Lumina to avenge itself on the Sultanate of Fire.

Tyburn booted the door open. Guards stood behind him, the closest carrying a set of iron cuffs. He bowed, ever so slightly. "M'lord, I have some questions for you."

K'leef didn't protest. The shock he'd shown in front of Thorn had completely disappeared. He looked calm and in control. Like a true noble. "Of course. You won't need the chains."

Tyburn nodded. "I'll have the cell made as comfortable as possible."

K'leef shot Thorn one last, desperate look before the guards led him away, leaving Thorn with the grim-faced executioner.

Tyburn casually searched the box of rings, perhaps looking for another one storing poison. "I wondered why he'd stopped wearing them."

"He ain't the assassin," said Thorn.

"The ring was his. He had the opportunity, and he had the motive. Am I missing anything?"

"Yeah, the real killer." Thorn was desperate. "What about this sixth brigand? You were sure he was behind this poisoning."

Tyburn turned and faced him. The dark eyes of his went cold. "I was, that is true. I made a mistake. I was so fixated on the man I was chasing that I forgot the first rule of the hunt: Beware of other predators."

"Yeah. My dad warned me to watch out for the wolf at my front *and* the bear at my back."

"Wise words." Tyburn smiled. "I'd like to meet your father one day."

"Maybe you ain't wrong. Maybe it is this sixth man. You just ain't found him yet."

"You're letting your feelings cloud your judgment. Do you think K'leef is the first person to betray a friend?"

"No, that ain't K'leef. He's got honor."

"Honor? The first refuge of liars and scoundrels." Tyburn looked over at him. "You've a lot to learn about the world, boy."

"So you think all this time he was just pretending?"

"Yes," Tyburn replied. "It's difficult for you to understand the stakes. You value friendship too much."

"Friendship is important."

"To some." Tyburn scratched his chin. "Given how Gabriel treats him, it makes sense that K'leef would try to poison him. The crystal goblets all looked the same, but it didn't really matter. If Gabriel had died, his father would have blamed the Shadows. If Lily had died, the Shadows would have held the Solars responsible. There would be war between the two countries all over again. K'leef would have saved his country with a few pinches of poison."

"K'leef thinks he was set up, to give the Solars and the Shadows a reason to attack the Sultanate," said Thorn.

Tyburn looked doubtful. "Interesting theory, but not as believable."

"Maybe the duke arranged it," said Thorn. "Just to keep K'leef from getting home. He'll end up an old man, a prisoner of the duke for life."

"No, he won't," said Tyburn. "By attempting to murder Lady Shadow, K'leef has committed treason."

"You can't mean . . ."

"K'leef's not going anywhere but Lamentation Hill," said Tyburn. "Where he'll be executed."

THIRTY-SEVEN

"**L**ady Shadow! Wait!"

Thorn ran across the courtyard. He'd been waiting all morning, and finally Lily was out, though guarded by Mary and three of her maids.

Lily stopped, and Mary frowned as Thorn skidded up to them.

He bowed. "Can I have a word, m'lady?"

Mary got in between them. She crossed her arms and snorted. "Don't you have errands, boy? Lady Shadow is far too busy—"

"It's all right, Mary." Lily touched her nanny's arm, and the old woman, most reluctantly, stepped aside. "What is it, Thorn?"

"In private."

Mary gave him a scowl, but Lily nodded and the two of them walked a few yards away.

Thorn glanced over at the Needle. "So they let you out?"

"Yes. Now that we've discovered the poisoner, there's no need for me to be locked up there anymore."

"You don't believe it's K'leef, do you?" How could she? K'leef was her friend more than he was Thorn's. "He would never hurt you."

"Tyburn says he might have been trying to poison Gabriel and the goblets got muddled up." Lily bit her lip. "Oh, Thorn, I don't know what to believe anymore."

"Please, Lily. He'll be executed in three days. You have to do something."

Lily's eyes were red-rimmed, and she looked so tired. "Don't you think I've tried? I've pleaded with Uncle Pan, but he says there's nothing we can do. I have to uphold the law, for noble and commoner."

"But what if the law's wrong? Then it must be right to break it."

Lily's gaze cooled. "I hope you're not planning anything stupid."

He almost blurted it out right then and there. But he held his tongue, despite himself. Instead he gave Lily an insipid smile, the sort of smile he'd seen a lot here in Castle Gloom. "Of course not."

"You're a terrible liar." Lily glanced back at the waiting Mary. "I have to go. Duke Solar's back and it looks like he's brought half of Lumina's nobility with him. I'll do what I can, but you'll have to give me time."

"K'leef ain't got no more time."

She took his hand. "Please, Thorn, let me handle this."

Thorn watched her go.

She couldn't save K'leef. She just didn't want to admit it.

It was up to him.

The rest of the day was spent preparing. He groomed Hades and fed him to bursting. The bat used up a lot of energy flying, and Thorn needed him to fly as far and as fast as he could tonight with two on his back.

Thorn gathered enough food for two days, and he collected the few crowns he'd earned as tips for grooming the horses. It wouldn't get them far, but if they reached the coast, he reckoned they could get a ship to take them south. The sultan would reward any captain handsomely for the return of his son.

Thorn had visited the underground cells earlier that evening. The jailer was a sallow-faced man who drank a lot and slept even more. K'leef was his only prisoner. Thorn handed over a stolen bottle of wine, telling the jailer it was a gift for his good work. The cork came out before Thorn had even left the room.

Thorn settled himself down among the bales in the stables, telling the other squires that he wanted an early start. No one noticed.

He waited until the moon was past its zenith. The castle fell quiet.

Thorn brushed off the hay as he stood. He hefted his rucksack.

This was it, all or nothing. Either they got away, or in a few days both of their heads would be up on Lamentation Hill.

Don't think about that. Think about saving your friend. Think about getting home. Think about anything but the touch of cold sharp steel on your neck.

Thunder glanced at him. Thorn wandered over and rubbed his forelock. "I'm gonna miss you, boy."

The big stallion stamped his hoof.

"I ain't got no choice." He looked around the other horses. Yes, he was going to miss this place. For somewhere that wasn't his home, it wasn't too bad.

Thorn searched behind the oat sacks and drew out a club, nothing more than a heavy lump of wood he'd taken from the log pile. He might need to use it, if the jailer wasn't asleep.

Thorn crept across the stables to the door and peered out. No one in the courtyard and the moon hidden behind heavy clouds. Torches flickered weakly on the walls. Perfect.

Down to the cells. Get K'leef, then across to Murk Hall and Hades.

Simple. Like all the best plans.

Thorn stepped into the courtyard.

A match light hissed into life.

The flame waved over a pipe and lit the hard contours of Tyburn's face. He puffed at the stem until the tobacco was glowing, then leaned back on his stool, which was positioned a few yards from the stable doors. He was unarmed.

"Go back to bed, boy."

Thorn looked across the flagstones. The door leading to the steps to the underground cells was no more than fifty yards away.

All that stood between him and that door was Tyburn, an old man. Thorn tightened his grip on the club. One good whack and the executioner wouldn't wake till lunchtime.

Tyburn puffed out a big smoky ring. "I'm not in the habit of repeating myself."

You just want me to do something stupid. It ain't gonna happen. I'll wait.

After all, Tyburn couldn't watch Thorn *all* the time.

Thorn chucked the club away and went back to bed.

THIRTY-EIGHT

"Water the horses, troll."

"Take those sacks over to the kitchens, troll."

"More wood for the fires, troll."

"Faster, troll, faster!"

Old Colm woke Thorn an hour before the other squires. Fetching, carrying, feeding, watering, and a dozen other chores that should take all day and Old Colm wanted them done *now*.

Thorn ran back and forth across Castle Gloom. He knew why they were doing it. Tyburn must have spoken to Old Colm.

Keep Thorn busy. Too busy to think about doing anything else. Anything stupid.

There was plenty of activity outside the castle walls as more and more people arrived. Tents sprang up, creating a city of dazzling cloth around the fair on Devil's Knoll.

Nobles loyal to House Shadow arrived, and their horses needed grooming and looking after.

And it wasn't just allies to House Shadow. White pavilions rose along the walls, lined between Troll Gate and Skeleton Gate. Paladins in their silver armor rode in and out of Castle Gloom as if they owned it already. Stonemasons began measuring for windows to be added to the Great Hall.

One more day until Halloween.

Two more days to save K'leef.

He just needed to come up with a new plan. If only he could rest for just a moment . . .

"Wake up, troll!"

Thorn jerked and looked around. He must have fallen asleep standing up.

The other squires smirked as Old Colm tossed Thorn his keys. "Get down to the armory, troll. Bring me up ten more blades. Take someone with you."

"Yes, sir." Thorn nodded at Wade, and they went down to get more weapons.

The guard at the armory waved them through, and Wade held the lantern as Thorn pushed open the door.

Sword blades glistened in the lamplight. Suits of full plate armor lined up in silent regiments. Spears were stacked like kindling, and sheaves of arrows filled old wine barrels.

"The training weapons are over there," said Wade. "At the back."

How big was this place? Like everywhere in Castle Gloom, there were tunnels and passages going off in all directions. They found enough weaponry to arm the Black Guard ten times over. A row of saddles, each made of sculpted leather stretched over wooden frames. Lances as tall as trees. Thorn knew that Gehenna didn't have enough men to use them all. The population had never been large, as the earth was too poor to grow anything more than the most meager harvests. That was why the Shadows had used the undead to bolster their numbers. Corpses were plentiful during wars.

Thorn grinned when he came to a rack of axes. There were single-handed hatchets, ideal for trimming branches off trees and limbs off men. Then he found a hefty double-bladed great ax. He reckoned one of these could take down a horse.

Ah. Now this is more like it.

He picked up a battle-ax. Easy to carry in both hands and the head was just like his dad's back home. He ran his thumb along a blade. Dad had taught Thorn about sharpening early on. Thorn had learned how to stroke the whetstone along the steel, making sure the edge wasn't too shallow—the metal would chip—and not so steep that it wouldn't bite deep enough. He put it back and ran his fingers along the row of ax handles, enjoying the way the wood slipped through his fingers.

Then, without thinking, his hand tightened around one.

Thorn lifted it, sensing its balance, as if his muscles knew it. He felt a familiar pattern press against his palm.

Strange . . .

"Wade, bring the lantern here," he said.

"I'm just trying to sort out these swords. Some help would be appreciated."

"Bring the lantern!"

"All right, all right . . ."

Thorn's nail circled the pattern. He shivered.

I've used this ax before.

He'd carried it a hundred times. He'd spent evenings at the fire sharpening it.

But that ain't possible.

Wade joined him. Thorn grabbed the lantern and held it up.

The carved pattern was an acorn—just like the one on his amulet.

"This is my dad's ax," he whispered.

"Are you sure?"

"Of course I am." The last time he'd seen it was on his dad's shoulder as he went off.

His heart beat fast. What did this mean? His dad would never have left his ax behind.

"Hey, what about the swords?" asked Wade.

Thorn checked the acorn again. Why bother? It *was* his dad's. The same hands that had carved the ax had carved his amulet.

Ignoring Wade, Thorn ran outside with the ax. Someone would know. Someone would tell him how *this* ax came to be here in Castle Gloom.

A few minutes later, he stumbled into the courtyard. The other squires were busy at work, attacking thick wooden posts with their blunt swords. Ten chops to the head and waist. Then the next boy. The courtyard echoed with the endless *thud thud thud* of steel on wood. Old Colm stood talking to Tyburn.

"This is my dad's ax," said Thorn.

He'd chopped trees down with it and even killed a wolf with it once.

No one paid any notice. Old Colm kept on talking, and the squires continued hacking.

Thorn marched up to the nearest post and swung the ax with all his might. It hit like thunder. "Tell me!"

The squires stopped. Silence fell over the whole courtyard.

Old Colm glared, his face lit up a livid scarlet. "You little troll! How dare you interrupt?"

Tyburn raised his hand, and Old Colm backed off. "What's on your mind, Thorn?"

"This ax belongs to my dad."

"And you want to know how it ended up here?"

"Yeah, I do."

"You want to have this talk right here, right now?"

Thorn's pulse pounded in his ears and he suddenly felt terrified. Did he really want to hear the truth?

"Tell me," he said, steeling himself.

"I got it off a brigand. He'd been part of a gang of six outlaws, lurking in Spindlewood. His companions were dealt with, but he escaped, dropping this ax as he fled. I've spent the last few months searching for him, this sixth brigand. I didn't find him, but I did find you, his son."

Those five heads on spikes on top of Lamentation Hill...

"What are you saying?" whispered Thorn.

Tyburn's gaze chilled him. "Your father murdered Lady Shadow's family."

THIRTY-NINE

By evening, everyone in Castle Gloom knew the truth, that Thorn's dad was the last brigand responsible for the death of the Shadows.

The other squires now wanted nothing to do with him. They whispered as he went past, or muttered threats, and occasionally one would trip him, or kick him as he tried to rise, promising worse to come.

Fine. He didn't care. He preferred working in the stables by himself.

Thorn stabbed his pitchfork into the hay. He hated them all. Everyone in Castle Gloom.

Except Hades. Thorn had gone to see him at Murk Hall, but the bat wasn't there. Thorn assumed he'd gone out hunting and just hoped he hadn't eaten some poor farmer's whole herd.

Life must be bad if my only friend is a giant bat.

What about Lily? Why hadn't she come to see him? Did she hate him, too?

Someone came to the stable door. "Hello? Anyone in here?"

Why couldn't they leave him alone?

It was Wade, the only squire still speaking to him. He strolled over, sat down on a sack of oats, and handed over a wrapped package. "Missed you at dinner."

"I ain't hungry."

"That's because you haven't tried this."

"What is it?" Thorn asked.

"Fruitcake. It's poisoned, so you can eat it and die and stop feeling sorry for yourself."

Thorn took a huge bite, half hoping it *was* poisoned and he'd die and they *would* all be sorry.

"It's good, isn't it?" said Wade.

"I suppose."

"If there's a fault, it's that the cake's a bit dry. So I brought this." He held out a small bottle. "Lemonade."

"Is that poisoned, too?"

"Have a sip and find out."

Thorn did, and the lemonade was acid sharp. But not *actually* lethal.

Wade took a swig and screwed his face up as the sour taste attacked his taste buds. "I'm sorry about your dad, Thorn."

"He wasn't like everyone says he was. He ain't no killer, Wade."

"If you say so."

He doesn't believe me.

Why should he?

"What are you doing here, Wade? The others won't like you taking sides with me."

Wade wiggled his nose. "Those lemons are deadly."

"Are you paying any attention?"

"To your whining? No, not really." He drew his fingers over his face. "Will you be at the Halloween Ball tomorrow?"

"I ain't interested in your stupid ball."

"C'mon. I've a spare mask if you're interested. You can get up to plenty of mischief wearing a mask."

"How can I be thinking about masks when they'll be executing K'leef the next morning?"

"Tyburn said—"

"Tyburn don't know nothing! The man's mind is so twisted with treachery he thinks the worst of everyone. The world ain't like that, Wade."

"Your world, maybe. Things are different here."

Thorn grimaced. "I should have known. He sees me and buys me, just like that. Why?"

"Certainly not for your good looks."

"Shut up, Wade."

"I was just saying that you're no—"

Thorn clamped his hand over Wade's mouth and listened. Growing up in Herne's Forest gave you sharp ears. You needed to know if the rustling in the bushes was a deer or a wolf. The difference mattered.

Now he could hear that something, or someone, was in the stables with them. Hiding behind the hay bales.

Thorn got up quietly. If it was a squire looking for a fight, he was going to get one. He slunk closer, taking care not to make a sound. Yes, definitely some creep lurking; he could hear their breathing and the rustle of cloth.

Thorn reached over and grabbed a fistful of hair.

"Ow!" Lily screamed as Thorn threw her across the floor. "What do you think you're doing?"

"Nice one, Thorn." Wade cleared his throat and stood up. "Well, I'd love to stay, but there are chores to do, errands to run." He performed a smooth, elegant bow. "M'lady." Then he dashed out.

FORTY

"What are you doing?" snapped Thorn. "Spying on me?"

Lily held up her arm. "Just look at that sleeve! Torn. I'm supposed to meet Baron Gaunt in ten minutes." She pulled pieces of hay out of her hair and tried to arrange her dress into something that wasn't a total mess. "You're an idiot."

"Why are you here, Princess?"

"Do I need a reason? I can go anywhere I like. These *are* my stables." She shrugged. "I wanted to see you. But you were talking with Wade, and you sounded so angry that I wasn't sure that you wanted to talk with me. So I hid."

"How did you get in here, anyway? I didn't see the door open." He peered around. "It's one of them secret passages, isn't it?"

Lily smirked. "Maybe."

"Could any of them help me get out of here?"

"What do you mean?"

Thorn checked the nearby wall. Was there a hidden door among the bricks? If he pushed the right one, would a tunnel open up? "Why am I still here? Now that everyone thinks they know what my dad did, no one wants me around." He pressed a few bricks. No luck. "Why not just let me leave?"

"Tyburn won't permit it." Lily looked conflicted. "I . . . I understand you want to leave, but you can't. Tyburn doesn't want you finding your dad and warning him."

"Find him? How does he think I'll find him?" That was stupid. Thorn had spent months searching for his dad, and all he had to show for it was several weeks as a slave and then this.

"You know what Tyburn's like." She glanced down at the bottle Wade had left behind. "Is that lemonade?"

Thorn handed it over. "Be careful. It'll twist your tongue and close off your throat."

Lily took a gulp. Then another. "Not bad."

He was impressed, despite himself. "It ain't too sour?"

"I like sour." She looked at him. "I'm sorry about your dad, Thorn."

"He's innocent."

"Men get desperate. They do desperate things."

Thorn scoffed. "That's Tyburn talking, not you."

Lily sighed. "Tyburn found my parents and brother. What was left of them. He followed the trail deep into Spindlewood. He found the brigands' encampment. He tried to take the assassins alive, but things got out of control. Five of them were killed, and the sixth fled, dropping his ax." She touched the black pearls around her neck. "My mother's jewels were found on them. What more evidence do you need?"

"I know my dad," said Thorn stubbornly. "He's innocent."

"Then he shouldn't have run away. Tyburn thought he was the poisoner, too, lurking nearby to try and finish the job he started. You even told us that you knew how to make life-bane." Lily frowned. "So he's probably long gone from here. On his way home."

Thorn knew her well enough now to know she was struggling with something.

"What is it, Princess?"

She glanced back at the door, making sure they were alone. "It doesn't matter anyway. Not now."

Thorn went cold. "What do you mean?"

"Tyburn knows where your family lives. You told him. Stour, a village on the edge of Herne's Forest."

"So?" Thorn felt dread start to well up inside him.

"So he's sent men there. Dangerous men. They'll kill your father the moment they find him. I'm sorry, Thorn. If I could stop them, I would—"

"Why *can't* you stop them? You're Lady Shadow! Tyburn works for you!" Thorn was on the edge of panic; he took deep breaths to calm himself. Surely his family was safe. Stour was a thousand miles across the sea after all.

"I can't! They left weeks ago! I didn't know!"

Thorn started pacing back and forth. Lily stopped him with a hand on his chest and met his gaze with a cold fury of her own. "Your dad's a criminal. He did what he did and has to pay for it. That's the law."

"The law?" He flung her arm away. "The law's an excuse you people made up. I'm sick of you nobles. You take what you want and never give anything back."

"That's not true! I look after my people." Lily glowered. "You wouldn't understand. You have only one family to look after. I have thousands."

"And when we try and look after ourselves, what happens?" Thorn closed his eyes, trying to shut down his rage. "My dad's a poacher, but all that means to me is he's tried to feed his family. Like I was trying to do when I shot that deer."

"Poaching's against the law."

"And starving isn't. My dad's lost enough from people like you." He held up his hand. "They cut off his first two fingers, did you know that?"

Lily stared at him. "What?"

Thorn continued. "First offense, you lose them. Second, it's your whole hand if you're lucky; your life, if you're not." He crooked his thumb. "That's why I shoot the way I do. Dad was the one who taught me, and he couldn't shoot the usual way."

"I met a man with some fingers missing. . . ." muttered Lily.

"It's a common punishment. Half the men back home have only eight fingers."

"Is your father good with animals, like you?"

"Better. Scared off a wolf just by whistling."

Lily dropped the lemonade bottle. It shattered at her feet, but she didn't notice. She just stood there, mouth gaping and eyes wild. "I . . . I think I saw him." She stared at Thorn. "You look a bit like him. The eyes are the same. Why didn't I realize? The hair. His is long, and yours is short, but the color . . . He also had a beard. It was as if he was trying to hide as much of his face as possible."

Thorn grabbed her arm. "You ain't making no sense."

"Remember that zoo we visited? Maximilian's Marvelous Magical Menagerie? I met a man there, looking after the animals. He had only three fingers on one hand." She shook her head. "If you hadn't walked off in a huff, you would have seen him!"

"No, it can't be. He'd be a long way from here. He ain't stupid." But there was a mixture of hope and fear sprouting in Thorn's chest.

"Tyburn told me he injured the man. It could be that's what's delayed your father. He'd have needed to rest up." Lily's brow furrowed. "And leaving's not that easy. There are many rivers between Gehenna and the south and only a few bridges, all guarded by my soldiers. Tyburn would have ordered them to keep a lookout."

Thorn gasped. "Tyburn's been watching the ports, too. He found me at Port Cutlass."

Could it be true? He almost didn't want to believe it. That his dad could be so close, and he not know. . . . Thorn tried not to let his hopes rise too high, but it was hard. "The fair was just a mile or two away. Come on, let's go look!"

"The zoo left, Thorn. Two days ago."

"Left? Why? Halloween's tomorrow." The zoo would have made most of its money then.

"I don't know, but they're gone. They were going south to the Sultanate for the winter."

What to do? He had to find that man and see if . . .

"It don't matter. I'll catch them on Hades. They can't have gotten far in their wagons."

"Hades?" The color drained from Lily's already pale cheeks. "Thorn, I thought you *knew*. Didn't anyone tell you?"

"Tell me what? Nobody speaks to me, Lily! What have you done with Hades?" He was frightened down to his core. The bat was all he had left.

"A couple of the Solar squires were fooling around. That moron Gabriel put them up to it. One tried to get up on the bat's back. The squire was thrown off and broke both his legs. He's Gabriel's cousin and . . . I didn't want to be the one to tell you this."

"Tell me what?" He was desperate now.

Please let Hades be all right.

"Duke Solar was furious. He complained to Uncle Pan and . . . Uncle Pan's weak. It's not his fault."

Ice ran through Thorn's veins. "Where's Hades?"

"He got rid of him."

"Rid of him? What do you mean?"

Lily bit her lip. "You know what I mean."

Thorn shoved Lily aside and ran.

Murk Hall was empty except for a few bats flitting high in the roof, as lost and aimless as Thorn.

They were looking for Hades, too.

A few minutes later, Lily stumbled in behind him. "I'm sorry, Thorn. I really am."

Thorn stared at the emptiness. He stared and stared. Stared until he felt dizzy, trying to gaze into the darkness, hoping to see the curve of a giant wing, the bristles of black fur, or the shape of a claw or fang. But there was nothing in the darkness now.

Hades was gone.

Lily hugged him.

How could it have gone so wrong? He stood stiffly in Lily's embrace, getting no comfort from her closeness. Hades was gone. The man who might be his father was gone. Tomorrow Lily would be gone. The day after that, K'leef would die, and where would that leave him?

"Let me go home, Lily."

She looked at him; their faces were inches apart. "Tyburn will come after you. I won't be able to stop him."

"Let me find my dad. He's innocent, Lily. I can't prove it, but I know it. Just like K'leef."

Lily wiped a tear from his eye and nodded. "Then you must save them both."

"There's nothing I can do for K'leef. Tyburn doubled his guard."

"There are ways in and out of the cells that only I know about, Thorn. I'll help you. Take K'leef and go."

"You'll do that, for me? For K'leef?"

"You're my only friends, Thorn. You must know that."

He did, now. "I ain't got none better." Then he grabbed her hand as an insane idea sprang into his head. "Why don't you come with us?"

Lily laughed. "It'll be hard enough escaping with Tyburn chasing after you. If I go, you'll also have Duke Solar and his paladins on the hunt. No, I'll stay and do my duty."

"You'll be Solar's prisoner, Lily. You said so yourself."

"But there will be peace." She sighed. "The menagerie will be headed for Port Charon. The ship sails tomorrow night. Your father, if it is your father, will want to take that ship. It passes near Herne's Forest on its journey south."

And if I don't reach him, he'll head home, not knowing that Tyburn's men are waiting for him.

Thorn still hesitated. "What about the scarred man? You ain't safe here, Lily. Come with us."

"Not safe? The scarred man has a very unique face, so he should be easy to spot, if he is foolish enough to come within ten miles of here. I have my Black Guard. Baron Sable and all the other nobles of Gehenna, every one of them has sworn to protect House Shadow to the bitter end. And the Solars won't risk me getting a hair out of place. Finally, there's Uncle Pan. He's always taken care of me." She smiled, seeing the disbelief on Thorn's face. "He may not be the hero he once was, but he still cares about me and my welfare." She stepped back and fixed her dress. "Get two horses saddled. You'll be leaving in a hurry."

Thorn still held her hand. "I have to say good-bye, but I don't know how."

"Like this." Lily kissed him. Her lips lingered on his long enough for him to take in her breath and her scent. It was dark and of roses. Then she stepped away.

"Good-bye, Thorn." Lily joined the shadows and was gone.

Once again, Thorn didn't pack much. Food and water for them both, some blankets, and besides that, he just went with the clothes on his back, a bow, and a quiver of arrows. They needed to move quickly if they wanted to catch up with the zoo. And save his dad. *If* the man was his dad.

If, if, if . . .

And if he wasn't? They were still going home.

It was an hour after midnight when the stable door opened and a cloaked figure entered.

Thorn watched silently from the darkness.

The figure searched around, then snapped his fingers.

The lanterns hanging from the rafter flared into life.

Only one person Thorn knew could do that. He stepped out. "I've been waiting."

K'leef lowered his hood and smiled. Then he crushed Thorn in a bear-like embrace. There was muscle under that padding of flesh. "Thank you."

"Thank me when we're home."

"I can almost feel the sand between my toes already. My father will fill your pockets with rubies for this, Thorn."

"That ain't why I'm doing it."

"I know, but it's better to have gems in your pockets than air."

"Sounds like the sort of thing my grandpa would say."

K'leef spread out his arms. "I must look ridiculous. Dressed in this . . . color."

He was wearing a squire's black hand-me-downs, just like Thorn.

"It looks all right." Thorn didn't know much about fashion. He led out a beautiful pearl-white mare. "Your horse, m'lord."

"Isn't this Gabriel's?"

"So?"

"They'll hang you, Thorn."

"They'll have to catch me first." Thorn led out Thunder. He was going to take Tyburn's own horse. The executioner owed him that, at least. "Did Lily say anything about how to get past the gates?"

"Yes. We're to take Skeleton Gate. There are only two guards there at this time of night, and she left them a barrel of ale." K'leef didn't look confident. "Getting out is one thing, but the castle's surrounded. There are thousands of people camped outside because of Halloween. Someone's bound to spot us."

"Not if we go via the City of Silence," said Thorn. "No one has camped anywhere near the graveyard."

"And for good reason. You know the stories, about Halloween being the night the dead walk out of their graves."

"Halloween's *tomorrow*, K'leef, and by then we'll be a long way from here."

Thorn looked around the stables for the last time.

This weren't meant to end like this. Me sneaking out like a thief.

He wasn't sad about leaving, not really. He wanted to get far away from the cruel people who had killed Hades. But he did have one regret.

He wished he could write. He wanted to leave Lily *something*.

He took off his acorn amulet. Thorn couldn't remember a time he hadn't worn it. He hooked it over a nail.

K'leef smiled sympathetically. "Let's go home, Thorn."

FORTY-ONE

Halloween morning dawned bright and clear. Mary declared there wasn't a cloud in the sky and it would be a beautiful night for the masquerade, deep with countless stars and crowned by a crescent moon. Lily dragged herself through a miserable series of pointless duties. Nobles were greeted. Presents accepted. The kitchens visited, and the cooks and chefs congratulated on the roasting sheep and pies and endless platters of cheeses, cold meats, cakes, and tarts. Now she stood up on a stool, arms spread out to either side like a scarecrow while Mary, pins locked in her lips, made a few more adjustments to her ball gown.

Three maids fussed and whirled around the room collecting ribbons and threads. Each was more excited than the other. The whole castle celebrated the masquerade, and most would have preferred to spend all year preparing their dresses and making their masks.

"We've cleared the bats out of the Stygian suites," said Mary. "Lord Ebon and his family are staying there tonight."

"Lord Ebon?"

"Yes. You know, the one who had that unfortunate vampire problem a few years ago?"

"Didn't Father stake half his family?"

"I wouldn't mention that. He's still very sensitive about it."

Lily looked around her room and at the chests filled with her belongings. Three massive oaken crates held all her clothes, and there were smaller ironbound boxes for her jewelry and other valuables. Half the furniture was already on wagons, the rest covered in sheets to keep off the dust and cobwebs. Mary had it all listed in her red ledger, now open on the dressing table.

"I can't believe I'm actually leaving," Lily said. "What would Father think?"

"He'd think you're safe. For all his faults, Duke Solar will protect you."

Lily had once thought that magic would save her country. She had the potential to be a great sorcerer—more powerful than anyone else here, maybe even more than the duke. But what she'd experienced with Rose had scared her to her very soul. Magic wasn't a gift; it was a curse. She would never use it again.

Now she realized the best way to save Gehenna was to leave. Lily was the last Shadow.

She wished she was dead. "Maybe they're right. I can't protect my people. Maybe the duke and his paladins will do a better job."

"Rulership wasn't meant for you, Lily. You're just a—"

"Girl?"

Mary scowled. "What I was going to say was that you're just a *child*. By the Six, I know I couldn't cope. Organizing a handful of silly maids is more than enough for me."

"Organize silly maids? You run Castle Gloom," said Lily. "Ever since Mother died it's been you, doing everything."

"I wouldn't say *everything*."

"It's true. I've passed your room late at night and seen the candles burning. You hunched over the red ledger, scratching away at sums and lists and who's delivered what and how many sacks of flour goes to which village. How did you learn it all?"

"'Twas easy, child. I just watched your mother."

Lily stifled a sudden spike of sadness. She'd relied so much on Mary her whole life and hadn't really noticed. It was like air—you never think about it but need it more than anything. You only miss it when it's gone. "You'll take care of things here when I'm ... when I'm not around?"

"What nonsense is that? I'm coming with you. Never heard anything so ridiculous." She patted the ring of keys hanging from her belt. "It'll be a relief not to carry these anymore. Let the steward run things from now on."

Lily squeezed her nanny's hand. "Thank you, Mary."

Mary added a few more pins to the folds. "Heard a strange thing this morning. The guards were all in a flutter. About the sultan's son."

Lily put on her most nonchalant expression. "Oh?"

"He's escaped."

"Gosh," said Lily. She glanced down at Mary and met a fierce, accusing gaze. She decided to inspect the ceiling. For cobwebs and such. "That *is* strange news. Look, I think the cleaner's missed a bit."

Mary continued. "Disappeared. *Poof,* like a cloud of smoke. The jailer's beside himself. Swears he saw the young K'leef reading a book at midnight. Then, at dawn, he brings breakfast and the cell's empty."

"K'leef is a sorcerer. He might have used magic."

"You know as well as anyone that the cells are barred with cold iron. No magic can get in or out." Mary shrugged. "And he took Thorn with him. Thought you might want to know."

"Really? Thorn and K'leef have left? That is news. To me. Because how would I know that? At all? I think it's—*ow!*"

"Sorry, did I stab you with this little needle? Oh, dear. My eyesight isn't what it used to be."

"You're a horrible old woman."

Mary took out a small wooden amulet and dangled it in front of Lily's nose. "Thorn left this behind. I wonder why."

Lily laid it on her palm and drew her fingernail over the delicate acorn design. Thorn's dad had made this. It was a single piece of wood, its surface oiled and shiny by constant touching. It meant everything to Thorn, and there was no way he would have forgotten it. She held it up. "Put it on me."

"Lily . . ."

"Please, Mary."

Lily lifted up her hair as Mary knotted the string. The amulet rested just below her neck, where everyone could see it. "I'm glad they got away," she said.

Mary frowned. "It won't do either of them any good. I saw Tyburn gallop off an hour ago."

"He'll have a hard time catching them. They had a night's head start." Lily paused. "That's assuming they left around midnight. Not that I would know anything about that."

"Those boys won't get far, Lily. Them escaping like that only makes things worse."

"I doubt it. K'leef's due to be executed tomorrow, remember?"

Mary paled. "You're right. Maybe they *will* get away. Let's hope so." She collected a fistful of pins from the dressing table. "Now turn around. We need to fasten your train and only have eight hours left to do it."

FORTY-TWO

"**T**hat's the third patrol in as many hours," said K'leef. "Do you think they're looking for us?"

"What kind of fool question is that?" Thorn answered. "Of course they are."

"But you planned for that, right?"

Thorn twisted around. "How come it's suddenly all up to me?"

"I'm a noble, Thorn. I delegate."

"You mean pass the hard work down to us peasants?"

"Well . . . yes."

They lay in a ditch thirty yards off the main road, eyes on the Black Guard horsemen galloping past. Thorn rested his chin on his fist as he watched the horses kick up leaves and mud in their haste and disappear around the bend.

"They're headed south to reinforce the crossing points," said K'leef. "How are we going to get out of Gehenna now?"

"I don't know. Yet." And why had he stolen Gabriel's horse? The beast was so white it practically glowed. If any of the horsemen had even glanced to the right they'd have spotted it, standing among the trees and utterly failing to blend in with anything.

He'd stolen it to spite Gabriel. Which now seemed pretty stupid. He'd stolen Thunder to spite Tyburn. Which made him stupid twice over.

He glanced up through the canopy. The sun was out, rare enough here, and tipping over to the afternoon. Another two hours and the shadows would lengthen; another hour after that, darkness would hurry down out of the sky. Their head start had evaporated into nothing.

That was the problem with escaping at night. Sure, you could creep out without being seen, but you had to move slowly. Galloping through woods in the dark didn't promise extra miles; it promised a stumble, fall, and broken neck.

"We need to venture farther into the woods. Stay away from the road." He got up and brushed the leaves off his tunic.

"But that takes us farther from the crossing." K'leef gathered his gear and remounted the white horse. "I studied the maps of Gehenna once. The only way across the river is Bone Bridge, and it's at the end of this road."

"And it will have fifty guards on it. No, we stay southbound and cross the river downstream. Either we find a boat or just wade across."

K'leef shook his head vigorously. "I can't wade across. What if I fall in?"

"So what? You just swim to the bank."

"Swim? When would I have learned to swim? I grew up in the desert, Thorn."

"You are not making this any easier." Thorn mounted Thunder. He jerked the reins and faced into the deeper woods. "We're wasting time."

The ride took longer than Thorn had planned, and the sun was dipping behind the horizon by the time they reached River Styx.

K'leef sat on the white horse, staring at the churning white waters. "I'm not crossing that."

"I'll admit it is a *little* fast-flowing," offered Thorn.

A tree trunk, ripped off the bank somewhere upstream, spun past and smashed against the rocks that jutted across the river's width. The crack of the shattering wood was louder than mountain thunder.

K'leef gulped loudly, and his horse skittered back from the bank. Its eyes rolled with terror, and it pulled fiercely against its reins.

"That horse is just like Gabriel," said Thorn. "Spoiled and a coward."

K'leef managed to bring it under control and brought it next to Thunder. The black warhorse stood as immobile as rock on the river's edge, but Thorn felt a tremor through his flanks. Thorn patted his neck. "You can swim that easy, can't you?"

Thunder snorted. It sounded like a *maybe*.

K'leef searched along the bank. "Let's try farther down. Maybe we can find a kindly fisherman with a boat. Or a couple of beautiful mermaids to carry us across."

"We ain't got time. Lily said the ship sails tonight. We've got two hours, maybe three, to get to Port Charon and find my dad."

"If it *is* your dad."

"It makes no difference. We cross here. Throw me your reins and I'll wrap them around my saddle pommel. Thunder will lead. You just hang on." He nudged Thunder forward. The horse hesitated, then slowly, carefully, picked his way down the bank.

The noise of the river was deafening. It shook Thorn's bones, and the water was freezing cold. He gritted his teeth as Thunder sank in farther, down to his chest. Broken twigs and branches flew past, and the horse fought against the fury of the current and the uneven, stony riverbed. Thunder slipped and neighed as he struggled to regain his footing. Thorn gasped as water crashed over him. He shook it out of his eyes and panted. His fingers were locked around the reins. He looked back.

K'leef sat pale and terrified on the white horse that was tossing its head and tugging to break free. It bucked and K'leef bounced up and down on the saddle. Then he caught Thorn looking at him and gave a grin that did nothing to hide the terror in his eyes.

White foam blinded Thorn, but he reckoned they were about twenty yards across. Another fifty to go.

Maybe sixty.

"Thorn!"

K'leef's shout came too late. The panicked white horse had pulled back hard on the reins. Thunder whinnied, slipped, and fell, taking Thorn under with him.

The water roared in Thorn's ears. Its weight was crushing, and all he could do was grip Thunder's saddle. His hands locked around the pommel as Thunder floundered. A branch whacked his back; Thorn gasped and swallowed water. The swift flow threatened to drag him off Thunder.

Thunder burst up through the surface, Thorn barely hanging on, coughing violently.

"Thorn! Help me!"

Soaked and bedraggled, Thorn swung around.

The white horse was swimming back toward the riverbank. Without K'leef.

Thorn heaved Thunder around as he spotted K'leef, spluttering and half-submerged, clinging to a rock. Blood ran down his face, and his fingers were slipping off the water-smoothed stone.

Thunder plowed into the worst of the rapids. Legs braced wide, he put his muscles and his warrior heart against the endless attack of the water. All Thorn could do was hang on, whispering encouragement. Thunder's legs trembled with the effort, and they were still yards from K'leef.

Thorn looped the reins around his left hand and dropped off the saddle.

The force of the water threw him against K'leef's rock. It knocked him this side and that, and Thorn felt his arm being torn out of its socket. He spread out his other arm as far as it would go. "Grab it!"

K'leef, worried about letting go of the rock, hesitated for just a moment before throwing his whole body toward Thorn. Even then their fingers barely met.

But that was enough. Fingers hooked together, then locked into a solid grasp.

Thunder didn't need telling. The indomitable warhorse fought the raging river, dragging both boys closer and closer to the riverbank.

It seemed like forever, and just when Thorn thought he couldn't hold on anymore, pebbles scraped his knees and he felt the relentless pressure of the water recede.

They were out. Back to the bank they'd started on.

All strength spent, they crawled out on their hands and knees. K'leef collapsed face-first into the ground with a long, pitiful moan. Thunder shook his mane and then sniffed at the grass and settled down for a snack.

Thorn wiped his face. They'd lost the white horse. He looked across the river. The bank opposite wasn't that far away, but they couldn't reach it.

He'd never get to Port Charon. They were trapped on this side and, sooner or later, they'd be caught by one of Tyburn's patrols. His dad would take the ship south, unaware of the killers waiting for him back in Stour.

Once again, Thorn had failed.

FORTY-THREE

They made a miserable camp. Neither boy could get a fire going, even with Thorn using his woodcraft, and K'leef trying with his magic.

K'leef stared at the damp pile of unlit twigs. "We've got food, haven't we?"

"Yeah. I packed sausages—a string of twelve, and each one a feast. Then I managed to smuggle out half a chicken and six of Mary's spice buns. A bag of apples and even a few oranges."

"Excellent. Take it out, I'm famished."

Thorn sighed. It was deep and it was despairing. "It was all in the saddlebags of Gabriel's horse."

K'leef groaned. "So what was Thunder carrying?"

Thorn handed over a soggy parcel. "See for yourself."

K'leef opened it up, revealing a lump of hard cheese and a waterlogged loaf, now reduced to mulch.

K'leef stared at it. He sniffed. "I want to go home. Really very badly."

So both sat there, shivering, and shared the cheese.

"I hate this country," Thorn declared. "Why would anyone want to live here? There's no sun. It's always drizzling. The earth is so stony you can't grow nothing but weeds, and . . . and . . ."

"Everyone's out to kill us?" suggested K'leef.

"I was going to say it's too cold, but thanks for reminding me about the death sentences hanging over us."

The trees swayed in the cold wind. Bats awoke for their night hunt. They gathered in the air above the two boys, swelling one moment, then dispersing as they chased flying insects and small animals scurrying in the undergrowth.

"And bats. I hate them most of all." Thorn tried to swat one, but it darted away. "If I never see another bat again, it'll be too soon. What sort of country breeds bats, anyway? They ain't no use to no one."

"Thorn . . ." K'leef's attention had drifted upward.

"What?"

More and more bats spilled out of their nests. The sky was black with them, an immense mass of fluttering leathery wings and shrieking mouths. They streamed into a swirling cloud, excited and expectant.

An inhuman, ear-piercing cry swept across the treetops.

Thorn's heart jumped ten feet. "It's not possible. . . ."

A vast winged shape, trailed by an endless stream of bats, covered the crescent moon and plunged their camp into total darkness for a fraction of a moment as it flew over.

But Thorn had seen it clearly enough.

Hades! He leaped onto Thunder, not bothering with a saddle or bridle.

"Hey, Thorn, wait!" shouted K'leef, but Thorn didn't stop. He had to follow the giant bat before it was out of sight.

They galloped through the dense woods, Thunder weaving his way between the trees and under their branches while Thorn searched the sky.

Suddenly, Thunder neighed and slammed in his hooves. He skidded, plowing a deep furrow through the earth as a high-pitched scream erupted in front of them. He stopped a foot away from crushing a small girl dressed in a threadbare shift with a blanket over her scrawny shoulders.

Thorn stared. He knew her. "Maggie?"

She pulled a tangle of hair from her face and squinted. "My dad isn't giving you no refund, if that's what you're after."

"What are you doing here? Shouldn't you be at Port Charon by now?"

She shrugged. "My dad don't want to pay the toll to cross the bridge. So he's gonna arrange boats to take him across. On the cheap."

"Where's your dad?" asked Thorn, almost laughing at Maximilian's penny-pinching.

She pointed. "There."

Thorn dismounted and stumbled forward. Light shone through the trees, and he could hear voices singing.

A camp sprawled across three or four clearings. There were wagons hidden among the trees, and tents had been pitched within ditches and up against boulders. A fire dominated the largest clearing and there feasted the roaming folk, maybe two dozen of them. Three iron spits turned over the flames, each skewering a fat-sizzling piglet, and black iron pots steamed on the burning wood.

Max, the zoo owner, danced around the fire, laughing and waving a bottle. Thorn ran up in front of him. "That man who looked after your animals, where is he?"

Max stopped and stared, drunk and bleary-eyed. He blinked as he searched his memory for faces. "No refunds!"

"I don't care about refunds! How many fingers did he have?"

Max blew a loud raspberry. "Fingers?"

It was hopeless. Thorn wouldn't get anything out of him until he was sober, and that wasn't going to be anytime soon.

Thorn searched every face in the crowd. He didn't recognize anyone.

Had he been wrong? Was this just a wild-goose chase? Maybe it hadn't been his dad after all.

Then Hades came.

He flung out his wings as he settled down into a clearing beside a single, crudely painted wagon with a big wolfish dog sitting at its steps.

Thorn approached. He pushed past a web of branches and brittle twigs, unable to take his eyes off the giant bat.

A man came out of the wagon. He scratched the big dog between the ears and approached Hades, who sniffed loudly and opened his jaws.

Thorn stopped. Hades had never let anyone but him get that close.

The man tossed up a skinned rabbit. Hades snapped it out of the air and gulped it down. The man stroked the bat's cheek, and Hades replied with a growl of pleasure. The man had only three fingers.

Thorn entered the clearing, his mouth so dry he could barely speak. "That's my bat."

The man turned to face him.

A pair of bright green eyes met Thorn's. Green eyes identical to his own. The face broke into a smile, then a grin as the eyes dampened with the promise of tears. The nose was slanted to one side and a scar crossed from jaw to temple. When Thorn had last seen that scar, it had been fresh, livid and red, but now it was pale and cold.

Without saying anything more, Thorn walked up and embraced his dad.

FORTY-FOUR

"**Y**ou've grown. Someone's been feeding you well," said Thorn's dad when they finally pulled apart. Then he winced. "Sorry, son. That's a stupid thing to say. I've thought so hard about what I was gonna say when I got back home—had it all ready in here." He tapped his chest. "Now, when I see you, it's all gone."

"It don't matter," said Thorn. "I'm sorry, Dad. Sorry I let you down. I should have done more."

"Let me down?"

Thorn felt a lump in his throat. "When them guards came. It was me who killed that deer. I tried to find you, honest I did. I looked and looked, but you weren't nowhere and then—"

"Hush, boy." His father took Thorn's chin so they were eye to eye. "You found me, a thousand miles from home, I don't know how. I'm proud of you, Thorn. You're a better son than a man like me deserves."

"Don't say that, Dad."

A few minutes later, they sat inside the small wagon, enjoying hot rice and beans from a bowl, Thorn dry in borrowed clothes. The room contained a few belongings Thorn recognized. A hooded cloak made by his mom, and the belt embroidered by his sister Ivy. A longbow rested on the bed, and up against the door stood a quiver of arrows, fletched with white goose feathers.

Hades waited outside with his face at the window. He'd hissed at Thorn at first, and there had been a moment, brief but intense, when Thorn had thought the monster was going to attack him, angry at having been abandoned. But once Thorn gave the bat's furry chin a tug, Hades had nuzzled him, then snapped his fangs and demanded another ready-skinned rabbit.

"I thought he was dead," said Thorn.

His dad smiled. "You'll have to ask Max about that. Someone sold the bat to him, with the warning that he couldn't stay around Castle Gloom. Apparently the beast was in trouble."

"So that's why you left early. I almost missed you." It must have been Pan. Instead of killing Hades as Duke Solar wanted, he had merely sold him, probably for another box of junk. For once, Thorn was pleased about something Pan had done.

Thorn studied his dad. His hair had more white in it than yellow now, and his skin was more deeply wrinkled—and scarred—than he remembered. He wore a beard, wiry with gray. No wonder Lily hadn't spotted the family similarities at first—they were well hidden.

There was a knock and in came a big roaming man. He had to bend down to get in and his gold earrings twinkled as bright as his eyes in the candlelight. The beard on him was thick and decorated with gold rings. He dragged a boy along behind him. "We found this one. He with you?"

K'leef stumbled in, huffing and puffing. "Thanks for waiting, Thorn. Remind me to abandon you in a dark, spooky, zombie-infested forest one day."

Thorn's dad nodded. "Thanks, Treader."

Thorn pushed over a stool. "Sorry, I thought you was right behind me."

"I wasn't. Is that beans?" K'leef took the bowl from Thorn's hand and stuffed four big spoonfuls into his mouth in as many seconds. "So this is your father?"

Thorn slapped him on the back. "Dad, this is K'leef. He's my mate."

"Call me Vyne." Thorn's dad stood up and shook K'leef's hand. "We met at the fair, didn't we? You were with that pretty girl."

"That's right. With Lily."

"As in Lilith Shadow?"

Thorn's stomach rolled. He had to ask the question, yet he was afraid of the answer. "Where have you been, Dad?"

Vyne chewed the end of his mustache. "Listen, son. I want you to know something. I did things I ain't proud of. I guess I need to live with that."

"I don't care."

"Don't lie to your old man, Thorn."

What should he do? He'd just found his dad, and he didn't want anything to spoil their reunion. But he needed to know.

"The Shadow family . . ." Thorn swallowed hard, but the words were already hanging in the air. "Did you kill them?"

Vyne didn't say anything for a long while. Instead he searched Thorn's face, as though judging if his son could handle the answer. Then, finally, he spoke. "Banditry's a dirty business, son. Very dirty."

"What happened?"

Vyne stood up. He paced to the doorway and looked out across the camp. Was he afraid to meet Thorn's eyes? Eventually he turned and picked up his longbow. He plucked the bowstring with his thumb, his brow creased with unease. "I'd soldiered in the past and I knew there was work here, what with the Shadows and Solars having been at war since the beginning of time. Turns out I was wrong." He laughed. "Lord Shadow and the duke were at peace! If not exactly peace, the borders were quiet. What was a man to do? I was all for going home, but then I got an offer. Of a day's work. An ambush."

"Someone hired you to attack Lord Shadow?" said K'leef.

"I didn't know who the target was going to be, and I wouldn't call it an attack exactly. I was hired along with five others, all hard, dangerous men.

You show up with six armed men and any fella will give you what you want. No need for violence. The threat's enough. Still, it shames me to think I'd fallen to robbing men who'd done me no harm." Dad looked weary. "But I'd been away from home too long to come back empty-handed."

"It wouldn't have mattered to me. It wouldn't have mattered to any of us. We just wanted you back," said Thorn.

"It would have mattered to *me*, son. A man who can't provide for his family ain't much of a man."

"But something went wrong?" pressed K'leef.

"The man who'd hired us wanted to come along. He told us a merchant owed him money and would take the road through Spindlewood with a strongbox filled with gold. I thought it was too good to be true, but I was desperate—we all were. We cut down a tree to block the road and waited."

Thorn's heart quickened.

"The moment we stopped the carriage, I knew something was wrong. The sky went dark and the trees shivered. I swear, ice grew from the branches."

"Magic," said K'leef.

"Our employer just gestured at the carriage and it burst into flame. Black flames, I tell you. The whole thing went up just like that, carriage and horses. We was hiding a hundred yards away, but the heat shriveled the leaves all around us. You could smell the stink of burning flesh. And the screams . . . they'll haunt me forever."

Thorn swallowed. It was almost too hideous to take in.

His dad shook his head. "That's no way to die. If you have to kill a man, it should be sword against sword, face-to-face. Give him a fighting chance. You meet him on a battlefield, and that's how it is. This was pure evil. I ran down to the carriage, quick as I could. The boy and the woman were dead, but the man still lived."

"You saw Lord Shadow?" asked Thorn, eyes widening.

"Yes, I did." Vyne frowned. "Blackened, burned, his skin . . . well, you can imagine. He didn't have no business still breathing. I reckon it was just sheer stubbornness. I dragged him free and did my best to beat out the flames, but it was sorcery—the fire ate him no matter what I did." He looked at Thorn, his eyes wet. "I tried, son, believe me, I tried."

Lily's father. Thorn ached, thinking how she must have felt when she learned the horrible truth. How she must still feel. He'd gotten his dad back, and it was as if Thorn's life was starting all over again, but Lily would have to bear that emptiness forever.

His dad grimaced. "The others were afraid of what they'd done. But that didn't stop them from looting the wreckage once the black flames finally died out. I wanted no part of it. I gave Lord Shadow some water. I don't know if it helped at all. Then the other man came, the one who'd hired us." He closed his eyes. "Lord Shadow raised his hand and spoke. 'Pain,' he said. At least that's what it sounded like. Then our employer kneeled down, took Lord Shadow in his arms, and slid a dagger into his chest."

FORTY-FIVE

So that was how Lily's family had died. Thorn's belly knotted itself as he imagined the screams, the burning flesh. Lily thought they'd been burned after they'd been killed.

She was lucky she didn't know the truth. At least she'd been saved that.

K'leef had sat cross-legged on the floor throughout, listening intently. "Let me guess: you were allowed to keep Lady Shadow's jewelry as payment."

Vyne nodded. "He set us up. With that jewelry it would be clear to anyone that we'd been behind the attack. Tyburn found us the next day. He took off one man's head with a flick of his sword. He had guards at his back, but he hardly needed them. I could see the way the fight was going, so I jumped out the window." He touched the side of his torso. "I got an arrow in my ribs while I was at it. An inch or so to the right and we wouldn't be here talking. Still, I managed to stay on my feet and run into the woods. It was easy to lose them once I was among the trees."

Thorn smiled. He couldn't help but be proud that his dad had escaped the great and terrible Tyburn.

"I was found by these roaming folk. The arrow wound had become infected, and I was burning with a fever. I hadn't eaten in three days. They looked after me, and bit by bit I regained my strength. I knew they were working their way south after the big fair at Castle Gloom, so I thought I'd stick with them then slowly make my way home."

"What about the man who hired you, the sorcerer?" asked K'leef. "What did he look like?"

"Well-dressed, rich, that much was obvious. Fancy clothes, if a bit wine-stained. He stank of alcohol. He had a warrior's build, though it had turned to blubber, and his face was all scratched up."

The scarred man. The one Thorn had seen at Graven. The one who'd killed Rose. And now he knew he was behind these murders, too. Thorn was looking at a jigsaw and could see a picture forming; he just needed a few more pieces. "Would you recognize him if you saw him again?"

"No, it's not like that. It wasn't his real face I saw."

"What do you mean?"

"It was a mask."

K'leef frowned. "Why wear a mask?"

"Why else? He didn't want us to know who he was. That way, if we were caught, we wouldn't be able to identify him."

"What sort of mask?" Thorn asked.

"A broken one, made outta stone. What I first thought were scars were the cracks."

A broken mask? Why wear a broken mask?

Unless the mask itself was special . . .

Thorn punched the wagon wall as the pieces fell into place. "We've been fools! All this time we've been thinking the scarred man was some powerful sorcerer, but he's not—he's a nobody. An *anybody*, if what Lily told us in the Shadow Library was true."

K'leef interrupted. "That's ridiculous, Thorn. Your father just said he saw him cast black flames against Lord Shadow. That's not the work of a 'nobody'; that's a very important somebody indeed."

"Don't you get it, K'leef? It's not the person, it's the *mask*," argued Thorn. He knew without a doubt that he was right. "Was it made of *black* stone, Dad?"

"That's right. Like polished marble."

Richly dressed in clothes covered in wine. Alcohol-soaked. A hideous, smashed-up mask. Thorn had seen it, held it, even. At the fair, the night Rose had died.

The night the "scarred man" had killed her, too.

"Obsidian," said Thorn. "The Mask of Astaroth. He must have found it and put it together."

"Who?" asked K'leef, confused.

Thorn continued. "Lord Shadow wasn't saying 'Pain.' He was pointing at his murderer when he spoke. He was saying his name."

"Name?" said Vyne. "He knew his murderer?"

Thorn jumped up. "I've got to get back to Castle Gloom. Lily's in danger. We've left her alone with him, and she doesn't know!"

"Who, Thorn?" asked Dad.

"Pan. That's what he was saying. *Pan.* Lord Shadow was killed by his own brother."

There was a moment of stunned silence while they all absorbed this dreadful information.

Then, "With Lily dead, he'll be the next Lord Shadow," said K'leef. "And with the mask he'll be unstoppable."

"That's what he was doing in Graven: raising the dead. Testing out his powers," added Thorn. The very man he expected to protect Lily was planning to kill her!

They hurried down the steps and back into camp. The music still played, and men and women danced by, but Thorn could only think of the distance back to Castle Gloom. A day's ride on a horse, but on Hades? An hour? Maybe two?

A man stepped out from behind a tree, but Thorn barely noticed him. Just another roamer.

The man drew his sword as he approached Vyne, and Thorn turned as the steel glinted in the light. The sword rose up. "Look out, Dad!"

The man rammed the pommel into Vyne's temple, and Vyne collapsed with a groan.

Thorn blinked, unable to believe who stood in front of him.

Tyburn!

"No!" Thorn threw himself at the executioner, but Tyburn sidestepped and Thorn crashed into the ground, whacking his head against a mud-covered rock.

Eyes bleary with pain, Thorn tried to focus on what was happening.

Tyburn stood over the unconscious Vyne and nodded with satisfaction. "I knew you'd lead me to your father, sooner or later."

FORTY-SIX

Thorn's skull throbbed. He touched his forehead and his fingers were bloody. "You . . . were right behind us?"

Tyburn clamped a pair of iron cuffs on Vyne. "It's easy for a man to track his own horse." He then inspected Thorn's injury. "Nothing too serious."

"Not that it matters, right?" Thorn snapped.

"I suppose not."

The roaming folk had gathered around. No one intervened; they all knew Tyburn, and it wasn't wise to interfere in the business of an executioner.

But not everyone was wise.

Maximilian barged his way to the front of the watchful mob. "What's going on?" He looked Tyburn up and down, clearly unimpressed. "No refunds!"

K'leef spoke up. "You've got this wrong, Master Tyburn. Thorn's father didn't kill the Shadows. It was the earl."

"Forgive me if I don't believe you, m'lord."

"Let my son go." Vyne struggled to his feet. "You've got me, and let that be the end of it."

"That's not how it works. Thorn aided a traitor—K'leef—so all three of you must suffer the same fate." Tyburn glanced at him. "I'll make it quick, boy. You won't feel a thing."

K'leef joined Thorn and put his hand on his shoulder. Thorn didn't know whether to laugh or cry. They were all going to die together, but K'leef didn't seem afraid.

"You're a blind fool, Tyburn," said the Sultanate boy. "You've left Lily unprotected, just when she needs you most. All so you could chase us through the woods."

Had anyone ever spoken to Tyburn like that before? Thorn seriously doubted it.

K'leef wasn't finished. "Go ahead, put our heads on spikes. That's all you're good for. But know this: Lily will be dead by morning, and you will have failed. Then . . . what is the point of you?"

Thorn could see there was something—hesitation, perhaps; maybe doubt—in Tyburn's eyes.

"You'd better explain your thinking," said the executioner. "What do you claim the earl is up to?"

"He hired this man"—K'leef gestured to Thorn's dad—"and five other men to ambush Lord Shadow. Lord Shadow, the most powerful necromancer in the New Kingdoms. Did you never stop to wonder how six half-starved brigands could kill such a sorcerer?"

Tyburn looked unsure. "Lady Shadow's jewelry was found on them. Tracks led from the site of the murder straight to their hideout."

"How very convenient," said K'leef.

Tyburn shook his head. "Earl Pan is a drunk and feeble fool. He doesn't have the stomach for anything but wine, and he does not have the power. Everyone knows that he has no magic."

"He has both the stomach and the power," said Thorn. "He's found the Mask of Astaroth. I saw him with it at the fair." Thorn was careful not to mention that Lily saw him with it, too, when she probed Rose's memories. He continued. "The mask must have been smashed when Astaroth was first defeated. Pan put it back together, and he's using the magic stored in it. That gives him all the power of the ancient necromancers, the greatest sorcerers of House Shadow. Lily's dad never stood a chance. Pan's been using it all over Gehenna. He's the scarred man I saw in Graven, commanding the zombies." Thorn faced Tyburn. "Lily's my friend and she's in terrible danger and that's the whole truth. If you don't believe me, then cut my head off right here and now and be done with it."

Tyburn frowned. "It just doesn't seem possible. . . ."

Thorn's heart sank. He didn't believe them.

Then help came from the most unlikely source.

"They're telling the truth." Maximilian had his hand raised. "I sold the mask to the earl."

"What?" exclaimed Tyburn.

"I thought it was junk! How was I to know?" said Maximilian. "Last year, just before Halloween, I showed the earl this chest of, er . . . rubbish that I'd gotten off a nomad from the Shardlands. The earl started drooling, I swear. He took these pieces of a mask, made of obsidian, I think, and pushed a hundred sovereigns into my hand. How was I to know it actually *was* magical?" He kicked a stone angrily. "If I had, I would have asked for double."

Thorn turned to Tyburn. He had to believe them now.

But Tyburn wasn't listening. Not to them, anyway. He cocked his head toward the path.

Thorn knew better than to speak now.

Fire crackled. A piglet's skin hissed on the spit. The wind rustled the leaves.

Wait . . .

Hoofbeats. The jangle of armor.

Tyburn drew his sword.

A scream broke the night's quiet. A roamer stumbled back from the crest that hid the camp from the road. He fell and slid down the leafy slope.

A crossbow quarrel jutted out of his back.

"Get down, boy!" Tyburn threw himself over Thorn, knocking them both to the ground as quarrels thrummed through the air and Black Guard riders charged into the camp.

FORTY-SEVEN

Crossbowmen emerged from behind trees and shot off another volley; the air hissed with their deadly missiles. The riders wheeled around, slashing left and right with their swords. More men screamed and died. The gypsies ran, some for safety into the trees, others to grab weapons.

Tyburn slapped a key into Thorn's hand. "Go free your father."

"I told you he was innocent, but you didn't—"

"Get on with it."

A horse trampled through the bonfire, kicking flaming branches everywhere.

Thorn, head down, sprinted to his dad and unlocked the manacles. Vyne rubbed his wrists as he glanced around frantically. Then he grabbed Thorn's arm and started to pull him toward the nearest wagon. "Slide yourself under and stay there, no matter what happens."

Thorn twisted out of his father's grip and picked up a thick fallen branch. "I want to fight, I can—"

"*Now,* Thorn!"

Horses whinnied and spun as the riders searched for their targets. A horseman saw Thorn and charged. Thorn didn't have time to run. He raised his branch, knowing it was useless.

Suddenly, the horseman's reins burst into flames. His mount, startled by the fire, reared and threw him off. Thorn ran up and smacked the branch into the man's helmet. The rider went limp.

Thorn grinned at K'leef. "Thanks. I owe you. Now if you can do that another ten times, we might just make it out of here."

The Sultanate boy, leaning against a trunk and ashen-faced, gasped for breath. "I could barely do it the once." But the exhaustion didn't stop him from grinning back.

A white-fletched arrow zipped overhead and took a crossbowman in the throat.

"Run!" shouted Vyne as he loosed another.

Thorn took the rider's sword and handed it over to K'leef. "D'you know how to fight?"

K'leef stared at the weapon. "Not in the slightest."

"You'd better start learning real quick."

"What about you? Don't you need this?"

"I've something better." Thorn ran. Straight to Hades. The beast was flapping his wings with excitement and tearing deep grooves in the earth with his claws. He twitched his shoulders, eager for Thorn to get on.

"You really are a bloodthirsty fiend, aren't you?"

Thorn leaped on.

Hades surged upward. He rose over the trees, and Thorn gripped for all he was worth as Hades arched backward, readying for a dive.

"Stop showing off and get on with it!" Thorn scolded him. "The fight's down there!"

Men screamed as Hades swooped over the camp. The monstrous bat grabbed one in his claws as he flew past, lifted him into the air, and hurled him over the treetops.

Thorn's dad swung an ax now that his arrows were spent. Even K'leef was fighting, waving his sword desperately at a pair of crossbowmen. Tyburn didn't fight. He slaughtered, chopping men down with gruesome ease.

Hades plunged down in among the soldiers, jaws open wide and fangs glistening. Horses screamed and men tumbled. They were of Castle Gloom and knew, and feared, the monster. A few crossbowmen shot a ragged volley at him, then fled.

Hades beat his wings and growled as he settled himself among the carnage.

It was over, Thorn's first battle. And he had survived it.

Bodies lay here and there, black-clad soldiers and roaming folk. Streaks of blood ran within the mud and a few men moaned, injured but breathing. A few riderless horses wandered aimlessly in the ruins of the camp.

His stomach churned. A roaming man lay in the dirt with a crossbow in his chest. His expression, frozen in death, wasn't one of fear or pain, but surprise.

Thorn dismounted, but his legs seemed to have turned into rope and he wobbled. They'd tried to kill him. If a crossbow quarrel had been an inch or two straighter, he'd be lying in the dirt, too.

Hades looked over the dead men, salivating. Thorn knew what *that* meant.

"Hades, I don't think that's—"

Hades bit off a head. He crunched down, then spat out the helmet.

"Ah, well. Waste not, want not," said Thorn with a sigh.

Tyburn handed him a waterskin. "Fighting's thirsty work."

"This one's alive," said Vyne. He stood over a rider, the man Thorn had clubbed. The horseman groaned as he sat up and struggled with his helmet. When it came off, Thorn saw the bloodied face of Cornwell, the captain of Troll Gate.

Thorn liked Cornwell. He always tipped the stable boys well.

Tyburn squatted down in front of the captain. "You'd better explain what you're doing here."

Thorn stood there and offered the man his water. What else could he do?

"You've a strong arm, young Thorn," said Cornwell.

"Give me words, Captain," warned Tyburn.

Cornwell shrugged. "The earl said you and the boy had freed K'leef. I was ordered to deal with it."

"You believed him?" asked Thorn.

"Does it matter? He gave an order, and I followed it."

K'leef looked at them. "Now what?"

"Get back to Castle Gloom," said Thorn.

"We'll ride," said Vyne.

Tyburn shook his head. "We'll never make it in time. Not on horse-back." He looked meaningfully at Thorn. "It's up to you, boy."

Vyne looked horrified. "If you think you're going off to fight the earl by yourself, you can forget it. I saw what that man did. He just snapped his fingers, and black flames ate his brother and his family. Arrows ain't no good against sorcery."

"I've got to go back to Lily."

His father met his gaze. "She's that important?"

"Lily? She's stuck up and proud and totally full of herself. And *real* annoying. I can't stand her, sometimes."

His dad smirked. "So I guess you like her a lot, then?"

"Yeah. I guess I do," said Thorn. "She ain't got no one else, Dad."

"I think you might need these." K'leef handed him a bow and fistful of salvaged arrows. "There aren't many ballads sung about princesses and peasant boys, you know."

"K'leef, I—"

"But there are plenty about princesses and *heroes*. You go save her, Thorn."

"Thanks." Then he whispered, "Got any idea how?"

"The mask," said K'leef. "It's both Pan's strength and his weakness.

With it, he's everything; without it, he's nothing."

"Understood."

Thorn tugged the thick fur at the base of Hades's neck and the bat reluctantly dropped his second helping of head. Thorn looked down from his seat. "Dad . . ."

"You get going, son," he said, his face marked with pride and not a little fear. "I'll see you again soon."

Thorn wanted to stay with them longer, but it was getting late.

He just hoped it wasn't too late.

THE CITY
OF
SILENCE

FORTY-EIGHT

"Knights wear armor," said Mary as she added another layer of jewels to Lily's hair. "Ladies wear gowns for the same reason. To conquer."

"And they're just as cumbersome." Lily straightened and stretched, trying to get some space between her lungs and the bone corset of her dress.

The underskirts were linen. Then came velvet and silk all covered in precious gems and embroidered with miles and miles of thread, creating legions of demons, devils, ghosts and ghouls and bats, clouds of them. The bodice's ribbed frame was made of sculpted leather covered with silk.

She wore her hair up and that had taken all day with three maids working on it. Her mother's diamonds were entwined with small roses made out of glass and mounted on a spiky tiara of iron. Dusty silver shimmered in the iron so it looked as if it had starlight trapped within it.

"What's that?" said Lily, staring at the small pot and brush Mary had in her hands.

"Paint for your lips."

"I know, but it's *red*," complained Lily. "Don't you have anything darker?"

"Plenty of vampires in your family." Mary held up the brush. "Pout."

Lily did.

Mary turned her to face the mirror. "Have a look."

The kohl smeared around her eyes transformed their grayness to silver. The lips were the color of fresh blood.

"Now the Mantle," said Mary.

The Mantle of Sorrows slipped over her like a high-collared coat with a train that turned to tendrils of mist yards behind her. It was cold and caressed her skin, as if the layers of material she wore were finer than tissue.

As solid as smoke, as real as a dream.

"A true princess of darkness," said Mary, admiring her in the mirror. "No, a queen." Then she fussed over the pleats. "How does it feel?"

"Heavy."

Mary carried over a loaded tray and set it down on the dressing table. "Pick one."

The masks, both horrific and beautiful, looked up at her from the tray. Leering devils and skulls and monsters, their eyes blank, waiting for her to give them life.

"Pick one, Lily."

Which suited her?

She was Lily. She was thirteen and loved climbing trees and had once had a small puppy named Custard.

She was Lady Shadow. She was heir to Castle Gloom. Her ancestors had been masters of dark magic. She could summon the dead.

Lily and Lady Shadow. They were utterly different but each the real her.

"This one." Lily picked up a mask made of glass. Trapped within it was black oil that constantly moved, sometimes hiding, sometimes revealing the face underneath.

That was her mask for tonight.

Mary nodded. "That'll do fine."

Pan waited, shuffling uneasily, in the antechamber.

"You are a vision, Niece." He bowed.

Lily returned his bow with a curtsey. "It's been a while since I saw you in armor, Uncle."

He tapped the polished breastplate. "I could barely fit into it. Last time I wore it was at the Battle of Ice Bridge."

"Father told me all about it. He said you were a great warrior."

"Great? No, I was merely good. That was the day Tyburn made his name. Held the bridge against the trolls till dawn. Then your father arrived with reinforcements and banged out a spell or two, and that was that." He tapped the sword on his hip. "Your father saved the day again and got all the glory. I just stood on the cliff edge and watched. As always."

She hated it when he spoke so bitterly. "Where's your mask, Uncle?"

He seemed to shake himself awake. Then, very carefully, he drew out a mask from under his cape. "Do you like it?"

It was the mask she'd seen him with the night of Rose's death, the broken one. He'd put a few more pieces together, but it was still ugly and deformed. She hated it but didn't know why, exactly. It wasn't just that it was riddled with cracks. "It's . . . interesting."

"I've spent a long time repairing it. Bit by bit. It's been a labor of love, in a way." Pan caressed it with his fingertips. "Do you know what I love about masks? They let you be the person you want to be, rather than the one you are. Look at this." He pulled at his jowls. "Look at it. Sagging, sickly. Pathetic."

"Uncle . . ."

"But when I put this on"—he settled the obsidian visage onto his face—"I am transformed."

He stood straighter. He squared his shoulders and raised his head. "There, that's better."

Even his voice was deeper, stronger.

Cold, even. Enough to make Lily shiver.

Pan held out his hand. "It would be an honor, Niece, to accompany you to the Halloween Ball."

FORTY-NINE

The steward banged his staff upon the hard marble, and it echoed across the crowd. All the faces, all the masks, turned toward her.

"Lady Lilith Shadow, heir to Castle Gloom. Lady of Dreams and Nightmares. Child of darkness and guardian of the Twilight."

Baron Sable bowed low. "M'lady."

This was a true dance of light and darkness. There were thousands here from Gehenna and Lumina, both in black and white.

The Gehennish wore masks that were beautifully grotesque. They were grinning devils, ghosts, ghouls, and skeletons from the grave. They dressed in cobwebs and in bones and ancient shrouds.

The guests from Lumina—Solar's kinfolk—could not have been more different. Their costumes dazzled. Women wore gowns of silver, and the masks were all coldly perfect. They portrayed angels and handsome heroes and were of the finest porcelain and crystal. Some wore thin gauze, unwilling to hide their beauty beneath anything but the most transparent of materials.

Pan cleared his throat. "Lily, they expect you to dance."

"I'll dance when I feel like it."

"Lily . . ."

Lily made her way down the steps to the hall itself. It was hot and stuffy in here. Too many people. Too many candles and too many mirrors, gifts from the duke. She wanted to escape.

She missed her friends. She missed K'leef. She remembered how the two of them had whirled across this very floor. The shocked looks on the Solars' faces. It had been brilliant.

She missed Thorn. It surprised her how much she missed him.

He was loud, cheeky, and independent. He did things his way and didn't care what anyone else thought.

He did what was right.

Now they were gone forever. She only hoped they'd gotten away safely.

A servant in a red demon mask offered her a drink. Lily pushed past and headed out one of the side doors into a small courtyard.

Rose-covered walls enclosed it. Weeds and small flowers grew out of the cracks in the paver stones. Black petals floated upon the water of a small fountain basin.

Lily removed her mask. She was tired of pretending to be something she wasn't—ruler of Gehenna.

I could stay here until it's over. Who'd notice?

They all would. She couldn't escape who she was.

There was a splash from behind her.

"Who's there?" Lily asked. Typical. She couldn't get away for even a minute.

Her heart sank even lower when Gabriel appeared from beside a tree.

"Shouldn't you be in there, dancing?" He tossed another stone in the fountain. "Oh, I forgot. You only dance with prisoners and traitors."

"What do you want?" Lily asked.

Diamonds had been sewn into his tunic, and his cuffs were ringed with pearls, hundreds of them. A necklace of platinum hung from his neck with a golden centerpiece of a blazing sun.

They sat face-to-face. He sneered as he saw Thorn's acorn amulet. "How typically cheap and nasty. There is nothing beautiful in Gehenna. Don't you have anything like this?" He touched his own necklace.

What would Thorn say? "You can dress it in silk and jewels, but a pig is still a pig."

Gabriel clenched his jaws as a blush rose on his cheeks.

Heirs to rival houses. Enemies for generations. A thirteen-year-old girl and boy.

"Where's your mask?" Lily asked.

"I'm wearing it. Can't you tell?"

He was perfectly handsome with skin smooth and unblemished, his hair lustrous. His suit shimmered. The buttons were diamond studs clasped in silver and gold.

But it was the way he spoke, softly and without that usual sneer, that made Lily pause. "What do you mean?"

"This isn't what I really look like," he said in a serious tone. He pointed at the water in the fountain basin. "Look in there."

Lily couldn't trust that he wasn't playing her for a fool, but he had piqued her curiosity. "What will I see?"

"The truth?"

Lily peered down.

In the reflection, Gabriel's hair was mostly missing. His skin was not smooth, but pockmarked and sickly. His clothes hung loose over bony limbs and a sunken chest. Small shoulders and a thin neck seemed to struggle to hold up his head; his jaw was big and held crooked, tarnished teeth.

Seeing Lily's reaction, Gabriel laughed, and it was harsh and sad. "If you think I'm ugly, you should see my sisters."

"I didn't say you . . . Wait, it's all an illusion?"

"Yes. The Shadows command the magic of darkness; we Solars command light and can make you see only what we wish you to see. This . . .

trick has become as automatic as breathing—it doesn't even fade when I'm asleep. But it takes all my power to maintain it."

"Why do it, then?"

"I . . . need to be the sort of son my father wants," said Gabriel.

"He's not happy with you as you are?"

He huffed sarcastically, but before he could say anything, Pan appeared at the door. Gabriel straightened his tunic and swept his fingers back through his thick, shiny blond locks. "And don't keep me waiting much longer," he said dismissively before he reentered the hall.

"Getting along as famously as ever, I see," said Pan. "It would be helpful if you at least tried to make friends with him."

Friends? Lily doubted that would ever happen. But now she saw Gabriel in a new light—literally. Or perhaps she just pitied him now.

She kept staring at the water, watching it gently ripple back and forth.

Pan joined her. In the reflection, his mask looked like a real face, real but horribly scarred.

She frowned, suddenly uneasy but not sure why.

What will I see?

What had Gabriel just said?

The truth.

She saw another face in the water. Rose. Reaching up toward the surface as she drowned . . .

A man's face looked on, impassive. With scars—no, *cracks*—and a pair of black holes for eyes.

The scarred man.

Lily gasped involuntarily.

Pan grabbed her arm. "Anything wrong, Niece?"

I've got to get away.

Lily tried to smile. "No, everything's fine. I think we should get back. I . . . feel like dancing. Gabriel's waiting."

His grip tightened. "I don't think so."

"Uncle, you're hurting me."

He laughed. "Yes, yes, I am."

The blackness thickened around Pan, pouring out from the folds of his long cloak. Tendrils rose up and clasped Lily's limbs, lifting her and pushing her against the wall.

"What—what are you doing?" she asked, panicking now.

He whispered in her ear. "Lily, I thought you were smarter than that."

FIFTY

Pan had practically raised Lily. He'd taught her to read and write and looked after her when she'd been sick and her parents were too busy. He'd told her stories of his adventures as a young man.

He was her hero.

Now he wanted to kill her. Like he killed Rose. It was—

"Let her go!" Gabriel's shout interrupted her thoughts. He locked his arm around the earl's neck and wrenched him back.

Gabriel trying to save her. Her uncle wanting to kill her. The world had gone *insane*.

The shadowy forms holding her vanished, and Lily dropped to her knees, gasping for breath.

Pan twirled around, grabbed Gabriel's head, and slammed it against the wall. He did it again, then let the unconscious boy drop to the ground.

Lily fled toward the door to the Great Hall. Shadows surrounded the doorway and slammed it shut. She grabbed the handle and pulled, but it wouldn't budge.

"It's no use," said Pan.

Lily banged her fists on the door. "Help! Help!"

"Who's going to hear you, Lily? No one. They're all too busy enjoying themselves. Come now, I will make it quick and painless." He looked down at Gabriel. "For you both."

"Uncle, you're not making sense." Lily couldn't fully grasp what was happening. Pan was using real magic. How? "I don't understand."

Stall him. Someone will come out here soon, looking for us. They have to. . . .

"What's to understand? I am merely claiming what is rightfully mine. I will be Lord Shadow, as I was always meant to be. Tonight begins a new reign, Lily. The reign of Pandemonium."

"You can have Gehenna. I don't want to rule. I never have."

He shook his head as he stepped closer to her. "It's not that simple, I'm afraid. No one will see me as legitimate ruler while you still live." He flexed his fingers, gave Gabriel a kick. "Strangled by Duke Solar's son, while you bashed his head against the wall. How utterly perfect."

"There'll be war," said Lily, forcing herself not to cower.

"Exactly. All of Gehenna will rally around me. Your death will inspire them. Then I will reveal the extent of my power. Armies of undead. Legions of zombies and skeletal troops. All-conquering. The age of the necromancer will return."

"No one has that power, Uncle."

He tapped his mask. "Astaroth has."

"Astaroth?" She stared at the deformed, cracked face before her. She'd said it herself, back in the Shadow Library. How a common farmer could be a great sorcerer, just by wearing the mask. "You found the Mask of Astaroth?"

"You have no idea how many years, how many fortunes I spent looking for it. To think I found it in a box of junk. Broken, to be sure, but I recognized it instantly." He caressed his stone cheek. "He's still here, Lily. He tells me things. He gives me power, all the power I ever dreamed of."

"Did Father know you'd discovered it?"

"I gave him a chance, Lily. I really did. But he wouldn't listen. He said the mask was evil and I should destroy it." He slammed his fist against the stone wall. "He was jealous. Jealous that I would be more powerful than he was. He would not let me reclaim my right to rule Gehenna. He would not step aside, so I removed him."

Removed him? She felt a wave of dizziness as shock, rage, and sorrow swirled inside her.

It was Pan all along.

"I will make Gehenna great again. All the other houses will bow before me. Your death will ignite the flame, Lily. You will achieve more by dying than you ever could have by living." He chuckled. "After all, you are just a girl."

Gabriel moaned softly and blinked. He was regaining consciousness, but he still looked shaken and weak. Whatever happened next was up to her.

"My father loved you, Uncle."

Pan twitched. There was a savage jerk and his hand jumped to his mask. His fingers trembled against the straps.

Was he trying to take it off?

Was the mask controlling him?

Pan threw his head back and groaned.

He's fighting it.

"You won't hurt me, Uncle." She said it forcefully, trying to believe it herself. "If you really wanted to do it, you would have killed me by now. But you can't. We share the same blood."

Her words seemed to give him renewed strength. Pan straightened and gave a hollow, dreadful laugh. "I'm afraid you are dead wrong. I already *did* kill you. Only it turned out to be your foolish maid, Rose. I have been aching to kill you for months now, ever since I slew the rest of your family." His face took on a hideous leer. "Your brother and I shared the same blood, too."

Lily was nauseous; it felt as though Pan—no, *Astaroth*—had punched her in the stomach. She realized she truly was facing her own death.

Before she could catch her breath, he continued. "Tonight I have the entire Solar family here along with their relatives. Once I've killed you and Gabriel, I will summon an army of undead to destroy our greatest enemies."

"What army?"

"This is Halloween. The night when the barrier between the land of the living and dead is at its thinnest. I've tested my powers already, by raising zombies and ghosts in villages and graveyards throughout Gehenna. Tonight I'll do something not seen in hundreds of years: I shall summon thousands."

But where could he hide so many? Oh no. It was obvious. The biggest graveyard in all of Gehenna was just a stone's throw from here.

"The City of Silence. That's where they are."

"Yes, I will use our own ancestors." Pan flexed his fingers. "It is time to die, Lily."

Tentacles of black spread over her. She tried to scream, but the cries were absorbed by the darkness enveloping her. Lily tore at the living shadows, ripping them off like cobwebs. Pan forced her down to the ground, where she couldn't prevent their spread.

She saw that Gabriel was awake, held down by tendrils of blackness only a few feet away from her.

She had to get away. Otherwise she was dead.

The Mantle of Sorrows rippled, as if sensing her fear, her confusion. It rolled over her, back and forth like waves upon the night's shore. Pinpricks of power dug into her skin.

Lily forced her mind to be calm. She concentrated on the darkness. It was Pan's weapon, but it could also be her salvation. And escape.

She didn't know the way. She could be lost forever, but she had to risk it.

Lily clutched Gabriel's hand. "Hold on. Do not let go."

The darkness thickened until there was nothing else. It entered her; she entered it. They merged into one.

And Lily slipped into the Twilight.

FIFTY-ONE

Something was wrong with Hades.

Instead of sailing the winds, he was fighting for every yard, gasping for each breath. Foam was dripping from his mouth.

"What is it, boy?" The bat was drifting left—south—his right wing working harder than the left. Then Thorn saw the blood.

"Down, boy, let's have a look. There, by that pond."

Hades hissed, as if reluctant to admit his weakness, but in the end, he relented and swerved downward.

Boy and bat landed. Hades tripped and skidded out awkwardly as his wings failed to reduce his speed. Thorn was almost thrown over his head, but he grabbed Hades's big ear and managed to hang on.

Hades screeched with annoyance.

"If you're going to crash, then what do you expect me to do?" Thorn soothed the irate bat and ran his hand over his chest. "Let's see what's wrong."

Blood matted the fur.

Suddenly anxious, Thorn examined the beast's chest more softly. His fingers touched a stump, almost buried into Hades's left shoulder. Hades growled but let him continue inspecting.

The blood was thickest here, and he probed as gently as he could.

One of the crossbow quarrels was wedged deep in the shoulder. It had snapped, so only a few inches of the shaft still stuck out. The flying must have made it worse, the rolling action actually pushing the quarrel in deeper.

"You stupid bat! Why didn't you tell me you were hurt?" Thorn looked closer. He tried to get a decent grip but could only get two fingers to the stump. It wasn't enough. The quarrel was too far in and too slippery with blood. He needed a knife to cut the wound open and pliers to ease out the broken shaft.

Hades coughed. His whole body shook violently, and blood sprayed out of his nostrils. Thorn hugged him and through his thick fur felt the heart struggling, not steady and heavy, but fluttering. "Stupid, stupid animal . . ."

Hades licked his face, smearing it with slime and blood. Thorn didn't care. The bat and boy rested head against head, and Thorn felt each breath weakening and the gaps between them getting longer.

They were miles from anywhere. It was too far to fly back to his dad, and Castle Gloom was nowhere in sight.

He'd never reach Lily, not now, and not even on the fastest horse in the world. Thorn's chest trembled with a held-back sob. He wasn't going to save her, or Hades.

Thorn washed the wound and padded it with leaves. He tore off his shirtsleeve to make a bandage, but as soon as he finished wrapping it around, the cloth was soaked with blood.

Hades nudged him. Thorn rubbed the big monster's chin. "I won't leave you, don't worry."

Hades pushed him harder. He struggled to beat his wings.

"Stop it! You're only making it worse!"

Hades glared at him. The beast rose up straight until he was higher than Thorn, and he spread out his wings. The moonlight shone down on the giant bat, and the blood glistened like Lily's black diamonds. Hades gazed up at the moon and opened his mouth, his fangs shining silver bright in the cold ghost light.

"You won't make it," Thorn said, his voice catching in his throat.

Hades roared his defiance. The trees shook as birds and bats fled in terror, and a deer bolted from the undergrowth. Far out, in the deepest of the woods, a wolf howled.

Hades peered down at Thorn, his eyes blazing with a terrible fire, a fire that would burn like an inferno before it went out.

Thorn kissed the bat's bloody cheek.

He climbed back on, and they rose into the night sky one last time.

FIFTY-TWO

It was as simple as walking through a door. One moment, Lily was in the courtyard, the next she stood . . .

Elsewhere.

"Where are we?" asked Gabriel, his fingers achingly tight around hers.

"The Twilight. The place of restless spirits." Lily looked around. No one living had visited it in a hundred years. "It was the only way we could escape."

Gabriel gasped. "You used magic?"

"Jealous?"

A black sun shone in cracked sky. Its rays fell not on stone or rock, but on dreams and nightmares.

"The sky's broken." Gabriel stared into it, awestruck. In the brittle gaps cold, sparkling lights stirred and blinked. "What are they?"

Lily pulled him along. "We don't want to find out."

Walls of twisted misery stood beside streets of sighing wishes. Lily trod on pebbles cast by unhappiness and felt the farewell kisses upon her soles.

"How do we get out of here?" said Gabriel.

"Hush. I'm trying to think."

"We're lost."

There was a mournful wind. But she thought she could hear something else. "Shh."

Gabriel jerked his head up. "I hear it, too."

Something moved among the stones of sadness on the uneven, rubble-strewn ground. Something small and bouncing. And yapping.

"Custard?"

The puppy barked as he bounded toward them. One more spring and he was in Lily's arms, licking her face. In the living world, he'd appeared as insubstantial as smoke when Lily had conjured him. But here, in the Twilight, he was as solid as any living creature.

"Good boy, good boy." She laughed and gave him a huge squeeze.

"Is that your dog?" said Gabriel. "But he . . . died."

Custard noticed Gabriel and growled.

"I know, Custard. I had to bring him along," said Lily. "But I need you to be nice."

Custard looked at her, his big eyes shining. He yapped a question.

"I said, be *nice*. Gabriel needs our help." She put him down. "Do you know the way out?"

Custard chased his tail.

"No. The way *out*."

He darted back and forth, wanting her to play.

"Another time, Custard. The way *out*."

"This is so useless," snapped Gabriel. "Here, let me do it."

"You touch my dog, and it'll be the last thing you ever do."

Gabriel scowled. "Fine. You deal with the mangy mutt."

Custard flattened his ears and growled.

"Yes, Custard. He's a very, very naughty boy." Lily held the puppy's face. "Now, pay attention. Show us how to get out of here. Right now."

Custard barked and set off.

"Follow him," said Lily.

"Are you serious?"

"Got any better ideas?"

Gabriel didn't say anything more. His eyes widened as he stared ahead of them.

They were faint, but Lily spied the uncertain outlines of figures moving in the distance.

Who were they? She wanted to shout out, but something constricted her throat. Fear.

They came closer. Dozens of them.

Gabriel stifled a scream.

"Specters," she whispered.

The bitterest of spirits. Specters were the remnants of all misery, despair, and sorrow. They'd coalesced out of every foul memory of those who'd died unhappy and every dream of those with lives unfulfilled. There were plenty.

Custard barked. He darted in among them, snarling and biting. One lashed out and swept the puppy away.

"Custard!" Lily shouted.

The specters surrounded them on all sides.

She tried to back away, but it was too late.

They caressed her with icy fingers. The chill sank through Lily's skin and into her bones, deep into her soul.

Her world was cold and brittle. As it had always been.

The unwanted daughter.

The unwanted ruler.

The unwanted.

It was all the coldness of her childhood. Every loneliness. Every unloved moment.

"What do you want from me?" Lily screamed at them. Tears froze on her cheeks as she felt their dreadful despair.

Gabriel sank to his knees.

She could leave him behind. They'd take what they wanted from him and maybe she could escape.

No. She wouldn't abandon the living in this place. Not even Gabriel.

The thought cleared her head. She put her hands under his arms and lifted him, and they pushed their way through the wall of phantoms.

A hill rose up before them, and at its summit stood a shimmering doorway.

The way out. It was a simple matter of putting one foot in front of the other for another hundred paces. Custard joined her and wagged his tail with excitement.

A sea of specters followed right behind. She could tell they sensed her plan and were angry. Their anger seemed to renew their strength.

Hands grabbed her sleeves. One after another held on to Gabriel. The boy stared at her, terrified, suddenly aware of what was happening.

"Let him go!" Lily screamed. The doorway waited just yards ahead. Through it the night sky, shining with stars. She could feel a breeze.

They were almost out!

The specters doubled their attacks. They piled onto Gabriel's back, dragging him to his knees. They clutched at Lily's arms and legs and tore at her face.

There are too many!

Inch by inch, they wore her down.

Custard pulled at the Mantle of Sorrows, trying to drag her along.

"Get back," Lily muttered, barely able to speak. She tried to fend them off, but she was too weak; she couldn't even raise her arm. She knelt down beside Gabriel.

She wanted to close her eyes and sleep. Just drift off. It wouldn't matter. Nothing mattered now.

Yes, just close my eyes.

Her eyelids drooped.

All strength fell away.

"Please," she whispered as her life faded. "I never said good-bye."

To Mary, Old Colm, Wade, and others. It was hard to remember the names. K'leef . . . Thorn.

And three most of all.

Dante.

Mother.

Father.

"I never said good-bye."

Fingers wrapped around hers. They were firm, strong, and steady. "Stand up, Lily."

It was a gentle command, but Lily obeyed. She stood.

The specters cringed. They retreated.

Lily couldn't see through her icy tears, but someone had taken hold of her hand.

"I . . . I need to get Gabriel," she said, grasping the Solar heir roughly by his collar.

Lily willed her leaden legs to move, just another few more feet, dragging Gabriel along.

The specters howled and her ears were flooded by the most hideous, evil screams—and that gave Lily the strength for a last surge. She dove toward the starlit doorway.

The darkness ripped with the sound of tearing steel as Lily and Gabriel broke through. They both collapsed face-first into the grass, Gabriel unconscious, and Lily sobbing. Her fingers raked the earth.

She'd done it. She'd walked out of the Twilight and back into the real, living world.

They lay among tombs. To Lily's right was a statue of a skeleton in court robes. Custard—more ephemeral now—bounded in and out among the gravestones, his little voice howling.

They were in the City of Silence.

Thank the Six.

"Lily . . ."

She looked up and saw a man before her.

It can't be.

His face was elegant, his eyes as gray as hers. His clothes were black, but he was no living thing. He smiled. "Lily. I've missed you."

Lily choked. She stared at him, her heart thundering. "Father?"

FIFTY-THREE

"We don't have long," said Iblis Shadow.

"Father, please don't leave me."

He smiled. "Never."

Lily tried to hug him, but there was nothing there. Her arms went through him and he disappeared to re-form a few feet away. It wasn't fair, to see him but not be able to hold him.

"I'm sorry, Father," said Lily. "I'm so sorry I wasn't there. I should have been with you."

Her father shook his head, smiling faintly. "I thank the Six you weren't."

"I could have done something. I could have saved you, somehow."

"You must look to saving yourself. That is what matters now."

"I want to see you all," said Lily. "Where is Dante?"

"They are here, too, Lily. Your mother and brother. They always will be. This is our home."

"Why can't I see them?"

"You don't need to. Can't you feel them, in your heart?"

"My heart aches, Father."

"Because it is so full. That is no bad thing, Lily."

Lily couldn't stop her tears.

Just then, the shadows began to shake. The deep blackness in the door-ways of the tombs trembled.

"Pan has entered the Twilight," said Father. "He is searching for you. He'll be here soon."

"Can't you stop him?"

"He wears the Mask of Astaroth, lord of the undead. I am bound to do his bidding now. It'll be up to you."

"Me? I don't have that power."

"You entered the Twilight. You communicated with the spirit of Rose. You called me from the lands of the dead. Your blood is blackest of all, Lily."

"I . . . I don't even know where to start," she said.

"You start now, daughter."

"Begone, foul spirit!" someone shouted from behind her. "By the Prince of Light I command you!"

Er . . . what?

Gabriel stood facing her father, his right palm up. "I said, *begone*! Return to that pit that spawned you!"

Gabriel's hand glowed—a little. Sweat dripped off his face.

"Will you stop that?" Lily knocked his hand down. "And who are you calling 'foul spirit'? That's my father you're talking about!"

"But he's a fiend from the outer darkness!" Gabriel extended his hand again. "Begone! By the power of the Prince of Light, *begone*!"

"Stop it, Gabriel! I'm really starting to regret saving you!"

The darkness within the broken doorway of a mausoleum pulsed and a desperate, hideous keening erupted forth. A chill wind, the wind of death and horror, blasted out.

Lily's Mantle of Sorrows fluttered.

"Prepare yourself," said her father. "Pan comes."

FIFTY-FOUR

Specters spewed out of every dark hole.

They crept from the empty doorways of the tombs. They crawled through the moon shadows of the gravestones and slithered out from under the moss-stained statues.

Here in the living world, the specters struggled to maintain their solid forms and instead were a seething, oily mass of limbs and snarling faces. A bone-chilling wind surrounded them, and the grass shriveled beneath their feet.

"It's hero time, Gabriel. Banish them." Lily backed away.

"I want my daddy," said Gabriel. He crawled behind the nearest tombstone.

Yes, now would be the perfect moment for a last-minute rescue. Duke Solar at the head of his paladins. Or Tyburn. Or faithful Baron Sable and his sons. She'd settle for Old Colm and his big stick.

But there was no one but them.

A loud, metallic shriek rose over the hissing crowd of specters. A hole tore open in the air.

Pan stepped out of the Twilight.

Smoky darkness surrounded him. The mask seemed to suck in all light, making the eye holes darker and deeper than anything Lily had ever seen. It was as if she was staring into the night sky at the end of time, when the last star had burned out.

"Sweet niece," hissed Pan. "Waiting for me in the City of Silence. How considerate."

Lily's father moved between her and Pan's mob of spirits. "Brother, what has happened to you?"

"Step aside, Iblis. My business with you is over."

"Aren't your hands bloody enough? Leave her be, Pan. Find some pity in your heart. Lily has done nothing to you."

"She is in my way, just as you were. It is my destiny to make Gehenna great again," said Pan. "Now *step aside*. Or do you think I cannot hurt you any further?"

Pan held out his hand, then twisted it into a fist.

Iblis cried out. He sank to his knees and started to fade.

"Father!" She couldn't lose him again! "Stop! You're hurting him!"

An evil laugh fell from Pan's lips. "Look to your own pain, Lily."

Lily felt a wave of heat and leaped aside. Black flames ripped across the ground and smashed against the tombstone right behind her. The stone melted like wax, revealing a cowering Gabriel.

Lily scrambled to her feet. "Run!"

Gabriel pushed his way ahead of her.

Pan laughed. "Find her, my slaves. Find her and kill her!"

A thousand spectral voices roared across the City of Silence.

FIFTY-FIVE

"I'm going to die," Gabriel sobbed. His face was wet with tears, and his nose dripped with trails of snot.

"I'll kill you myself if you don't shut up," said Lily as they huddled behind a tall mausoleum. "Now wipe your nose and get on with the task at hand."

He took the corner of the Mantle of Sorrows and blew.

Lily gritted her teeth. But she had bigger problems. She tried to take control of her own rising panic, and think.

Could she reenter the Twilight and sneak back into Castle Gloom?

No. That's exactly what Pan would expect her to do. He'd have specters waiting for her there, too.

Endless walls of black fire surrounded them. Smoke covered the City. Pan was burning everything. It didn't stop his ghostly minions, of course.

Think, Lily. Think!

"I can't stand it anymore!" said Gabriel. He jumped out into the open. "Help! Help!"

"Shut *up*!" Lily hissed. "They'll find us!"

"Help! Help! Someone please help me!" He waved his arms frantically. "Help!"

Specters bounded toward him through the flames. They scuttled over the roofs of mausoleums like spiders, all jagged limbs and skull-bare faces. They grabbed Gabriel in their claws, hoisted him aloft, and dragged him away.

The flames thickened and drew closer. Lily glared at the figure on the other side of the wall of fire. Pan.

"Coward!" Lily screamed. "Coward! Why don't you come here and finish me yourself?"

The flames vanished, leaving the City of Silence wreathed in smoke.

"Well said, Niece," said Pan. "You deserve a better death than your father's."

"Dante and my mother, too. Or were they too unimportant to count?" Her Mantle of Sorrows shimmered. It fluttered and the black stirred like oil on water. Lily blinked her tears away. "They loved you, Uncle. *I* loved you. Doesn't that mean anything?"

"How many times have I told you, Lily? A ruler can have no friends. No favorites. You must be willing to sacrifice anything, anyone, if you want to rule."

Ash filled the air. That was Pan's kingdom. Just ash.

"Can you feel it, Lily?" Pan held out his hand, fingers gently caressing the space between them.

Lily gasped. The pain in her chest was crippling. Her blood pounded in her head.

The specters crept closer. Their chill coated the ground with frost and Lily's feeble breath came out as a white cloud.

The spirits touched her, and the ice of their emptiness sank into her again, turning Lily so cold she felt her blood begin to freeze. Her skin turned blue.

How could she beat them? There were too many.

Send them back into the darkness.

She was a Shadow; what else was that but pure darkness?

Lily reached out and dragged patches of shadow and dark spots into the folds of the Mantle of Sorrow. It was hard, and the effort burned her fingers, not from the heat, but from the cold. Still she pulled.

The specters snarled. They hesitated.

Pan urged the spirits forward. "What are you waiting for? Finish her!"

Lily drew her cloak around her. To her amazement, it dripped darkness that crept along the ground. The shadows searched, trapping any specter they came across. Lily was like a fisherman; her shadows were her nets.

The folds of the mantle drew in the ensnared specters and they were consumed. Their howls of pain echoed in her cloak as if it were a gateway to some unfathomable eternity.

"Finish her!" ordered Pan again.

Lily stood up. The darkness surrounded her, but she wasn't afraid. She'd never been afraid of the dark.

The spirits screamed. Some turned and fled, scuttling over the smoldering ruins on their hands and feet. But wherever they trod, the mantle's shadows took them, dragging them, flailing, howling, into the forever.

Pan thrust his finger at her. *"Finish her!"*

The remaining specters, knowing they could not escape, turned to face her. There were dozens, all foul and deadly, and they started toward her, slowly at first, then faster and faster as they charged.

Lily threw her cloak across her like a barrier, and all the specters vanished into it.

Only their fading, echoing screams lingered.

The Mantle of Sorrows shivered. It undulated around her, dozens of yards long and moving of its own accord. Then it settled. It shrank back to its normal size, and was still.

Lily collapsed to her knees.

What . . . what just happened?

She'd done it—used her magic—but it had taken all her strength. She trembled, and all she could do was curl up and retch. The Mantle of Sorrows had the heaviness of iron and she could barely move under its crushing weight.

"No, that's not possible. . . ." said Pan. He stared around him, bewildered. Then a deep, monstrous growl rolled out of his mouth. "Awake, awake, you sleeping dead! I command you!"

The earth began to crack. Inside the tombs, ancient bodies stirred to life. Bony fists beat at their doors.

Pan wore the Mask of Astaroth, the lord of the undead, and here they were, fighting in a huge graveyard. How many people were buried here? Thousands? Tens of thousands?

In a few seconds, Pan would have resurrected his army of corpses and then it would be over. For her, for everyone.

"The mask . . ." Lily muttered. "You're nothing without it."

Pan stood over her. "Yes, I admit it. But who's going to take it from me?"

Lily grinned, despite the pain. "That'll be him."

There was the creak of wood from behind Pan. He spun around to see the figure Lily had just spotted.

Thorn stood facing them, bow drawn. He looked along the shaft of his arrow. "Yeah, that'll be me."

His thumb freed the bowstring. It thrummed.

Pan threw up his arm to protect his face, but a second too late.

Steel arrowhead met stone mask, and the stone shattered.

FIFTY-SIX

"You came back to save me," said Lily, exhausted but never so relieved. Or happy.

Thorn was with her again.

He leaned on his bow. "It didn't look like you needed it, but I thought I'd *help*."

"How'd you get back? I thought you'd be halfway to Stour by now."

Thorn's face fell. "Hades brung me."

Lily looked at the bat, lying motionless halfway down the slope. "Oh no, Thorn . . ."

Hundreds of lesser bats swirled around Hades, and Lily and Thorn had to beat them off to reach him.

Blood soaked his body. Sticky strands hung from his mouth, and his eyes were barely open. His breath didn't have enough strength to stir a blade of grass.

Lily felt his life fading. It was a small, weak match light surrounded by the encroaching darkness of death.

The magic still held her in its feverish grasp. She could wink that light out and replace it with a colder, eternal glow. She had the power to turn

Hades into something not alive but perhaps more powerful. . . .

A true king of the underworld.

Thorn took her wrist. "No, Lily. Don't do it."

"Why not? I could bring him back from the dead."

"But he wouldn't be Hades anymore. Not really."

Horsemen galloped out of Castle Gloom, both her Black Guard and Solar's paladins.

Sure, now *they come.*

She put her hand against the beast's chest. She shouldn't be so quick to use magic. While there was life, there was a chance. "We'll save him, Thorn," she said. "I promise."

Thorn nodded and stroked the bat's bloody fur.

It was Baron Sable who reached them first. He jumped off his horse, sword drawn, with his men behind him.

He stared in horror at the ruins.

Tombs were broken open. Gravestones lay cracked on the blackened grass. Ribbons of smoke twisted around them, and the earth hissed. Bodies had half-crawled from their graves and now lay slumped in their rotted funereal garb.

"By the Six . . ." he muttered.

Pan lay unconscious on the ground. Gabriel walked up to them unsteadily, looking around him as if he'd awakened from a nightmare. Which wasn't far from the truth.

"Baron," Lily ordered, "have one of your men summon the surgeon and the apothecary *right now.*"

"Are you injured, m'lady?"

"No, Hades is. I want him saved, Baron."

Baron Sable snapped his fingers, and one of his men turned around and galloped back to the castle. Sable took Lily's arm, supporting her. "What happened?"

"My uncle killed Lord Shadow and the rest of my family. He tried to kill me, here."

Sable shook his head. "Your uncle? How's that possible? He has no magic. . . ."

"The evidence is before you."

Duke Solar looked down at a grave body and kicked it aside.

Lily glowered. "That's my great-granduncle Soriel, Duke. Please pay him some respect."

"Necromancy. That much is obvious," said the duke, his mouth twisted in disgust. "How was the earl defeated?"

Lily put her hand on Gabriel's shoulder. "Your son did it."

"I did?"

"Yes, you did. You were incredibly brave."

Gabriel stared at her, jaw hanging. She could practically hear the cogs in his brain grinding.

"Isn't that right, Thorn?" asked Lily. "Gabriel used his magic to destroy the specters and beat my uncle."

"Uh, yeah," said Thorn sourly. "He's a real hero. He certainly didn't run around the graveyard screaming and sobbing and wetting his pants."

"My champion." Lily kissed Gabriel's cheek. And whispered, "If you tell the truth . . ."

Gabriel nodded vigorously. He straightened his tunic. "I could see Lady Shadow was in danger, and I offered her my help. As any gentleman would do. Really, the spell was most simple to one of my blood and training."

Duke Solar looked down at his son. "Really?" There was something in his eyes that Lily hadn't seen before. Pride?

Gabriel bowed. "Really, Father."

Sable pointed at Pan. "Chain him and drag him down to the cells."

Orders were given and the crowd began to disperse, still not clear about exactly what had happened.

Thorn joined Lily near the horses. "Why'd you let Gabriel take the credit? Sounds real stupid."

"If they knew I was using magic, they'd all seek to destroy me, Thorn.

Now's not the time. And I can trust Gabriel to keep his mouth shut. Did you see the way the duke looked at him?"

"Yeah. I almost vomited."

"Gabriel's a hero, but he owes it all to us." Lily jumped up into her saddle. "That's a debt I might call on one day."

Thorn looked at her with caution. "You're a strange and scary girl, Lily Shadow."

Lily smirked. "That's a compliment where I come from."

"I bet it is." He handed over pieces of obsidian. "You'd better take these. If you want my opinion, you should chuck them down the deepest pit you can find."

Lily had a better idea. She tucked the broken mask into the folds of the Mantle of Sorrows, and the black garb closed around it.

FIFTY-SEVEN

The next few days were a whirlwind of activity and wild stories in Castle Gloom.

Pan was the assassin. He'd learned magic secretly so no one would suspect anything. Gabriel had saved Lady Shadow and Gehenna. There were already songs being sung about him.

The Solars had gone home. They hadn't even waited till sunrise before riding off. That left Thorn and the other stable boys with plenty of idle time. Thorn spent it at Murk Hall.

Hades was perched high on a broken column. He unfurled his wings and glided down, the air hardly stirring, and settled beside Thorn.

"Let's have a look at you."

Thorn pulled out the healing salve the apothecary had given him. The stinky goo would have cost him a year's wages, but suddenly his money wasn't good enough. He was getting everything for free.

Sure, the stories would all be about Gabriel—the nobles always got the glory—but there were enough folks in Castle Gloom who knew who'd *really* saved Lady Shadow. It seemed Lily had mentioned something to Mary. Mary had then told the cook. And the cook had told everyone.

Hades snarled as Thorn opened the pot. Its contents stank.

"Stop being such a big coward and come over here."

Hades widened his mouth to make sure Thorn got a good view of his lethal fangs.

"So you want to play rough? All right, but don't say I didn't warn you."

Thorn grabbed the monster's ear and pulled. Hard.

Hades yelped, then butted Thorn playfully.

Thorn peeled off the bandage for a look at the wound.

Black stubble was growing back where the fur had been shaved off. The stitches looked good, and the redness around the puckered flesh was now a healthy pink. Thorn started rubbing the salve over it, holding his breath as much as he could.

"Yeah, it really is stomach-churningly foul, isn't it?"

Lily arrived with Custard scampering at her heels.

The ghost puppy was back for good and up to his usual mischief. Even more so now that walls and doors didn't stop him. Not that it mattered; everyone was spoiling him. They loved having a ghost back haunting Castle Gloom.

I'll never get used to this place.

"How are you, Hades?" she asked.

Hades opened up his vast, sail-sized wings.

Thorn sighed. "Stop showing off." He added a second layer of goo. "Surprised to see you here."

"I needed to get away. Baron Sable's taking care of things."

"Things?"

"Returning the engagement gifts, for starters."

"So it's true? The wedding's off?" He glanced over. "I can see you're real upset."

Lily sniffed loudly. "Utterly heartbroken."

"I still don't get it. I thought the duke *needed* this marriage."

"That was before he found out the man who'd organized it all had tried to start a war between House Solar and House Shadow. That was before K'leef escaped. Now that the sultan has his son back, the first thing he's going to do is get revenge for all the raids the duke has made into his lands. Duke Solar's going to be very busy next year. And he'll need Gabriel beside him."

"Since Gabriel's proved to be a powerful sorcerer, right?"

Lily smiled. "I wonder if Gabriel realizes what he's in for."

"Why doesn't he tell his father the truth?"

"My guess is that Gabriel has repeated the story about how he defeated Pan so often that he truly believes he *did* do it."

"You can put a saddle on a cow, but that still don't make him no horse," said Thorn.

"I suppose that's one of your grandfather's sayings?" said Lily. "Sort of makes sense in a stupid way."

Thorn grinned. "And thanks, about my dad. I never got the chance to tell you. I really appreciate what you've done."

"That was Tyburn's idea. We haven't had a huntsman in Castle Gloom for years, and your father's an expert woodsman."

Dad was sailing home right now, with letters from Lily and plenty of gold. He'd collect Mom and the rest of Thorn's family and then return in the spring. Gehenna was going to be their new home.

Who would have thought it?

Thorn tied the bandage back in place. "It's all sorted, then."

Lily's brow furrowed. "No. There's one thing left to do."

Of course.

Tyburn had been down to the blacksmith earlier today, with an ax. He'd spent an hour sharpening it.

Tomorrow was Earl Pan's execution.

FIFTY-EIGHT

The bats knew. Flocks gathered on the bare trees that clung to the mossy boulders on the slope. The morning mist, too, waited, reluctant to raise the shroud of white it had spread over the gorse and dark heather.

Weeds covered the old, unkempt path, forcing Lily to step carefully as she continued up Lamentation Hill. It was hard work in her thick, embroidered skirts and jewelry, so she was breathing heavily when she reached the top.

And found two men waiting.

Tyburn, his hand resting on the haft of an ax.

Pan, trembling.

A few yards farther was a stone. Low, flat, and stained. The weeds had been stripped off so it looked unnaturally tidy compared to the rest of the summit.

How did it feel when you laid your cheek against the cold stone?

Against the Traitor's Pillow?

Her uncle shivered in a yellowed shift. He looked small and pathetic. His eyes were red—not from drink, not this time, but from tears.

I want to cry. But I can't.

I am Lady Shadow.

She needed to be strong. "Earl Pandemonium Shadow . . ."

Her uncle flinched as she said his name.

I am Lady Shadow and I do not cry.

Lily continued. "Earl Shadow, by your own admission you are a traitor. There is no greater crime than to betray your liege lord. A man who was not just your ruler but also your brother. There is only one penalty for such a crime." She looked at her uncle, but he wasn't really there. She gazed right through him, as if the job was already done. "Are you ready to die?"

FIFTY-NINE

Pan seized Lily's hand. "Please, Lily. You're not like this. I know you. You know me. Lily, think about all the things we've done together. Who taught you how to read and write? Who read you stories every night, *every* night, because your parents were too busy? I soothed your nightmares, child. The first words you ever spoke were to me. To *me*." His fingers tightened. "Please, Lily. I made a mistake. It was the mask. When I wore it, it made me do terrible things. Things you know I'd never do. Please, just give me one more chance."

Everything he said was true. There had been times he'd been more of a father than her real one.

How can I kill my own kin? How can I do something so evil? So unnatural? Because I am Lady Shadow.

She had to remind herself. Lady Shadow. Ruler of Castle Gloom.

She had to show them she was strong. That no one was above the law. That she would dispense justice to both the great and small.

Lily slipped her hand from Pan's. "Tyburn?"

The executioner glanced down at the Traitor's Pillow. "On your knees, m'lord." He spoke quietly, plainly. There was no joy or triumph in his voice.

He was the executioner and this was his job, no more, no less. How Lily envied him. She was the one who had to decide who lived or died. All the guilt was hers.

Pan knelt down. "Here?"

Tyburn nodded. "Rest your cheek against the stone. Stretch your hands out on either side to steady yourself."

Lily couldn't breathe. She could imagine the cold granite against her cheek, as if it was her lying there.

After his death, then what? Would she summon his ghost one day, like she had summoned Custard?

Pan put his head down. "Like . . . like this?" He sounded like a small child, unsure of the simplest things. Pan gripped the stone until his fingers went white. "I'm so sorry."

Tyburn lifted the ax. "Close your eyes, m'lord. If you want."

Pan squeezed them shut.

"M'lady?" asked Tyburn.

He has to die. He killed my father, mother, and brother. He killed poor Rose.

The other great lords will fear me all the more if I execute him. They will be reluctant to raise their hands against me, because, if I can do this to ones I love, what horrors would they *suffer?*

All of this, with the simple swing of an ax.

Given such a choice, would any other ruler hesitate? Would Duke Solar? Of course not. Not for a second.

And that was reason enough.

"Wait."

She met Tyburn's questioning eyes. Lily shook her head, and he lowered the blade.

"Stand up, Uncle."

Knees wobbling, Pan got to his feet. He stood there, cringing. "What's going on?"

"Run," said Lily. "Run far away."

"You're . . . letting me live?"

"Live? I suppose so," she said. "You're a traitor, Uncle. Everyone in the New Kingdoms knows it. Who will shelter a traitor? Everywhere you go you'll be despised, spat upon. If that's living, then, yes, I'm letting you live."

Barefoot, dressed in his thin shift, Pan shuffled away from the Traitor's Pillow, looking back to say, "Thank you, Lily. Thank you."

"I didn't do it for you." Lily pointed into Spindlewood. "Run and never come back."

Pan nodded. He stumbled over the roots and sharp stones, then he ran, frantic to get away from the hill. The bats launched themselves after him, their shrieks mocking his cowardice. Then they and Pan were lost in the mist, their cries the last thing trailing behind them.

It's over.

A weight rose off Lily's shoulders as Pan disappeared. "Did I do wrong, Tyburn? Should I have executed him?"

Tyburn rested the ax on his shoulder. "That all depends on what sort of ruler you wish to be, m'lady."

SIXTY

Mary unlocked the doors into the Eclipse chambers. Lily stood beside her with the red ledger under her arm.

"I don't see why I have to do this," said Lily.

"K'leef was your guest, that's why," said Mary. "And his father has asked for his things to be returned."

The rooms hadn't been entered since K'leef's arrest. Now her friend was back home, and they'd received a letter from the sultan thanking them for saving his son. The letter had come with a gift, a ruby the size of Lily's fist.

"I'll collect K'leef's belongings, and you tick them off." Mary opened up the first chest and sighed as she stared at the pile of silks. "This could take a while."

Mary called out the number of shirts, the number of boots and cloaks and tunics and gloves, and Lily steadily crossed them off. Then came the jewelry. Mary opened up K'leef's box of rings. "Right . . ." She picked them out and spread them over the table. "Sixteen rings. All amber."

"Says seventeen here." Then Lily remembered. The seventeenth was the hollowed ring they'd found in the pond. The ring that had contained the poison. "Pan swore he wasn't behind the poisoning."

Mary hesitated. "I wouldn't listen to anything that traitor has to say. I still don't know why you let him live."

"He said he only did evil things when he wore the mask. He didn't have it anywhere near him on the night of the feast."

"Lily, what's the point of this?" Mary poured the rings back in the box.

"And how did Pan know K'leef's ring had poison in it?" continued Lily. "It doesn't make sense. He would have had to search every ring, check them. They were all up in this room, and you're the only one with the keys."

Mary cleared her throat. "Right. Now, the bracelets. There are four gold ones. . . ."

Lily put the quill down. "You checked them, didn't you? It's your job."

Mary arranged the rooms and listed all the belongings. *All* of them. It was all up to her. Lily looked at her first and oldest friend. "That day he arrived. I told you to put him in the Eclipse rooms."

Mary faced her. "I . . ."

Lily shook her head, trying to rid herself of the idea forming in there. No, it wasn't possible. But the thought refused to dissipate. There were two people with access to K'leef's belongings. K'leef himself, and the person with the keys to each and every room in the castle. Mary. Lily trusted her. Everyone trusted Mary.

"So you counted out the rings and all the jewelry, like you always do. If anything went missing, it would be up to you. How did you know?" Lily held Mary's hand. She couldn't help but notice how clammy it was.

"That K'leef's ring was hollow? That it had poison in it? Oh, grow up, Lily."

"So you took the poison and poured it into Gabriel's cup. Didn't you?"

Mary tried to back away, but Lily held her.

"Lily . . ."

"Didn't you?"

Mary broke free. She stumbled against the table, knocking over the jewelry box. The rings scattered everywhere.

"Why, Mary?"

Mary's jaw hardened. "Why? Why do you think? You lost your parents, your brother, and you think that's the greatest pain a person can ever suffer. You're wrong. You don't know what pain is until you've lost a child. My sons, they were just boys with stupid dreams of being heroes. They should have been catching fish and chasing girls, but instead they went to war and never came back." She sat down. "I wanted the duke to taste the same pain I felt, what it was like to lose a child. I saw the ring, I knew what was in it. Do you not think your father and mother had similar rings? Of course they did. I poured some poison into a paper fold and carried it with me but left the ring here. I swear I didn't know what I was going to do with it until I saw Gabriel at the feast. How could I let my sweet girl marry a monster like that? You're a daughter to me, Lily. You're all I have. I didn't use very much. Just enough to make Gabriel sick. That's all."

Lily stood there, eyes closed. "You almost started a war, Mary."

"I'm sorry, Lily. I'm truly sorry." Mary looked about her, frightened. "What . . . what will you do?"

What *could* she do? If she admitted it to anyone, Mary's life was forfeited. She'd lost so many members of her family already; she couldn't lose another.

Instead, Lily put her finger to her lips.

Mary nodded and smiled widely with relief. She moved to embrace Lily. "Thank you, my girl, thank—"

"You forget your place, *servant*."

Mary curtseyed so very low. Her voice cracked as she spoke. "Forgive me, Lady Shadow."

Lily turned her back on her. Her heart ached more than ever.

Lily put the Skeleton Key in the lock. The doors groaned open.

Custard barked and ran in.

Candles spluttered to life and gradually light spread across the Shadow Library.

She walked up to the table in the center of the main chamber. Custard sniffed a stack of scrolls, his small black nose wrinkling with suspicion. He bit at one, but his phantom jaws went straight through it. He looked at it, momentarily surprised, then gave a little puppy shrug and dashed off, his high-pitched yaps echoing down one of the many passageways.

A book slid off a shelf and floated across the room. It settled itself upon the table in front of her.

A figure appeared in the space between the darkness and the light.

"I'm sorry I'm late, Father," said Lily. "You don't mind Custard, do you?"

"He is good company." The ghost smiled. "For our first lesson in magic we shall study Dagon Shadow, one of our family's greatest necromancers." He touched the spell book, and the pages flapped open. "Let us begin. . . ."

ACKNOWLEDGMENTS

Phew. Writing's a lot of work. I wouldn't say it's hard—it's the best job in the world and even the worst day of writing is pretty great, but it does take a lot of effort.

And help.

Many people helped me create the world of *Shadow Magic*. They gave me their time, their devotion, and their love, which is needed by each and every writer, especially during those moments at the desk when the screen's blank and you just don't know if you should have given up the day job.

Huge thanks to Ruth and Alison. I needed to put them first as they have worked hardest. Harder than me. This book, whatever quality it has, is all down to their endless patience and enthusiasm. I just hope they remain equally keen when I send them the sequel.

Next is my wife, Rachel. She tells it to me straight, and the work I do is inspired by her—always has been and always will be. She is the reason I became a writer.

I have to thank my girls. They've been along every step of the way, reading chapters hot off the printer, helping develop the characters, and also giving the series its title. It has been a true family effort, and I hope they're not sick of me constantly asking them for opinions about everything. Because I'm going to ask for plenty more.

My passion for fantasy and reading was nurtured by my family, so I will be forever thankful to my parents and sisters for sharing that passion.

I have to acknowledge the huge effort of Sarah Davies, my epic agent of the equally epic Greenhouse Literary Agency. She's tough, but fair. As an agent should be.

I must mention the awesome Disney Hyperion gang. It's my home, and I couldn't have asked for a better one. Dina Sherman is the very first person I ever pitched *Shadow Magic* to, and she gave me hope that it could be something special and strange, in a good way. One person I cannot thank enough is my editor, Stephanie Lurie. I've wanted to work with her from the moment I put pen to paper. Now I do, and it really is rather excellent.

I save my biggest thanks to the readers, old and new, be they schoolchildren, booksellers (especially George, Jen, and Nell, all early fans of Lily, Thorn, and Hades), librarians, bloggers, or reviewers. Writing's a funny old business, but it's home to some of the best people I know. Long may that continue!